ABOUT THE AUTHOR

Penny Freedman has taught Latin, Greek, English, Drama and
Linguistics in schools, colleges and universities in London,
Kent and the West Midlands. She has also been a theatre
critic and an amateur actor and director. Her earlier books,
*This is a Dreadful Sentence, All the Daughters, One May Smile,
Weep a While Longer, Drown My Books, Little Honour, Where
Everything Seems Double* and *Chronicles of the Time*, featuring
Gina and Freda Gray and DCI David Scott, are all published
by Troubador.

THE SCOTTISH PLAY

PENNY FREEDMAN

Matador
Unit E2 Airfield Business Park,
Harrison Road, Market Harborough,
Leicestershire. LE16 7UL
Tel: 0116 2792299
Email: books@troubador.co.uk
Web: www.troubador.co.uk/matador
Twitter: @matadorbooks

ISBN 978 1803136 011

British Library Cataloguing in Publication Data.
A catalogue record for this book is available from the British Library.

Printed and bound by CPI Group (UK) Ltd, Croydon, CR0 4YY
Typeset in 11pt Book Antiqua by Troubador Publishing Ltd, Leicester, UK

Matador is an imprint of Troubador Publishing Ltd

For Zoë, who shares Pitlochry and chose the victim

and

Remembering Basil, who liked to keep me company
while I wrote this book

Apologies and Disclaimers

First, I have to offer my sincere apologies to the Angus police force. Presenting them as somewhat lackadaisical was the only excuse I could provide for the involvement of a senior officer in the Met in their investigation. I know nothing but good of the Angus force, and all the police officers I have created here are entirely fictional.

I have taken liberties, too, with Glamis Castle, imposing my own geography on it, and planting a marquee and a guest house in its grounds. Freda's views about the décor of the castle are entirely her own.

There is no Curtain Theatre in Perth. The theatre described here is invented – as are the people who work there. The Aphra Behn theatre and its staff are also inventions.

The School of Oriental and African Studies is a real place, but no Virginia Gray teaches there, and I have no reason to cast any slur on its hiring practices.

Finally, I am very grateful to Naomi Perry for her eagle eye on legal questions. She has saved me from some blunders, and where I have chosen to overrule her expert advice in the interests of a better story I am entirely culpable.

Chapter One

THIS CASTLE HATH A PLEASANT SEAT

My daughter is getting married.

Marianne Beatrice Gray is marrying Jonathan James McCleod *in Glamis Castle*.

I am so unsettled by this last phrase that this is the first time I have brought myself to write it down. It is not just that it feels rather naff to be borrowing somebody else's castle to get married in, but *Glamis?* Really? Does nobody else associate Glamis with its most famous thane – a man so ill-omened that actors go into superstitious meltdown at the speaking of his name?

I know, of course, that the historical King Macbeth (d 1057) bore no resemblance to Shakespeare's creation – he of the bloody dagger, seduced by a trio of bearded witches and a sexily ambitious wife into murdering his king and embarking on a reign of terror. King Macbeth had no connection to Glamis, did not murder his predecessor, and appears to have enjoyed a long and peaceful reign before being killed in battle by an invading English army with no excuse for unseating a perfectly good king. There was a king murdered in Glamis castle, but that was Malcolm II, not Duncan I, and anyway that castle was not the Glamis castle which is going to host our nuptials. So, what am I worrying about? What logic lies behind my fears?

Well none, I suppose, except that these puny historical 'facts' are mere feathers in the face of Shakespeare's Macbeth, who strides among us, dagger in hand, moving inexorably towards regicide, mass murder and mayhem, and when the saintly King Duncan arrives at Macbeth's castle and comments on its *pleasant seat* and the happy little birds building their nests among the stonework, we all know what is coming, and recognise a whopping great dollop of dramatic irony when we hear one. I am not a superstitious woman but why would you take the risk?

I am surprised at Jon, actually. I can see that he wouldn't be likely to be superstitious, but he doesn't seem like a man who would want to get married in a castle either. I can only assume that he sees this as Annie's day and is willing to give her whatever she wants. She has, after all, turned her life and her career upside down to go to live in Scotland with him, so I suppose that's the deal. What his parents think I can't imagine – a consultant physician and a university librarian, quiet Presbyterians, given to modest understatement rather than drama and display.

One of the more irritating elements in this Scottish wedding is Andrew – Annie's father and my long-ago husband. Not only has the aristocratic distinction of the castle seduced him into offering to pay for the whole shindig, but he has discovered his inner Scottishness. His forebears, who I have always understood to be many generations of Kentish yeomen, must originally, he claims, have been Grays of the clan Stewart, and thus firmly in the ambit of those *Wha Hae Wi' WallaceBled*. So, he will be wearing a kilt. Fortunately, it is to be a civil ceremony, so I shan't have to watch him prance down the aisle in it with Annie on his arm, but it is going to be exquisitely embarrassing all the same. There will be plenty of kilts around – Jon and his father will be kilted, as will a number of their friends and relations, I imagine – but they know how to do it. If a grown man is going to appear in public wearing a skirt and long socks – not to mention the sporran – then he needs to have been inured to it more or less from birth. Jon and his father will carry the look off with aplomb; Andrew will not.

And then there are the boys. – Andrew's two boys aged eight and ten, and Annie's eight-year-old nephew, Nico. They will be in kilts, too – particularly difficult for Nico, who has dual English/Italian identity already without adding Scottish into the mix. Weddings are difficult enough for boys at the best of times. Little girls get wildly excited, but they do at least see the point of the occasion and they like to keep their dresses clean, whereas for boys there are only two options: boredom or subversion. Dress our three little Sassenachs in kilts and we will get guaranteed flashing – at least one of them will be wearing no underpants.

I haven't seen Annie's dress – she may not be superstitious about the murderous associations of her chosen venue, but she has put an embargo on anyone's seeing the dress. I gather, though, that she is challenging the men's tartan finery with something classically simple. Something off a Grecian urn is what she has in mind, I think, to judge from Freda's bridesmaid's dress, which I have seen. She has sent me a photo, and I can see that she is intended to be a sort of attendant nymph to Annie's artfully draped goddess. Simply divine.

And what am I going to be wearing? Please don't ask as you're likely to trigger a panic attack. I know what I want, and I am willing to pay lavishly for the right thing. I want something that will be a rebuke to Andrew's borrowed finery and a reproach to the floral pastels that his current wife, Lavender, will surely be wearing. I want an outfit that is simple but striking, expensive but understated, elegant but youthful. Exhaustive research and exhausting shopping expeditions have not yielded the magic garment, in spite of my willingness to pay through the nose, and I am coming to the conclusion that I am the reason why. Simple, striking, expensive, understated, elegant, youthful – I am none of these things. I am a dumpy little woman in her fifties with unmanageable hair, and no outfit is going to change that. But my daughter, I tell myself, is going to look like a Greek goddess, and as Lady Redesdale liked to reassure her daughters, the attention-seeking Mitford girls, *Nobody will be looking at you, dear.*

Reading this over, I realise that I have omitted to say that I am very pleased that Annie and Jon are getting married. I have always liked Jon and I used to be afraid that Annie's moods and egotism would drive him away. Then, when Annie announced that she was abandoning her hard-won place in a Gray's Inn barristers' chambers to follow Jon to Scotland and start her legal career all over again, I worried that this was the first step down the slippery slope to becoming a domestic helpmeet, until I reminded myself that this was Annie we were talking about – a young woman with an unconquerable ego and a vigorous sense of entitlement, which would save her from ever becoming the support act or the second fiddle. After ten years with her, I guess Jon knows that.

The other plus to all this that I have failed to mention is that David is coming with me. I won't bore you here with the vagaries of my more than ten-year relationship with Detective Superintendent David Scott of the Metropolitan police, except to say that in all that time – whether we have been on or off – it has not been the sort of relationship in which we accompanied one another to formal social occasions. This will be the first time that David has been my *plus one* – and he actually volunteered for the job. I am quite unreasonably pleased. I have been tackling social occasions on my own for the past twenty years, and it will really be very nice to have a notional arm to lean on. And given my misgivings about the venue, it never does any harm to have a policeman around, does it?

Chapter Two

STANDS SCOTLAND WHERE IT DID?

Scotland really was a very long way away from East Kent, Freda Gray reflected as she lay sleepless in her bunk, feeling the train eating up the miles. Though she wasn't sleeping, she had to be grateful that they hadn't decided to take a daytime train or – even worse – go by car. The thought of being trapped in a car or train carriage with a bored, fidgeting eight-year-old was too horrible to contemplate. She had favoured flying, but Mum was still nervous about the COVID risk at airports, so the sleeper was the compromise.

It was good, too, to feel the distance. Reading about the sixteenth century, which was her favourite period, she had always thought it was a bit absurd that Scotland and England wasted so much money and energy fighting over being separate countries. Two parts of a small island – why on earth hadn't they joined up earlier? Auntie Annie believed that Scotland was going to go independent now and re-join the EU, and now, as the miles went on, Freda thought, *Why not?*

The train was all right. They had had really quite an elegant dinner in the dining car, and the 'room' she was sharing with Nico had its own basin, but she was in a bunk bed here, with Nico shifting around only inches above her. She couldn't kid herself that this was the Orient Express.

When she was younger, she thought, she had probably had enough imagination to transform this experience, but not any longer. These days she felt she confronted the world head-on, and it was hard work.

The movement of the train left her feeling slightly sick in the morning, and the train breakfast seemed unappealing. Then at Edinburgh station there was a lot of hanging about while Ben picked up a hire car to drive them to Glamis. The plan – adopted without consultation with her – was that after the wedding they would drive north and take a ferry over to Orkney, because Nico wanted desperately to see Neolithic sights. When she had protested, Mum had pointed out that Freda was getting the fun of being a bridesmaid, so Nico deserved a treat too, but frankly, being a bridesmaid was not that much of a treat. Three years ago, she would probably have loved it, but she was fifteen now, and a feminist, and marriage and weddings, in her view, were problematic. And then, the opportunities for embarrassment were mega. Friends had terrified her with information about what was expected of a bridesmaid – in her case, the only bridesmaid. Auntie Annie had said that all she had to do was to walk in behind her and then take her bouquet when she handed it to her. After that she could sit down. That sounded all right, but the girls had said that Jon would have to thank her in his speech, and everyone would turn to look at her, which meant she would go scarlet. And then the dancing. They said she would have to dance with the best man, who was Jon's brother, and she had never even met him. The only comfort was that the dancing was going to be a ceilidh and she had been to quite a few of those. Your partner didn't matter, actually, because whoever you started with you soon moved on to someone else. Still, it was going to be stressful, and not a treat, and then she was going to have to pretend to be interested in the Stone Age. She loved history, but history about people – their characters, motives, mistakes, tragedies. It was so odd to be interested in Neolithic people, where there were no individuals at all – just nameless, faceless people wearing animal skins. Nico, she decided, was turning into a weird little boy.

When they got into the car to drive to Glamis, Ben joked, 'They do still drive on the left here, do they?' But actually it did look a bit like a different country here. It was not just the landscape, the looming hills, but the houses, which were universally grey – a cold, grey stone which didn't look good on a dreary morning like this, with its grey sky and cool mist. You could see that people tried to brighten the houses up – there were hanging baskets of flowers in the places they went through when they came off the motorway – but there was a limit to what a hanging basket could achieve.

The castle, when they first caught sight of it, was amazing. She almost laughed because it was so perfectly a castle, so like a castle in a children's picture book, with its creamy walls and towers, and a host of little silvery turrets, and a mass of chimney pots, and crenelations (she thought that was the right word). The sun even came out a bit as they approached, making everything glow.

There had to be a disappointment, of course. When Mum had said that Grandpa had arranged accommodation for the family at the castle, she had imagined sleeping somewhere splendid, with a four-poster bed at least, but it turned out that they were staying in a place in the grounds, which was just an ordinary house. Well, not that ordinary – there was room for twelve of them to sleep there – but it was the same grey stone as everywhere else, and not a turret to be seen. And she was sharing a room with Nico.

The castle was just opening up to visitors, so Mum suggested taking a tour round before going for an early lunch. What a let down! There was this fabulous castle from the outside, and inside it was like a place lived in by a crazy collector. The rooms were huge and there were loads of them, but somehow they managed to feel cramped because there was so much *stuff* in them. Portraits were crammed onto every wall that wasn't already bristling with helmets and shields, and the living rooms were packed with frantically patterned carpets and sofas, with tables, cupboards and bureaus lined along every wall, all covered in ornaments of all kinds. And none of it was beautiful – or if it was, you couldn't see it because it was swamped by all the other stuff. No-one in this family, she thought, had ever taken anything to the Oxfam shop.

As soon as Nico got bored, she was ready to leave too. In a way she felt quite cheered by not liking the castle interior – it meant she was less disappointed about not sleeping there. And fortunately the wedding wasn't happening inside the castle. Not knowing what the COVID rules were going to be, Auntie Annie had planned for everything to happen outside, in a big, airy marquee, which was already up on one of the lawns, and was being festooned with ribbons.

They ate lunch in the castle café – sturdy sandwiches for Mum and Ben and her, but Nico was allowed fish and chips because he wasn't going out for dinner in the evening. Then they went over to their house and waited for the others to arrive – first Granny and David, who had stayed the night with Granny's friends Eve and Colin in the Lake District, and driven on from there, and then, finally, Grandpa and Auntie Lavender and Arthur and Hubert, all looking thoroughly pissed off.

'You're looking very fresh,' Auntie Lavender said, as she non-hug greeted them. 'The sleeper was obviously the sensible idea. But some people love their cars more than their family.'

It was one of those *just joking* non-jokes, and Grandpa looked ready to hit someone.

9

Arthur and Hubert cheered up at the sight of Nico, though, and the three of them went off to rush around the garden, while Lavender sat down with a cup of tea, and Grandpa muttered about needing a proper drink and took himself off to see if the café was still open, and what it had to offer. Freda took advantage of Nico's not being in the room they were sharing to shower and change for going out for supper. They were going to Jon's parents. *Aileen says just a family supper*, was Auntie Annie's message, so she didn't need to be that smart, but she felt grubby from the travelling and was glad to find that the controls on the en suite shower were easy to work. She didn't have anything very smart with her since she had packed for tramping round Neolithic burial sites probably in the rain, so she put on her best jeans and a top she quite liked and thought that would have to do.

Jon's parents lived between Glamis and Perth, where Auntie Annie and Jon lived, and Grandpa had booked a stretch taxi to take them there and bring them back. There were five of them besides her: Granny and David, Mum and Ben, and Grandpa. The boys, thank God, weren't invited, and Auntie Lavender had volunteered to give them supper and put them to bed. 'After all,' she said, with her little *poor me* laugh, 'I'm a spare part at this wedding – Mother of the Pageboys is all I'm good for.'

They were uncomfortably quiet in the car because Grandpa's bad temper was putting a downer on everyone, but once they got to the McCleods' house he started making an effort – and it would be difficult to be pissy with the McCleods because they were just so nice.

Adults hadn't yet worked out the rules for sort-of-post-COVID greeting, she had noticed. She and her friends had celebrated June 21st with hugs all round, but the only hugger here was Granny, who hugged Auntie Annie and Jon in a *What the hell* kind of way, while everyone else made up for missing handshakes and kisses with extra-big smiles, which made them all look a bit weird, frankly.

The house was nice in the same way that Jon's parents were – calm and comfortable somehow – and they were led out into a tidy garden for drinks before they sat down for supper at a big table in a conservatory with all its doors and windows open. Still COVID rules, Freda thought, even though everyone here must have been vaccinated, apart from her. Was that what they were all thinking – that she was a danger to them? Ben was sitting on one side of her, and it looked as though no-one was going to sit on the other side of her until someone rushed into the room saying, 'Sorry, everyone,' and slid into the chair next to her. From across the table Jon said, 'Freda, meet my best man, my brother Alex,' and Freda realised that she had a big goofy grin on her face because the best man wasn't a man at all, but a boy – older than her, certainly, but still at school, she reckoned.

He had red hair, and arriving late and having everyone look at him had made him blush, but he had a good smile and he said, 'And you must be the bridesmaid' in a nice, unpatronizing way. He would be perfectly OK to dance with, and if she could catch him in a good light and not looking too ginger, she wouldn't mind sending a photo to her WhatsApp gang.

Like everything else about the McCleods, the meal was unfussy but really good. Mrs McCleod brought in two big dishes of lasagne and bowls of salad and a basket of bread. 'They're roasted vegetable lasagnes,' she said. 'I wasn't sure if we had any vegetarians, so I played safe. Do just dig in.'

Once all the passing and the helping was done and they were settled with their food, Alex said to her, 'I'm guessing you've just not taken exams.'

Flattered at being taken for sixteen, she half wanted to lie and maintain the pretence, but it seemed a bad way to start really, so she said, 'No, my exams are next year – GCSEs. Lots of pressure though, because there's so much catching up to do.'

It was her turn to ask about him, she knew, but she didn't want to get it wrong, in case he wasn't still at school. 'How about you?' she asked. 'Should you have been taking exams of some kind?'

'Highers,' he said. 'They're like your A levels. I've got my place at university all right, but we didn't cover the whole syllabus in any of my subjects, so I don't feel all that well prepared.'

'What are your subjects?'

'Maths, Physics, Chemistry and Biology. I'm going to be another medic, I'm afraid.'

'I didn't expect you to be so young,' she said. 'When Jon said his brother was going to be the best man, I thought...'

'I know. We're half-brothers, actually, but we never say that.'

'Really? That's like me and my brother.'

'How old is he?'

'Eight. Nearly nine.'

'Does he worship you?'

She couldn't help giggling. 'I wouldn't say so,' she said. 'I think he does look up to me in some ways, but he doesn't like to admit it.'

'Jon is fourteen years older than me. I've admired him for as long as I can remember.'

She hesitated, trying to find the right words. 'So did Jon's parents, like, get divorced?'

'Oh no. Jon's mother died when he was very young. Car accident. Jon was actually in the car, but he wasn't badly hurt. So Dad was left with a two-year-old to look after and Grandma here came to live with them and helped.' He leant back in his chair so that Freda could see a tiny little white-haired woman, who was talking to Jon, on her other side, and whom Freda had hardly noticed.

'Then Dad met my mum – Aileen – and they got married, and she became Jon's mum, really. They'd been married for eight years by the time I was born. I've never asked, but I've always thought that she wanted Jon to feel that he had all her love – until he was old enough to cope with a sibling.'

'Did he mind when you came along?'

'Apparently not. I remember him as being endlessly kind and patient.'

'A good preparation for being a husband, then,' Freda said.

He laughed. 'Marianne seems good fun,' he said.

She was always startled when people called Auntie Annie by her proper name, but she knew *Annie* was only allowed from Granny, Mum and her and Nico.

'Oh yes,' she said. 'Definitely a fun aunt.'

She thought about how Granny and Mum rolled their eyes about Auntie Annie's drama queen tendencies, but she didn't think Alex needed to know that.

'How about you?' Alex asked. 'How did you feel when your brother came along?'

'Excited at first. I was six, so I thought of him as being a sort of super doll, I think. Then I got a bit bored with him, but now I quite like teaching him things. He won't be at his best this weekend because he's going to be with the other pageboys – my grandpa's sons, and technically my uncles! Families are complicated, aren't they?'

She knew that she had introduced this diversion because she didn't want him to ask about her father. She had got her answer to that question off pat by now – *My mum was in a relationship when she was a student, but it didn't last. I don't see my father. Ben has always been my real dad*. It was some way from the truth, though. She knew that what had happened to her mum could be called rape now, but she wasn't going to tell anyone that.

She was saved, anyway, from any questions because Aileen sent Alex out to the kitchen for more wine and spring water, and Freda was free to look around at other people's conversations. She saw Jon's talk with his grandma differently now, knowing that she had looked after him when he was small, and she could see how fond they were of each other. Aileen McCleod, on Jon's other side, was talking to Grandpa. He had stopped being grumpy, of course, and had his charming face on, saying something that made Aileen laugh. He had spent some time in Perth in the 1990s, when he was advising the Scottish government on something about human rights, and he had some story about English/ Scottish misunderstandings. On the other side of him was Mum, who seemed to be chatting happily with David, and at the top of the table was Duncan McCleod, managing a conversation with Auntie Annie and Granny – something that needed quite a bit of skill, Freda thought, since they got on one another's nerves at the best of times, and tonight Auntie Annie was probably quite strung up about tomorrow. What calm people Jon's family were; you would never guess at the trauma they had suffered, losing Jon's mum, and all the possible stresses with Duncan marrying again. Her own family could make a drama out of the smallest thing, and there was always someone ready to have a tantrum. And she knew she was just as bad – she had never forgiven Grandpa for that time when she was staying with him and Lavender, and the business over the dog. Ben was actually the calmest person in their family, and he was Italian, and Italians were supposed to be emotional and dramatic. It made her smile, as she looked round the table, to see how the McCleods were quietly keeping the Grays under control. She could only hope that they would manage to do that tomorrow.

Chapter Three

FAIL NOT OUR FEAST

It feels early when I wake but I am not sure whether that is just the effect of the unfamiliar northern light, so I lie and listen for sounds of movement in the house. Silence. David, never a lark, is still deep asleep beside me, so I lie quietly and commit the time to thought – it will probably be my last chance in the challenges of the day ahead. Last night was very soothing, I must say. The McCleods may not be exciting company, but they are, crucially, the kind of people who make you want them to think well of you. Their quiet, polite consideration defies even the most hardened social deviants to do anything other than behave well, and it was quite amusing to see the unruly Grays fall into line. Even Andrew behaved himself, chatting charmingly with Aileen McCleod and not attempting to muscle into the limelight when Duncan stood up to propose a toast to the happy couple. Ellie didn't bristle with suspicion every time I so much as looked at Freda, Freda never once looked at her phone, as far as I noticed, and I was particularly impressed by the performance of uncomplicated mother and daughter affection that Annie and I put on under Duncan's gentle direction. Who would have guessed that I usually give Annie fifteen minutes tops before she decides to be affronted by something I have said, and another ten before she storms off? Interestingly, I felt that the shared endeavour of putting on a good act did actually bond us together. A case of *Fake it till you make it*, I think.

So, I do have hope that the McCleods can help to keep things on an even keel today. With my qualms about the venue, I can't help wishing that he wasn't called Duncan. It does feel particularly ill-omened, even though kindly Dr McCleod seems an unlikely candidate for murder. After all, King Duncan is kindly too, isn't he? Kindly and rather stupid. Is it possible that anyone could hold onto a throne in those brutal times when he was so blithely unaware of treachery around him? *He was a gentleman on whom I placed an absolute trust*, he says of the treacherous Thane of Cawdor, just before taking into his arms the Thane of Glamis, who is already plotting his death. And Lady Macbeth, of course, runs rings round him with her extremely unsubtle flattery. Delighted by her charming castle and lovely hospitality, he presents her with a hostess gift of a diamond, no less, even as she is psyching herself up for drugging his guards and sending her husband in to put the knife in as he sleeps. Not a clever man.

Talking of psyching oneself up, I am considering how to pace myself in the day ahead. When did weddings become an endurance sport? Seriously, it could be added to the growing array of Olympic events. The nuptial pentathlon. Stage one, the dressing: here we test the strength and courage to straddle the yawning gap between imagination and reality as the view in the glass reveals that the outfit on which all hopes have been pinned has not made the entrant any taller or slimmer or younger.

Stage two is the ceremony itself, where tolerance of unbridled emotion and verbal nonsense is the important skill being tested, together with the ability to smile while wearing crippling shoes. Though I am an unbeliever, I have affection for the traditional marriage service. I like *For better for worse, for richer for poorer, in sickness and in health, and forsaking all other keep you only unto him/her as long as you both shall live.* What I don't like in civil ceremonies are the modern paraphrases. I particularly dislike the pledge of *unconditional love.* I don't think that's what the C of E vows mean. They envisage bad luck that may befall you – sickness and penury. I suppose *for better for worse* can be seen as a sort of catch-all, but in the context, I think it was intended to cover wars, revolutions and malicious Acts of God rather than the discovery that you have married a narcissist, sadist, psychopath, or simply a plonker. The irony is that often in these modern ceremonies the couples declare why they love each other, so why the unconditional love? If he/she turns out not to be the *kind, caring, funny, strong,* (supply your own adjectives as required) person you believed them to be, why on earth would you go on loving them? I find all of this so trying that I always emerge from the ceremony in a state of fizzing irritation. No gold medal for me.

Stage three of the pentathlon offers two challenges. It is the lunch, so you might think of it as a bit of an easy ride, particularly as sitting down eases the shoe problem. You would be wrong. For a start, lunch never happens immediately; there is always a seemingly endless spell of milling about, allowing for photos to be taken and so on. Most of those present will have made an early start and will be in danger of acute hypoglycaemia by the time they sit down to lunch. A performance-enhancing drug will be openly available at this stage, in the form of something white, fizzy and not quite cold enough. It is tempting to mainline on this in desperation, but those who fail to pace themselves will be vomiting into a flowerbed before the event is over. Food will be welcome and should sustain the participants for the speeches, which generally present a secondary challenge so acute that I would rather not talk about it just now.

The time was that this would have been the end of it. The happy couple would cut the cake, participants would have nothing more to deal with than the danger of losing a filling to the mass of dried fruit, icing and marzipan, the bride and groom would slip away to transform themselves into normal-looking people, would climb into their amusingly accessorised car, and drive away to the accompaniment of cheerful waves. Everyone else would take a brisk departure, setting their sights on the moment when they could kick their shoes off and lie on a sofa in the recovery position, to the accompaniment of something mindless on TV.

Not any more. Now there must be an evening event, with dancing, and it follows that there must also be some kind of activity to pass the time until the evening can begin. So, two more stages and a modest triathlon becomes the pentathlon. Actually, the last two stages may not be too demanding: the afternoon challenge may involve nothing more difficult than more smiling through the pain of your crippled feet, and for the evening dancing, competitors are permitted to change into comfortable shoes, so provided they have not exceeded their alcohol prescription and can still stand up, they should be able to get through the dancing challenge with nothing worse than trampled toes and a few blows to the head from flying elbows. The medals may not be awarded until the following morning, when the person who consumes a full English breakfast will get the gold.

Enough! I sit up and swing out of bed. *For God's sake, woman,* I berate myself silently, *it's your daughter's wedding. Get a grip and start smiling.* I shower and put on basic makeup and appropriate underwear, including the pull-in pants I would sooner not wear, but Lavender is looking particularly slim and I can't be the fat ex-wife. Then I put on a dressing gown, give David a shake, and go downstairs.

Here, the calm engendered by last night's gathering at the McCleods still seems to prevail. The boys have had their breakfast and been despatched outside, leaving the adults to their coffee and toast amidst the debris. Annie has just arrived and is drinking a smoothie, and when Ellie says she has a work schedule for the morning, nobody – amazingly – argues. Ellie, and only Ellie, will help Annie with her dress and hair, and I will do the same for Freda; Ben and Lavender will dress the boys and keep them under control. 'Whatever it takes,' Ellie says. Andrew, once he has arrayed himself for his highland fling, will go and harass the catering staff, and David, who has not been allocated a job, says he will wash up the breakfast things and, at Annie's request, will inspect the little summerhouse where the bridal party will be waiting before processing into the marquee for the ceremony.

'Absolutely no cobwebs, please,' Annie says.

When David says, 'Guaranteed, ma'am!' and she blows him a kiss, I have one of my periodic pangs of regret that I turned down his offer of matrimony several years ago. He would have made such a good substitute for my daughters' flaky father.

So, we all disperse, and the absence of the usual family friction so unnerves me that I think I may have to pick a quarrel with Freda just to make things feel normal. I don't, of course, and she doesn't give me the chance anyway. She is in a particularly blithe mood and gets herself ready with cheerful efficiency – no plucking at her dress, no scowling in the mirror, no fretting over her hair. She scoops her blond curls into a Grecian knot high on her head, and I assist with extra pins to secure it against collapse. Then she lets me zip her into her floaty little dress, slips on ballet flats, and sits down to apply mascara and pink lip gloss, and to tease out some tendrils of hair into tiny ringlets on either side of her face. Then she stands up and does a twirl in the full-length mirror. She is apparently satisfied, as she should be since she looks utterly lovely, but that is no guarantee of satisfaction in a fifteen-year-old.

'I hope Alex has got good legs,' she says, 'for the kilt.'

'I hope they all have,' I say, but I am beginning to understand the source of her blitheness. *He's eighteen*, I think. *Does he know she's only just fifteen?* But I have been here before and it didn't go well, so I just have to put my trust in the inherent decency of the McCleod family.

'Has Grandpa got good legs?' Freda asks.

'They were all right when I was last familiar with them, but that was more than twenty years ago,' I say. 'Talking of legs, I must go and put on tights and a dress, and then we'll have time to do the crossword on our phones.'

'Would you like some help with dressing?'

'You don't want to see me without my clothes on,' I say, and go to my room.

In case you have been wondering, I have found an outfit that will do. It is not the ideal that I was hoping for – I have had to resort to good old, tried and tested black and white – but it is cool, I think, and, apart from the shoes, reasonably comfortable. I zip myself into it and step into the shoes, which feel deceptively harmless at the moment, of course; that is the fiendish thing about smart shoes.

Freda and I go downstairs to the sitting room to do the crossword, and we are just finishing when others start to arrive. First come Lavender and Ben, dressed in floral pink and Italian grey respectively, with the three boys, scrubbed, slicked and kilted, and looking as solemn as choirboys. What combination of threat and bribe has been applied I don't know, but it is working for the moment. While they are being corralled onto a sofa to *sit quietly*, Annie appears in the doorway with Ellie hovering behind her. I know it is conventional on the first sighting of a bride to gasp, turn misty-eyed, and murmur *You look beautiful*, but I must say that Annie really does look spectacular, and I could go misty-eyed if I were that sort of woman. Like Freda, she has her hair up in a Grecian knot, giving her an elegant length of neck, and that combined with the artfully flowing draperies and four-inch heels gives her the height of a supermodel – or a supersized Homeric goddess.

'Pallas Athene, definitely,' I say.

'Not Aphrodite?' she says.

'I've always thought she was a bit of an airhead,' I say.

Then David arrives, looking irreproachable and really rather handsome, in a new suit and a buttonhole. I have been as much concerned about his outfit as I have about my own. It shouldn't be difficult for him to outshine Andrew in his fancy dress, but I do want to be sure that he is admired. He says that the guests are arriving thick and fast, and Andrew is greeting them.

'Time to go,' I say, and we make our way outside into a cool, bright morning.

We cross the lawn outside our house together and then divide, we who are only guests heading straight towards the marquee, while the bridal party takes a path between the trees towards their summerhouse, where they will wait in the wings for their cue.

In the marquee, a row at the front has been reserved for us. It is very odd the way civil ceremonies strive to ape church weddings in every detail apart from involving God, so we are on 'the bride's side', as though a hostile army was drawn up across the aisle. I slide along to the far end of the row, taking David with me. Andrew, busy greeting, will sit at the aisle end eventually, so this way I create as much distance between us as possible. Then I begin to relax. This is, I tell myself, a perfectly benign occasion, these people are all well-wishers, and nobody ever died of embarrassment.

Chapter Four

NOW GOOD DIGESTION
WAIT ON APPETITE

In fact, as things proceed, nothing is really embarrassing, if you discount Andrew's outfit. He is still a good-looking man, but he looks like an amateur actor wearing his costume for the first time at the dress rehearsal. Still, Annie's appearance with her entourage evokes smiles and sighs of satisfaction, Jon looks splendid, and they both make their vows with firm confidence. Jon recites *Let me not to the marriage of true minds* and Annie says Yeats's *The Cloths of Heaven*, making me well up at '*Tread softly, for you tread on my dreams*'.

Pouring out onto the lawn afterwards, we are given our doses of fizz, and I look around, realising that I know no-one here apart from the family. Andrew, I notice, is chatting with a group of people I don't know, and I judge them to be other lawyers, members of his chambers. I suppose. Does Annie even know them? I am not short of people to talk to since everyone seems to know who I am, and strangers come up to congratulate me on the beauty of my daughter and granddaughter. I smile graciously and ask them if they have come far. One woman I do recognise approaches me. She was Andrew's secretary in the days when he had an office in Marlbury as well as his London chambers. This was after our divorce, and I used her as a go-between, leaving messages for Andrew when I couldn't face speaking to him. She was gentle and tactful, and I was grateful to her. I am pleased with myself when her name jumps to my lips.

'Jeanette, hello!' I say, irrationally pleased to see her.

Her pale, rather anxious face breaks into a smile, and she tucks her hand tighter into her husband's arm and propels him forward to be introduced. 'I wasn't sure if you would remember me,' she says. 'This is my husband, Dennis. Dennis, this is Gina, mother of the bride.'

Dennis, obviously uncomfortable in his wedding suit, shakes my hand.

'Your wife was very kind to me at a difficult time,' I tell him. 'I was grateful.' I turn to Jeanette. 'It must have been difficult for you. You were naturally on Andrew's side, I'm sure, but you never let it show.'

'Well, it's not a question of sides, is it?' she says. 'But he was having a difficult time too, you know. And he was very good to me later on when we had – family problems.' She glances at her husband. 'Wasn't he, Dennis?'

He shuffles a bit and nods. Meeting me seems to have struck him dumb.

Actually, I am pleased when people say good things about Andrew; I don't like to think I was a complete fool to marry him.

'I'm determined to see the best in everyone today,' I say. 'Shall we go and consult that board and find out where we are sitting for lunch?'

Lunch is fine as I have been placed next to Nico, who enjoys his food and engages me in serious conversation about Neolithic sites on Orkney. It is not a subject I would normally warm to but I do like enthusiasm in the young and I don't often get a chance to talk to Nico. Then we have the speeches, which are admirable: Jon thanks everyone nicely and speaks sweetly about Annie (who is, of course, Marianne today) and Alex makes the obligatory jokes about Jon while avoiding the *nudge nudge, wink wink*. His jokes, in fact, are mainly against himself and his unsuccessful attempts, when young, to hoodwink his canny elder brother.

And then we are free. The entertainment planned for the afternoon is a tour of the interior of the castle, but Ellie and Ben saw it yesterday, Lavender doesn't trust her boys within range of glass and china, and in my fifties I have seen enough stately homes to last my lifetime. We retreat to the lawn outside our house, and Ben and Ellie start to organise a game of garden cricket with the three boys and Freda (who has decided that she can't bear to go inside the castle again, even though Alex has joined the tour). Lavender says she will watch, David says he would like a walk, and I say I can't walk anywhere until my feet have recovered from my shoes. I wave him off before getting the key to the house from Lavender and going inside to go to the loo, change my shoes, now that the formal stuff is over, and deposit my hat. Then, feeling a great deal better, I bounce back outside.

The game is underway, and I go to return the key to Lavender and join her on her bench, only to find that she is weeping silently but copiously into a handful of tissues.

'Are you all right?' I ask, in that idiotic way one does, to avoid the directness of *What's the matter?*

'She shakes her head and takes the tissues away for long enough to say, 'I really want to kill him.'

There is no need to ask who *he* is.

'I thought he was being relatively harmless today,' I say. 'What's he done?'

'Bringing her here!' she blurts, as tears threaten again. 'To his daughter's wedding – with the boys here – and me. It's so – insulting!'

And she buries her face in the tissues again.

'Did you know about her?' I ask.

'I found out three weeks ago, for definite. I knew something was going on – all that *working late* – and then one night he came home, and I could smell her perfume on him.'

'And he admitted it?'

'Oh yes.'

'Is she one of the lawyers? Which one is she?'

'You must have seen her. Pointy face, green dress, red hair – not her own.'

'A wig, you mean?'

'No!' She almost smiles. 'The red's not her own. Chemically assisted, I'm sure.'

I don't think I have ever heard Lavender be bitchy before, and I like it.

'She's years older than you,' I say, 'and nothing like as pretty. And I always think redheads in green are a bit obvious, don't you?'

Now she does manage a glimmer of a smile.

'Do you know how long it's been going on?' I ask.

'Since they were able to go back into their chambers last summer, after the first lockdown. I think it was revenge on me – he was breaking out from all those weeks of having Mummy and Daddy staying with us and him having to put on the perfect husband and father performance.'

'So that's over a year. Is it serious between them, do you think?'

'He says not.'

'But he's invited her to his daughter's wedding.'

'Exactly.'

'What do you want to do?'

'I want to kill him. Next best, I want a divorce.'

'And what about him?'

'He says I'm being ridiculous. That she doesn't make any

difference to our life, and we can carry on quite happily as we are. Of course that's what he wants – living in my house and spending my money while I look after his children!'

'So, he's not prepared to give her up? What's her name, by the way?'

'Bernice.' She wrinkles her nose in a way that I'm sure she learnt from her mother. *Not Our Class Dear.* Then she goes on. 'He says he can't break it off – she's so fragile and her husband doesn't understand her – she needs him to give her confidence – he makes it sound as though he's doing charity work!'

'Chutzpah is something Andrew has never been short of – or sheer, bloody, outrageous cheek. So, are you going to divorce him?'

'It's what I want, but there's the house. Daddy paid for most of the house when we got married – he joked that it was my dowry – and we've just got a small mortgage. Andrew says if we divorce, he'll be entitled to half the value of the house because he's been paying the mortgage. Daddy is absolutely furious at that idea.'

A mental image of their house presents itself to my inner eye and brings out the latent estate agent in me: *Imposing late 18th century dwelling set in extensive grounds, sympathetically improved and modernised, in immaculate decorative order.* Ellie and I like to call it *Aren't– We –Grand Hall.* The sums of money at stake here are eye-wateringly huge.

'I'm afraid it's a threat you have to take seriously,' I say. 'I got a rotten divorce settlement, and you will too, probably. He knows the best lawyers for it, and he's got a tame accountant – an old chum of his from school – who can fudge his accounts so that it looks as though he does most of his work *pro bono* and he's got hardly any income.'

'I know. So Daddy's against divorce and I've got no-one backing me up.'

'What does your father want to happen, then?'

'He wants to kill him!'

There is not much more to say after this, and soon afterwards the ball that is being used for the cricket game disappears into a thick bank of shrubs and the game has to be called off. Everyone goes into the house to clean up, and then we go in search of tea and wedding cake, being served on the lawn outside the marquee.

Those who have been on the castle tour look reasonably happy, so I feel the décor cannot be as terrible as Freda claims, and I am impressed by everyone's stamina as they stand around with their tea and cake, still finding something to talk about, and still reflexively keeping a polite distance from one another. The next stage is to be entertainment provided by young people from Annie's youth drama group. One of the ways she has tried to embed herself into her new community is helping with this group, which is attached to The Curtain, a small theatre in Perth. Perth has an impressive civic theatre of long standing, newly refurbished; The Curtain is intimate and experimental, and Annie has decided to champion it. As I am thinking about this, she comes towards me, bringing with her a young woman with a pierced eyebrow, unfestively dressed in black jeans and a black t-shirt with *Behind the Curtain* emblazoned on it.

'Isla, this is my mum,' Annie says, and then, 'Isla has brilliantly organised our entertainment, Ma.'

'You run the drama group?' I ask her.

'I do. And I'm very lucky to have Marianne to help me.'

'Except today you're on your own, I suppose – since she's been a bit busy.'

'Well, yes. My other helper is Alex. He used to be a member when he was younger, and this summer he's giving me a hand.'

'And he's been busy too.'

'Yes. Fortunately, Malcolm offered to come today.' She looks over to where a man seems to be in earnest conversation with Andrew. 'Malcolm Ross – he's the director of the theatre. He's very supportive of the youth group, and he offered to drive the minibus, which I'm really grateful for because I hate doing it.'

Malcolm Ross, I think, doesn't look like a man who drives minibuses. He is rather distinguished looking, with a thick head of wavy white hair and a matching beard. As part of the entertainment rather than a guest, he is in backstage black like Isla is, but the shirt looks as if it's silk, and if he weren't wearing sunglasses he would look exactly like a Velasquez portrait of a grandee. I'm not surprised that Andrew has sought him out for conversation.

'Tell me about the entertainment,' I say. 'Or is it to be a surprise?'

Isla and Annie look at each other. 'It's called *Something Wicked*,' Annie says, and I feel a strange fizzing in my head.

'*By the pricking of my thumbs*,' I almost whisper.

'*Something wicked this way comes*,' Annie finishes. 'Exactly.'

I can hardly believe this. We are standing in the garden of Glamis castle, and we are quoting *Macbeth*.

Isla says blithely, 'It was all the girls who wanted to do the wedding, so witches seemed the perfect theme.'

Really? This is my fault, I am sure. I went on so at Annie about the ill-advisedness of Glamis as a venue that of course she had to challenge me and my superstitions by bringing the weird sisters to the wedding. I have known Annie for thirty years – how could I not have seen this coming?

'A bold choice,' I say, smiling cheerily. 'Sounds fun. Excuse me, I must just …'

I have seen David arrive, back from his walk, and I speed over to him and grab his arm. 'Witches!' I say. 'The entertainment is all witches!'

'OK,' he says, and then looks at me properly. 'What's the problem?'

'Don't pretend to be stupid,' I hiss. 'Glamis and witches?'

'I thought we were over that,' he says. 'Nothing has gone wrong. Nobody challenged the bans. Everyone is behaving well. I'm not sure that anyone is even drunk – though Andrew is looking a bit flushed, I notice.'

'It's asking for trouble,' I say. 'Why do that? Fate doesn't need tempting – she's poised to do her worst already.'

'It's a group of kids being spooky,' he says. 'Don't get it out of proportion.'

The inside of the marquee has been reorganised, with the lunch tables and chairs arranged along either side, leaving a traverse stage space down the middle for the performers – a really tricky arrangement since the actors are bound to be side-on or with their backs to some of the audience most of the time. No doubt they would have liked to lower the marquee sides to achieve a spectral gloom, but COVID doesn't allow for that, so they have rather cleverly hung giant cobwebs along the sides, which suggest spookiness while allowing for air circulation.

We troop in, and I notice that most people have picked up a drink from the al fresco bar. I am sticking to tea. In a way I don't want to admit to, I feel I need to be alert and poised for action, though as the show gets started, I begin to relax. I was convinced that we were going to get act three of *The Crucible*, with hysterical girls screaming, '*I saw Goody Proctor with the Devil*', but it is actually quite harmless – as David said, a group of kids being spooky – a group of girls, actually, enjoying being bad and powerful. Why should I object?

It is a witches medley, with the younger girls doing bits of Roald Dahl and Harry Potter, and the older ones letting rip with songs from *The Wizard of Oz* and *Wicked*, to the accompaniment of keyboard and clarinet. The audience is mellow and indulgent, and it is all going splendidly until the finale, which is – of course – the Thane of Glamis's friends, the weird sisters. *You had to do it, didn't you, Annie?* I think. *You just couldn't resist.*

What they do isn't actually Shakespeare: they take the scene where the witches are preparing their spell and throwing newts' eyes and frogs' tongues into the pot, and they replace these ingredients with modern alternatives. The whole cast is involved, dancing round a wheelie bin, chanting their spell and throwing into it all things COVID. To give you a flavour of the thing, it runs from:

> *Jolly rainbows on the wall,*
> *Chuck them in there one and all*

to:

> *Mask from off your sweaty face,*
> *Phantom call from Track and Trace*

and:

> *Social distance, sanitiser,*
> *Jabby vaccines sent from Pfizer*

ending up with:

> *Variants from distant lands,*
> *Chuck them in and WASH YOUR HANDS!*

It is not great stuff, but the audience whoops and cheers, and there is a lot of banging on tables, so everyone is satisfied, and we all go out to replenish our glasses, while the band starts setting up for the ominous dancing ahead.

I am slightly dreading the dancing. I am fond of a ceilidh, where everyone galumphs around, getting it wrong and laughing happily, but this will be Scottish dancing. In Scotland. With kilts. I can see already that the kilted brigade are slipping off to their cars to change into their special dancing shoes, and while the English galumph flat-footedly, they will be leaping nimbly on their toes. People are not just collecting glasses, I notice, but taking bottles away with them. It does not bode well, but I get myself a large gin and tonic, and resolve to galumph with the best of them.

David does not dance. Like most Englishmen, he finds dancing acutely embarrassing, and I see no reason to force him onto the floor. Instead, I grab partners wherever I can find them – male or female, although this outrages some of our kilted friends – and throw myself into the fray, coming back to our table between bouts for refreshment. On my third or fourth break, I find David on his feet, staring into the corner of the marquee. This is where Andrew and his legal team have been sitting, but I see that most of them have melted away and Andrew is on his feet, confronting a tall, thin man, quite a bit younger than him, but made fogeyish by severely sleeked hair *a la* Jacob Rees-Mogg. Andrew and the JRM lookalike are shouting at each other, and Andrew's redheaded woman – Bernice – is hunched in her seat with her hands over her face. Then, as we watch, they start to fight.

Fight may be not quite the right word. I suspect that neither of them has been in a fight since they were at prep school, and it reminds me of the kind of fights that we girls used to have – all pushing and shoving and tugging at one another's clothes (we used to pull each other's hair, too, but the men's hair is less accessible). David says, 'I'd better deal with it,' and starts to make his way round the dancers. I follow because it might be fun.

David, I have to say, is brilliant. He must, I suppose, have broken up fights as a young policeman, but in his distinguished career as a detective in the Met he can't have done it for quite a while. Nevertheless, he doesn't flinch. He speaks, without shouting, as soon as he is close enough to be heard.

'Take your hands off each other,' he says, 'or I shall arrest you for causing an affray, and you'll want to think what that may do for your legal careers.'

They let each other go with very little reluctance, and I suspect that they are actually relieved. Neither of them wanted – or knew how to – deliver a killer punch, so they must both have been wondering how to get themselves out of this with some shreds of dignity. The JRM type straightens his jacket, glares at everyone and dives out of the nearest tent exit, fighting off the floating stage cobwebs as he goes. The redhead runs after him, calling, 'Henry, wait!' and Andrew stares round the marquee as if he is trying to assess how many people have noticed that their host has been in a brawl with one of the guests. He takes a step forward, as if he intends to mingle with the dancing throng, but he pitches forward and nearly falls, except David catches him.

'He's completely pie-eyed,' he says, not letting him go. 'We need to get him back to the house. Where's Lavender, do you know?'

'She didn't stay for the dancing. She took the boys back. She's babysitting.'

'Well, she can babysit him too,' he says, and getting a firm grip on one arm, he propels him outside.

I follow. Well, he did say, 'We need to get him back to the house', so I assume he thinks I can be useful, and the prospect of watching my part-time lover managing my sozzled ex-husband is, frankly, irresistible.

Outside, Andrew starts to struggle once the surprise of his capture subsides, but David has him in a very professional-looking armlock and marches him along at some speed, while I skip along beside them, feeling the dew seeping into my little dancing shoes. It is completely dark outside now, but the path across the grass towards our lodgings is marked by fairy lights, and David and I both get our phone torches on. Andrew is making quite a lot of noise, swearing fluently, if repetitively, and uttering threats of various kinds, so it is not until we get to the garden in front of our house that I realise that there is a group of people in front of us. I shine my torch ahead and can pick out the figures. It is our acting troupe, led by Isla and Malcolm Ross, and they are heading, I suppose, for their minibus, which will be waiting in the car park near our house.

I don't know whether this was a planned exit – it is ten-thirty by now, after all – or whether the adults spotted a potential brawl and hustled the kids out ahead of trouble, but I feel I should speak to them anyway. Brandishing my torch, I run ahead.

'Just wanted to say thank you so much for the performance,' I call.

The kids stop and shuffle a bit, Isla calls, 'Thanks. We really enjoyed it,' and gives me a wave before ushering them on their way, but Malcolm Ross comes back to meet us, catching a glimpse of Andrew before David marches him towards our front door.

'Emotional thing, marrying off a daughter,' he says, tactfully. 'Do tell him how much we all enjoyed ourselves, and thank him for his hospitality.'

'I will,' I say. Andrew won't welcome any reminder that he was not in a fit state to receive his guests' thanks at the end of the evening, but that will make passing on the thanks all the more fun.

David is standing at the door, waiting for me. 'Do you have a key?' he asks. 'Lavender may be in bed.'

I don't have a key. We were given three: Lavender took one so that she could bring the boys back when necessary, Annie took one because it is her wedding and she might want to do running repairs, and Andrew took one because he is Andrew, and he is paying.

'He will have a key,' I say, 'in his sporran, I suppose.'

And then, because the picture of David holding Andrew up while I scrabble around in his sporran strikes me as so wonderfully absurd, and I have had quite a bit to drink myself, I start to giggle.

'Gina!' David growls. 'I can't hold him much longer.'

'If Lavender is in bed, she's going to be disturbed by him arriving anyway,' I say, pulling myself together, and I ring the bell.

Lavender opens the door. She has changed out of her flowery dress into an equally flowery dressing gown, and she has bare feet, but I can hear the television burbling from the sitting room, so she was obviously not in bed. The most obvious thing about her, though, is that she has been crying.

David is brisk. 'He's a bit the worse for wear, I'm afraid,' he says. 'We'll just get him up to bed.'

There's that *we* again, and this time I am needed. The stairs are not wide enough to go two abreast, so David starts up them, yanking Andrew by his imprisoned arm and calling to me, 'Keep pushing from behind.'

So there we go, with David tugging and exhorting, and me shoving at Andrew's kilted buttocks. I could start giggling again but the pushing is taking up all my energy. Lavender, without saying a word, has gone back to the television.

We get him to the top, though there is an alarming moment when I think that both David and he are going to fall back on top of me, and we land him on the bed in their room, which is just to the left at the top of the stairs. There David takes his shoes off and I go and get him a glass of water from the bathroom.

'We should try to get his jacket off,' I say, and between us we roll him over and peel it off. While he is on his front, I loosen the back fastening of the frilly jabot he is wearing. All this stuff is hired, and God knows what state it will be in when it is returned, but I guess hirers are used to that.

Outside, on the landing, I say, 'Shall we call it a day? You don't want to dance anyway, and I think I've had it.'

David glances back at Andrew's room. 'Someone ought to be there to see the guests off,' he says, 'since we've lost the host.'

'Well it's not my job,' I protest. 'This whole thing wasn't my idea. I don't see—'

'I think I should go back,' he says. 'Just see everyone off safely. You can stay here.'

'Once a policeman…' I say. 'You have a pathologically overdeveloped sense of duty; do you know that?'

'You have mentioned it once or twice.'

'Well, go on then,' I say. 'But do me a favour – slip out without seeing Lavender. I don't want her to know I'm still here. I can't face another heart-to-heart tonight.'

In my room, I follow Lavender's example and strip off my dress and tights – whoever decided that women were to be punished by wearing these sodding things? Then I wrap myself in my dressing gown, make a cup of tea, and turn on the television. I don't bother to surf channels. There is some sort of sports discussion going on. There is nothing more boring than people talking about sport, but it is noise, and that is all I need to crowd out the noise in my head – the babel of voices from a day with too many people in it. I swig my tea, lean back and close my eyes.

Some time later I am stirred from my half doze by the sound of voices right outside on the landing. I open my door, and there they all are, still fizzing with the energy of the day – Annie and Jon on their way to their 'penthouse' suite on the floor above, Ellie and Ben heading down to the bedroom at the end of the landing to check on Nico, and Freda, dizzy with dancing and social success, and – possibly – love. There is no sign of David, though.

'Someone's taxi didn't turn up,' Ellie says. 'He's sorting it out.'

Oh David, do you have to be such a bloody boy scout?

I am not waiting up for him any longer. I take an unsatisfactory shower – the water pressure seems to be down – and then get into bed, switch off the light, and pick up the remote to turn off the television.

It is just as that noise fades that I hear Lavender begin to scream.

Chapter Five

HORROR, HORROR, HORROR

'David, can you come back? Now.'

As soon as Gina's call summoned him, David Scott knew two things: one was that only something deadly serious would have produced the wobble he heard in her voice, and the other was that whatever mess the Grays had got themselves into, he was going to be expected to sort it out. He made an abrupt farewell to the last couple who were still standing forlornly waiting for their taxi, and started to sprint across the grass in the direction of the house. As he ran, his mind whirled with possibilities. *Probably Andrew*, he thought, although he had been pretty nearly comatose an hour before. A fight with Lavender? She had obviously been crying when she had opened the door to them, and she didn't look as though she had much fight in her. Choked on vomit? He didn't think so – he and Gina had left him lying on his side – he ought to have been all right. As he neared the house and saw it loom in the darkness, his heart lurched. *One of the boys? Wandered off while Lavender was sunk in her misery? Please let it not be one of the boys.*

The front door was yanked opened as he reached for the bell. Gina was standing inside, wrapped in a dressing gown.

'Upstairs,' she said.

As they crossed the hall, he was aware of muted murmurs coming from the sitting room. Gina was dragging him to the staircase, but he glimpsed in passing the most bizarre of sights – the entire Gray family, it seemed, sitting round the room like patients in a dentist's waiting room, and virtually silent. He followed Gina up the stairs, turning left at the top, and into Andrew's room, where a dim bedside lamp was burning. Wordlessly she pointed at the bed.

'Turn the main light on,' he said.

In the sudden glare, he looked at the man on the bed. He was lying on his back now, but there was no sign or smell of vomit. Instead, there was a stream of blood down the right side of his face, starting from the eye socket, from which protruded the decorative handle of a small knife. He checked for a pulse, knowing he would find none.

'What happened?' he asked.

'I don't know. Nobody knows. Lavender found him when she came up to bed.'

He was automatically scanning the room for evidence. *No signs of disturbance. Not a fight. Doesn't look like a robbery. Has anyone touched anything?*

'How long ago?'

'I called you almost right away – so, less than ten minutes.'

'Has anyone else been in the room?'

'No. Only Lavender. I was the first to get here when she screamed. I kept everyone out.'

'Good. And you've rung the police?'

'I rang you.'

'I can't do anything. You know that. '

'I thought you'd know what to do.'

'I do. I'm calling 999. Come out of here now. I'm locking the door.'

He took the key from the inside of the door and locked it behind him. 'I'll ring from our room,' he said.

'Can I come?'

'It's your room too.'

She followed him into their room and slumped onto the bed. She looked small, bewildered, and somehow defeated. He had never seen her at a loss before, and it was unnerving. He dialled and asked for the police. It was odd to be a caller. He had listened to many recorded 999 calls – people always in a state of shock and fear. He considered giving his rank to the officer who answered, but decided that that could wait until later.

'My name is David Scott. We are a family party staying at the guest house in the grounds of Glamis Castle. One of our number has been stabbed. Killed.'

'And is anyone else injured?'

'No.'

'Is the assailant still armed?'

'Not as far as we know. The knife is still in the wound.'

'I see. Were you present when the incident occurred, sir?'

'No. He was alone. In bed.'

'I see,' he said again, although Scott doubted whether he did. 'What we'll do is, we'll send a couple of officers out to take a look at the scene. Where exactly are you?'

'The guest house for the castle. We've had a wedding there today. The house is adjacent to the castle car park.'

'Our officers should be with you in about twenty minutes. Please make sure that nobody interferes with the scene.'

Scott rang off and paced the room. He knew how it would go. A couple of uniformed constables would turn up, ask the same questions as he had just answered, possibly tape up the bedroom door, and put in a call for CID officers. With a murder like this, response would be fairly rapid, and they wouldn't wait till the morning, but all the same there was going to be a wearing night ahead, with everyone shocked and exhausted, and nobody able to go to bed. He thought he had seen Freda in the family group downstairs. Surely she, at least, could go to bed?

He looked at Gina. If anyone was going to take charge, it would surely be her, but she didn't look ready to do anything.

'I can't conduct the investigation, obviously, and the local police may not want me involved in any way, except as a fairly peripheral witness, but I might be able to be useful in setting the scene for them – it could save time. Can you pull yourself together and tell me exactly what happened after I left you here – up to the point when you phoned me?'

She looked round vaguely. 'Someone found a miniature of brandy in their minibar and gave it to Lavender. Do you think we've got one? I haven't even located the minibar.'

'Over there. Under the tea and coffee things. You're sure you wouldn't rather have tea?'

'Quite sure.'

He found the brandy, and was looking for a glass when she stretched out an arm.

'Give it here,' she said. 'Desperate times and desperate woman.' She twisted off the lid, took a long swig, coughed, and sat up straight.

'I'm ready,' she said.

'So, tell me exactly what happened after I left you to go back to the party.'

'I took off my wedding finery, made a cup of tea, and turned on the television. As it's Saturday night, it was sport, and I fell asleep.'

'You didn't hear anyone come upstairs?'

'Not until the family arrived and came crashing upstairs and woke me up.'

'What time was that?'

'A bit after eleven-thirty. I looked at my watch because I wondered if you were ever coming back.'

'And when you say *the family*, who do you mean?'

'All of them – Annie and Jon, Ellie and Ben, and Freda.'

'What about Lavender?'

'She didn't come up with them. I suppose she was still downstairs.'

'And everyone went to their rooms at that point? Remind me where everyone's sleeping.'

'Well, no-one's sleeping anywhere at the moment, are they?'

'You know what I mean.'

'All three boys are in the room down at the end. They asked to go in together – luckily because they actually slept through all the rumpus. Otherwise, they would have been next door to the scene of the crime. As it is, Freda is supposed to be in that room, Annie and Jon are upstairs, and Ellie and Ben are next door to us.'

'And you didn't hear anyone else come upstairs until the family came up?'

She gave him a long look. 'Yes, Detective Superintendent, as a matter of fact I heard someone creeping up the stairs, and I could tell by the way they were walking that they were carrying a dagger. Then I heard them go into Andrew's room, and after that the cry of a man being stabbed, before running footsteps back down the stairs. But I didn't think anything of it – just a joke I thought – and I went back to sleep. Is that what you wanted me to say?'

He allowed a pause, and then he said, 'I can't warn you strongly enough not to be sarcastic with the local police. It never goes down well, and it will go particularly badly coming from a snotty English woman. What happened after everyone went to their rooms?'

'I went and had a shower and got into bed. I'd given up on you. I was just turning off the lights and the television when I heard Lavender scream.'

'And how long was that after the others went to bed?'

'It was a quick shower. Less than fifteen minutes.'

He stood looking at her, and at what she was wearing. 'Is that what you put on when you took your dress off?'

'Yes. Why?'

He went across to the wardrobe, felt around among the spare blankets and pulled out a large plastic bag stamped with the details of a twenty-four-hour laundry service.

'It's going to be a long night, and you're probably going to want to put some clothes on.'

'When we have our naked frailties hid,' she said.

'What?'

'I'm quoting Macbeth – we've had the bad luck now, so why not?'

He pressed on. 'When you take off your night things, put them in here – and your wedding clothes.'

He passed her the laundry bag.

'Why? What for?'

'And Lavender should do the same. The police will want them for forensics.'

'Why? Why us two particularly?'

Was she being deliberately obtuse?

'Means, motive, opportunity. Hasn't it dawned on you that you and Lavender will be the prime suspects?'

'Oh come on! I can see that we had the opportunity, but it's years since I've felt like killing Andrew – and as for means, neither of us is in the habit of carrying a dagger.'

'You wouldn't need to. It was already there. Andrew provided it. Didn't you recognise it? It's a *skien du*. A highland dagger. It's the one he was wearing all day, tucked into one of his socks.'

Chapter Six

O, BY WHOM?

'OH MY GOD! OH MY ACTUAL GOD!'

Mia was gratifyingly impressed by Freda's news, especially considering that it was seven-thirty in the morning.

'Actually murdered? For real?'

'For real,' Freda said. 'He was – I'm not supposed to know, but Lavender let it slip – he was stabbed.'

'Oh God, Fre. That's horrible. Poor you. Are you all right?'

'Well, I didn't really like him much, and he didn't like me, so I'm not, like, heartbroken, but it all feels weird.'

'How can you not like your grandpa? I'd be in bits if mine died.'

'I know. It's just – you know, he's got – had – these little kids with Lavender, and I don't think he really liked being a grandfather, so…'

She stopped and thought. 'The thing is, I don't think anyone is really upset. They're all shocked, and we've been up all night being questioned by the police and stuff, so maybe it hasn't sunk in, but nobody's cried – except Lavender when she first found him. But the boys don't know yet – they were allowed to sleep – and I suppose they'll be upset.'

'The police questioned you *all night?*'

'They said the house was a crime scene and we all had to get out so the SOCOs could come in and investigate. SOCOs are – '

'Duh! I know what SOCOs are, Fre – Scene Of Crime Officers – I watch just as many crime dramas as you do.'

'OK. So we weren't allowed to take anything with us, and they brought in two mobile crime units – like vans – and we all had to wait in one and then go and be questioned one at a time in the other one. We had two policewomen with us all the time, so we hardly said anything because Granny sent a message round warning us that they were probably recording us. And even if they weren't, they were listening anyway. That was almost the weirdest thing – my family not talking.'

'What about when they questioned you? Was that scary?'

'It was all right. Except I misunderstood where they were going with the questions. They started asking about Grandpa, and whether he hugged and cuddled us a lot, and I didn't want to say he didn't like us much because, you know, *speaking ill of the dead* and all that, so I said, *Oh yes, he was like grandparents are*, and then they started asking whether he ever did anything *inappropriate*. I felt like saying, *Well, he once got someone to steal his dog*, but I knew what they meant, of course.'

'Like sex?'

'Yes. I think they were looking for motives and the only motive they could think of for me was if he had been like groping me or whatever.'

'Gross!'

'So then I had to switch and say that now I was grown up he didn't do hugs any more, but it was all a bit awkward.'

'But they don't really think one of his family killed him, do they?'

Freda didn't answer immediately. She moved a little further along the hedge behind which she had been sheltering to make her call.

'Fre? Do they?' Mia prompted.

Freda answered slowly. 'After we had all been questioned, they sent us off to spend the rest of the night in the marquee where the wedding happened,' she said. 'They gave us blankets – those red ones – so we look as though we're survivors from a disaster. Anyway, then we didn't have police with us – just someone on guard outside – they let me out to make this call. So, we were able to start talking. And it was all about keys. The house has a yale lock on the door, so it locks automatically, and we had three keys. Lavender had one, Auntie Annie had one, and she let us all into the house after the wedding, and Grandpa had one, so the point is, no-one can see how anybody else could have got into the house. So unless the SOCOs find obvious evidence that somebody else got into the house, you can see what the police think, can't you?'

'They think one of you killed him? OMG, Fre. OMG!'

Freda allowed Mia a few more *OMGs* and then gently detached herself. She could see David striding across the grass, and he was waving at her.

'There you are,' he said. 'Your mum was getting a bit anxious.'

'You mean she was going into panic overdrive, don't you?'

'Sort of. The boys are awake now, so she and Lavender have gone to the house to break the news. The SOCOs have nearly finished there, so we'll be allowed back in soon.

'What about… you know…?'

'Your grandpa? It's all right. They've taken him away.'

'So what happens now?'

'The police will let us know if we can leave. Most of us were planning to spend tonight here anyway, weren't we? Lavender has rung Andrew's brother, and he's driving up today. He'll take her and the boys home if the police are happy to let her go. I think there may be more interviews today but with any luck we can all go our various ways tomorrow.'

'So you think we'll still be able to go to Orkney?'

'I should think so.'

'Whoopee,' she said. 'Back to the Stone Age. My best thing.'

He laughed. 'Don't forget, archaeology is my hobby. You won't get any sympathy from me.'

'Is there going to be any breakfast, do you think?' she asked. 'Or is everyone too traumatised?'

'I'm doing that. I'm told there's a baker in the village who opens at eight, even on Sundays. I'm off there now to see what they've got. Do you want to come?'

She looked down at herself. 'I'm wearing pyjamas.'

'We'll call in at the house. I think they'll let you put on a pair of jeans.'

He was the most reassuring person, she thought, and wondered not for the first time why the hell Granny hadn't married him years ago.

Chapter Seven

WHAT WILL YOU DO?

So, this is how things stand. The police interview us all again – the same questions, hoping for different answers, I suppose. We are probably even less coherent second time around, since we have had no sleep and the adrenaline of shock has drained away, but eventually they tell us we are free to go – except we are not free to leave the country (by this they mean the UK, you understand, not Scotland) and they would like us to leave an address at which they can contact us. So not free, really.

We all had plans, mostly involving staying in Scotland, since we were coming this far and real foreign travel is still looking problematic. Now we can either go home and lie down in a darkened room or give ourselves a good shake and pick up the plans. Apart from Lavender, for whom life has been turned inside out, the rest of us opt for carrying on. Lavender and her boys are being carried off to his Oxfordshire farm by her brother-in-law, Charles, where she will have TLC, home-made cakes, and horses to comfort her; Annie and Jon will go off to honeymoon on Skye; Ellie, Ben and Nico are going in pursuit of the Stone Age on Orkney. But not Freda. Freda has other plans, but I will leave it to her to tell you about them. As for me, I had persuaded David to spend a few days in Pitlochry, a small town not far from here with a beautiful loch-side theatre, which this summer has an open-air performance space where I was looking forward to watching real-life actors actually physically in front of me for the first time in a year and a half. I am still going to do that, but David will not be with me. He has somehow negotiated his way into the murder investigation, and will be pursuing inquiries, on behalf of Police Scotland, in London and Kent. The wedding guests have all been allowed to go home, after giving statements, but the reasoning goes that if Andrew was not killed by one of his nearest and dearest, then it is more likely than not that he was killed by someone who knew him – someone close to home.

I shall stay in a luxurious hotel in a room with a balcony overlooking the loch, and I shall imagine myself to be enigmatic and mysterious, like the heroine of *Hotel du Lac*. Watch this space. I shall also be questioned by the police again, I have no doubt. They have me in their sights, just as David warned me. I have followed his advice in the interviews so far – avoided irony, made no jokes, have not been at all clever in any way – but they still ooze suspicion. And, quite unfairly, they seem to suspect me more than they do Lavender. Of course, we both had the opportunity – nearly an hour on our own in the house with him, I upstairs and she down. She claims to have been watching television, I claim to have been asleep. Neither of us has a witness, of course. Where Lavender scores is that she is so winsome, and I so very much am not.

They do know about Andrew's fight with Bernice's husband, and the likely reason for it. David will have told them about that, and you would think that that would foreground Lavender in the role of wronged wife rather than me, still nursing a grudge about our divorce two decades ago. Revenge may be a dish best served cold, but after twenty years wouldn't it just be crawling with maggots?

Actually, I can see that I might have been moved to murder yesterday, though I don't believe that anyone else would be able to imagine why. Except David perhaps. David knows that I feel responsible for Lavender, that I blame myself for cutting and running when I realised that Andrew had no idea how to be a husband, that it is my fault that he learnt nothing from marriage to me except to look for a more compliant, less demanding wife second time around. Given the guilt and Lavender's misery and the embarrassing fight with his mistress's husband and the emotions of the day and the amount of alcohol I had consumed, I suppose I could have done it. Knowing that he was lying in a stupor almost next door, with a convenient dagger stuck into his sock, I could have slipped in and done it, couldn't I? I am not an experienced killer, but I do happen to know that Christopher Marlowe, Shakespeare's more successful contemporary, had his promising life cut short, in what may or may not have been a drunken argument, by a single stab wound *above the right eye*.

I could have done it but people like us don't do that sort of thing, do we? All the same, I think I won't mention Kit Marlowe to my inquisitors.

Chapter Eight

MOST KIND HOSTESS

WhatsApp We Three
Lisa, Mia, Me
It's official Girls, there is a God!
No Orkney ruins. Staying here
IN GORGEOUS ALEX'S HOUSE!!!
Ring for lowdown!
☺!! XX

It had been, she thought, like something out of Jane Austen. Well, not so much the fact that they had all been lounging about outside the house eating a picnic lunch – mainly because, although no-one admitted it, none of them felt comfortable inside the house any more. The Jane Austen bit was Alex arriving with his mother, both of them so formally dressed that she wasn't sure whether it was because they were coming to a house of mourning or because they had been to church. By contrast, she and the rest of the family were mostly in jeans and T-shirts since holiday clothes were all they had with them and, sprawling on the grass as they were, they hardly looked as though they were in mourning at all, and had very obviously not been to church.

Aileen McCleod hadn't been fazed, though. She had walked towards them in her neat navy-blue suit, said, 'No, no, please don't get up,' as Mum started to push herself to her feet, and then sat down neatly on a corner of the picnic rug.

'Don't let us disturb you. You must have had a terrible night,' she said. 'Alex and I just wanted to say how very sorry we all were to hear such terrible news, and to see if we can do anything at all to help.'

Alex (in smart trousers, a grey shirt – and even a tie) sat down on the grass near Freda, since there was no more room on the rug. He gave her a smile, and for a brief, dreadful moment, she thought she might cry.

From an area to the side of the house came the sounds of the boys arguing, and Ben attempting conflict resolution. The scattered ruins of their lunch lay all over the rug, but at least they weren't here creating mayhem. Freda looked round the family group and tried to see it as the visitors would see it – Jon sitting back on his heels with Auntie Annie lying down, leaning against him with her eyes closed, Mum sitting hugging her knees, her face hidden by her big sunglasses, Granny, wild-haired, sitting with her legs stuck out in front of her, eating a strawberry. David was somewhere behind the hedge, talking on his phone – police business, she assumed. And she herself? How would they be seeing her? She wished she had had a chance to wash her hair, which was looking weird, she knew, from being in a topknot all day yesterday, and she knew how her face went when she was tired – pale and pointy looking – so really she couldn't have looked less attractive. Hearing her name, she tuned back into the conversation. Aileen McCleod was talking.

'... all your plans up in the air. Do you have any idea when the police will let you go on your way?'

'We don't. Soon, we hope, but there are no guarantees. It sounds ridiculous, I know, but the way things are, we seem to be the main suspects.'

Freda watched her mother as she said this, and saw how close to tears she was, in spite of the sunglasses.

'Well,' Aileen McCleod said, giving a look at Alex, 'We are here with a suggestion – just a suggestion – you must say no if you don't like the idea.' Here she glanced at Freda. 'But Alex is helping to run a week-long course at the theatre in Perth this week, and we know how much you all love the theatre, so we just wondered whether Freda would like to join the course. Marianne knows all about the young people's theatre group of course, so she can tell you it is very well run. She would be most welcome to stay the week with us and drive in with Alex each day.'

Some strange fizzing thing was going on in her head, Freda realised, and her heart seemed to have forgotten how to beat in any sort of steady rhythm, so she lost the opportunity to speak first, and by the time she was ready her mother was speaking.

'Oh, that's very kind,' she was saying, 'but we really hope to be away in a day or two, and we'll be off on our family holiday up to Orkney. We're all looking forward to it so much, spending the time together.'

Why did she do this? This *as a family* thing, always banging on about it? It was so annoying – especially when they had been stuck together for all those lockdown months, and had been, if Mum would only be honest, pretty sick of the sight of each other.

'Of course,' Aileen McCleod was saying, 'I wouldn't want to interfere with your holiday, and I do hope you're able to go and enjoy Orkney together. It was just an idea, in case you get delayed too long. You'll have ferry bookings and accommodation and so on. It may be difficult to postpone.'

Freda knew she had to speak now or lose her chance. She opened her mouth without knowing what was going to come out of it.

'I never wanted to go to Orkney,' she heard herself saying, and then stopped. She sounded like a whiney child. *Think Jane Austen*, she told herself. 'What I mean is,' she went on, 'the Orkney trip is for Nico really, because he loves the idea of the Stone Age sites. And I very much hope he will be able to go and won't be disappointed, but speaking honestly, I think he will enjoy himself more if he has his parents' full attention. I love history but I'm afraid I'm not terribly interested in the Stone Age, and I don't want to spoil things.' Here she thought she could be disarming with a bit of self-criticism. 'I must admit that when I'm bored, I'm not very good at hiding it.'

She looked from her mother to Aileen McCleod. 'So, I think it's a brilliant offer, and I would really like to accept, even if the rest of the family do go to Orkney.'

There was a silence. Alex was looking at his mother, who was looking at Mum, who had taken off her sunglasses and was looking at Freda. Freda looked at her grandmother. Eventually, her mother spoke.

'Well,' she said, putting her sunglasses back on and looking at Aileen McCleod, 'it seems there's nothing more to be said. You'd better take her.'

It was so rude that Freda almost gasped. She watched the reactions of the others. She thought she heard a little gasp from Aileen McCleod, Auntie Annie sat up and said, 'Ellie!', Jon and Alex exchanged a look which was just short of eye rolling, and her grandmother got to her feet as though she was ready to drag Mum off in disgrace.

Her mother looked round at them all, then seemed to sag. 'I'm sorry,' she said. 'I didn't mean – I'm sure she'll have a' and then she burst into tears.

Oh for God's sake. Why did her family have to be like this? Now, here, in front of Alex and his mother? Freda put her head down and started to rub at a stain she had suddenly discovered on the knee of her jeans, while she listened to the chorus – Auntie Annie saying, 'Do pull yourself together, El', Aileen McCleod saying, 'Oh my dear, the last thing we want to do is to upset you', and Granny – bless her – saying, 'I'm going to put the kettle on. We could all do with a cup of tea, I think. Freda, come and give me a hand.'

Freda jumped up and followed her. As they went inside, her grandmother gave her a gentle push towards the stairs. 'I'm giving you cover,' she said. 'Get your things together and make a quick getaway as soon as they've swigged their tea. Your mum will be fine once you've gone. She's just… you know …'

'Crazy?' Freda suggested.

'Her father's been murdered. He wasn't much of a father, but he was the only one she had. She's entitled to be a bit crazy.'

The thought came to Freda, not for the first time, that Granny was kinder about Mum than Mum was about her. Maybe that was always the case. Were parents always more forgiving about their children than the other way round? It made sense. Parents brought the children up, after all. If children had faults, then weren't their parents responsible – at least partly? So, admitting that your children were hopeless was admitting that you had been a hopeless parent. Really, why did anyone ever want to be a parent?

It was an effort to go back into her bedroom, seeing the police tapes still there on the door next to hers, and she swept up her belongings as quickly as she could. Most of her stuff had remained in her bag, so it was really just her night things and wash bag, her book and phone, and the bits and pieces on the dressing table. She wondered if Mum would give her any money. She and Nico usually got spending money on holidays, but none had been distributed yet. If Mum didn't offer, she would ask Ben. It would be embarrassing not to be able to pay for anything.

She took a last look round and then hauled her bag downstairs. Outside, the scene had changed. The boys were back, and Granny was distributing cartons of juice and biscuits to them. The adults all had mugs of tea, and David was talking with Auntie Annie, Mum and Aileen McCleod, while Ben, Jon and Alex were having some sort of male conversation where it was safe to assume that nobody would cry. Alex saw her and came over to take her bag.

'I wasn't sure if you'd gone to ground somewhere,' he said quietly.

'I am so sorry about the fuss,' she said. 'I would say, *We aren't always like this*, but I'm afraid we are.'

He laughed. 'I'm sure you're not,' he said. 'Not you, anyway. And you are entitled to some fuss. These are exceptional circumstances.'

'Yes,' she said. *Let him think that if he wants to*, she thought.

Departing was actually quite easy. A few brief hugs and promises to phone, and they were off to the car park, where they got into Aileen's blue Suzuki. Freda was surprised to see Alex get into the driver's seat, and Aileen caught her expression and laughed. 'It's all right,' she said, 'he's just passed his test. I'm lending him the car this coming week, so he'll be able to drive you into Perth and back.'

She got into the passenger seat, and Freda settled in the back, enjoying the smell of clean leather and fresh air. This was a car where nobody had left sweaty trainers lying around, or eaten a burger, or had even, she was prepared to bet, ever opened a bag of cheese and onion crisps.

She watched the countryside a bit, but mainly she watched Alex – the way his hands were relaxed on the steering wheel, and the way he occasionally caught her eye in his mirror and smiled. Next week he would be driving her to the theatre. She would be sitting beside him. He wasn't going to be her boyfriend, she knew that. He liked her, but not in that way, and she was pretty sure that Aileen (as she had now been invited to call her) would have reminded him that she was only just fifteen. Still, driving to and fro with him like that, she could dream, couldn't she? And for a moment she felt a thrill of happiness so powerful that she thought she would probably never be so happy again.

Chapter Nine

I'LL TO ENGLAND

The interminable drive down to London gave David plenty of time to mull over the case and his part in the investigation. It had been a neat piece of sleight of hand from the Scottish police to delegate the English side to him because, actually, that left them very little to do. The only obvious suspect they now had on their patch was Gina, stubbornly pursuing her holiday in Pitlochry although the theatre was closed, he had defected, and the police were breathing down her neck.

He had tried to warn her – but he did not believe she had taken in – how much the local police would like her to be the killer. However you looked at it, it was the case that she and Lavender were the obvious suspects. Both of them felt wronged by Andrew, and both of them had been in the house with him at the crucial time. Both of them knew he had the skien du in his sock, and it required relatively little strength to drive that into the eye socket of a stupefied man. You had to know what you were doing, but you only had to have read a few thrillers to get the idea. Lavender, of course, had a much stronger motive – Andrew had brought his mistress to the wedding and had been involved in a very public quarrel over her. The police knew that, but Lavender had looked so young and helpless, weeping gently, and never letting her voice rise above a whisper. Gina, on the other hand, did not weep or whisper. Even if she had heeded his urgent warnings about not antagonising the police, she would probably still have come over as hardboiled and unforgiving. Of course they would like to pin it on her.

They were more or less discounting the likelihood of the killer being local, on the grounds that none of the Scottish guests was known to Andrew before the wedding day. Even the McCleod family had met him for the first time the evening before. But playing devil's advocate, he argued to himself that the crime showed every sign of not being premeditated: the knife was not the murderer's own, and no-one could have predicted that Andrew would get into a drunken fight, and then need to be put to bed insensible. Any Scot would have known about the dagger as an adjunct to highland dress, he supposed, but they couldn't have known that there would be an opportunity to use it. So, had Andrew so infuriated someone in the course of the day that they were driven to kill him? He barely knew Andrew at all, had met him a couple of times at family birthdays. He didn't care for him, and Gina, of course, painted him as intolerable in every way, but nobody murdered a sleeping man like that unless he had done them serious damage, or was likely to.

Seeing signs to a service station, he turned off and went in for a cup of coffee. The murder was front page news in the Scottish papers, he saw, as he passed the news stand – *ENGLISH LAWYER STABBED AT DAUGHTER'S WEDDING: MURDER AT GLAMIS CASTLE*. Sitting with his coffee, he continued his reflections.

Of course, Andrew had upset several people on that day. He had invited Bernice Stafford to the wedding, after all, humiliating not only Lavender but Henry Stafford, the husband, as well. Stafford had insisted in his police interview that he had known about Bernice's affair with Andrew, and they were *working through it*, but that wasn't how it had looked when the two men were tussling with each other. Henry Stafford was, in many ways, a more likely killer than Lavender, and though he had alibis from several people who had seen him after Andrew had been taken away, and he returned to the party, the only person who claimed to have been with him the whole time in the following hour was his wife. She herself was a puzzle – unnaturally calm and self-possessed for a woman whose lover had just been murdered – though that could have been shock, of course. The two of them were at the top of his list of interviewees as soon as they were all back in London.

In the car and driving again, he turned his mind to keys. If someone outside the family killed Andrew, how did they get into the house? Not through the front door, he was pretty certain. He himself had slammed that door behind him as he left the house after depositing Andrew, and it seemed impossible that an outsider could have got hold of one of the keys. Andrew's key was still in his sporran, and Annie's key, as it happened, was in Jon's pocket, put there by her for safekeeping since brides don't carry handbags. Lavender had let herself into the house with her key when she returned to put the boys to bed, and produced it from her bag. In the morning, as they left for the ceremony, he had made it his job to check security, on the grounds that the Grays were a scatty crowd at the best of times, without the excuse of a wedding to think about. He was sure he caught Gina rolling her eyes as he made sure all the windows were closed and the ground floor ones locked, but he had ignored it and gone on to check that the back door was locked and the key in the lock inside. He was the last to leave the house through the front door, and he had slammed it shut. Both Annie and Lavender had used their keys in the course of the day, and Gina had borrowed

Lavender's key at one point, but Lavender was sure that the door was locked when she went in with the boys in the evening. And anyway, even supposing that the door had been left open or on the latch earlier in the day, it made no sense to think of someone going in and hiding there, waiting to murder. They couldn't have anticipated the opportunity arising as it did.

The puzzle was the back door. He had left it secure in the morning, but the SOCOs had found it unlocked, with the key still in the lock on the inside. Lavender insisted that she had not opened it on any of her visits to the house during the day, but she might have forgotten, or one of the boys might have opened it. As it stood, it looked as though this might have been the killer's route out, but his route in remained a mystery.

Unless, he thought. Unless somebody let the killer in. A picture formed in his mind of Lavender, tear-stained and rather drunk, opening the front door to Gina and him as they propped Andrew up on the threshold. He couldn't see Lavender as the killer, but could he see her as encouraging a willing man to be her champion? He could, he thought. She was a woman who expected the world to work in her favour, and when it didn't, she expected a man – father, brother, husband or gentlemanly volunteer – to put it right for her. That idea took him down to Kent, to her family. James Mitchell, the SIO on the case, had made it clear that he wanted to delegate the Kent end of the investigation – envisaging nothing more than routine interviews mainly with Annie's old school friends, who looked unlikely suspects. Lavender's family had not been guests at the wedding, of course, but he wondered...

And it was just as he was thinking this that his phone rang. The number was unfamiliar, but he decided to answer.

'Scott.'

'You still answer the way you always did, boss.'

The voice was a woman's, relatively young, and for a moment he could not place it. Then he said, 'Paula?'

'The very same. DI Paula Powell, Detective Super.'

'Are you handling the Kent end of the Andrew Gray case?'

'I am.'

'Great. That should make things easy. And I can concentrate on the London wedding guests while you cover the Marlbury ones.'

As he said this, it occurred to him that it might not be easy at all. Paula Powell had been in his team when she was a young DC – stroppy and hyper-alert for signs of misogyny from her male colleagues, but a promising officer. She had done well, and ought to be easy to work with, but there was bad blood between her and Gina which he had never really understood. Paula had been SIO on a murder that happened on Gina's doorstep in the strange period when she had taken herself off to the coast to indulge in what had seemed to be a mammoth sulk with the world. Gina had been helpful with the case, but the two women had emerged from it spitting tacks about one another, and both of them had bent his ear about it. Paula was not going to prove an ally, if he needed one, in deflecting suspicion from Gina.

When Paula spoke again, she sounded uncomfortable.

'Actually,' she said, 'I wondered if you could come down here in the next day or two. I could do with your seniority in dealing with Sir Nicholas Payton.'

'Andrew Gray's father-in-law? You're planning to interview him?'

'I am.'

'You're ahead of me then.'

'The thing is, he's a former Lord Lieutenant of the county, and when I tried to speak to him on the phone, he made it clear that I wouldn't do.'

Not just because she wasn't senior enough but because she wasn't male enough, Scott thought, but Paula wasn't going to say that.

'The thing is,' Paula went on, 'I can't come heavy with him because he's not a suspect – or a witness, really. He wasn't at the wedding. But he could be useful in giving us background gen. I'm not supposed to tell you this – DI Mitchell made it clear that you're not to be privy to anything to do with the family – but the friction between Lavender Gray and her husband seems to have been a lot to do with money – she told the local officers that. And in particular it was her father's money, which he had put into their house. So, it's a bit personal, and he won't want to talk about it, but DI Mitchell wants to know just how serious an issue it was. They're leaving the wife – *Lavender*, for God's sake – for a day or two. She seems to be getting the kid gloves treatment.'

'She's that sort of woman. Men want to protect her.'

'Great. I'm going to love her then.'

'Absolutely your sort of woman.'

'How does she get on with Gina?'

'Surprisingly well. But then Gina wants to protect her too.'

'That figures,' she said.

'I'm still in Scotland at the moment,' he said, 'but I'm driving home. I'll need to do some catching up tomorrow morning, but I could come down to see your man in the afternoon. You'll want to come too, won't you? Are you free?'

'I'll make sure I am. Thanks, boss.'

'Not your boss any more, Paula. You're the boss down in Kent.'

'That's me. See you soon.'

After she had rung off, Scott remembered that Gina had once told him that he should marry Paula Powell. She was turning down his proposal to her at the time, and she hadn't been serious, had she?

Chapter Ten

THAT WHICH SHOULD ACCOMPANY OLD AGE

My hotel is delightful, a model of the sort of discreet comfort that doesn't demand that you keep noticing it. Everything has been thought of, from a choice of duvet or blankets to complementary fresh tea, coffee and biscuits available in the sunny lounge at all times. The food is excellent, the staff are charming, the views over the loch to the hills beyond are stunning, and in spite of the ongoing drama of a murder investigation, I begin to relax.

My fellow guests are a restful lot. They are universally elderly, but with their well-cut, snowy hair, pink cheeks, and bright eyes they present me with a most benign picture of old age. Most of them could easily model for those glossy brochures in which smiling, slim, active people advertise upmarket sheltered accommodation, for which they obviously have no need. Some of the guests here are frail, and there is a good scattering of sticks and Zimmer frames, but the pervading air is one of a cheerful engagement with life.

I am interested in the couples – mostly survivors of lengthy marriages, I assume. They are, I observe, companionable and considerate, tolerant of slowness, deafness and the like, content to talk or to be silent. How have they achieved that?

I simply cannot imagine it. I always say that Andrew wasn't fit to be married, but perhaps I wasn't either.

I think the soft, well-educated accents help – not the braying vowels of the English upper middle class, but gentle Celtic consonants and musical vowels, which make everything – even a spirited political discussion (and I have heard a good few of those) – sound rational and calm.

I have not attempted conversation beyond conventional weather exchanges. Partly this is because the couples and groups seem to be happily self-contained, and I would just be an interloper, but more it is because I am afraid that I might let slip that I am a murder suspect. Asked what has brought me here, I could hardly claim that some nice hills and the theatre's offering of an open-air production of *Alice in Wonderland* have brought me five hundred miles, so I would have to explain about the wedding, and if anyone showed a glimmer of interest, I would be splurging out the whole improbable story. Because, you see, although this place has induced a kind of pharmaceutical calm in me, I am, below that placid surface, in turmoil.

David thinks that I am underestimating just how willingly the local police would have me be Andrew's killer, but I am not. I see quite clearly that the period of almost an hour when Lavender and I were alone in the house with Andrew is the crucial time, and that, given the choice between the helpless young widow that is Lavender and the sour old battle-axe that is me, they would like to cast me in the role of villain. Police officers do not (with the dubious exception of David) like me. I have met many in the course of the last thirteen years, and none of them has liked me – not even the Danish ones. However I may try to disguise it, they see me immediately as a clever clogs, they sense my assumption that they are unimaginative and rule-bound, they bristle at the deficit of respect. And it is my fault, I know. I am ridiculously arrogant about my own sleuthing skills, and absurdly dismissive of what David calls *good police work*. I have listened to him telling me that ninety-five per cent of cases are solved by detailed, repetitive forensic work, and officers going painstakingly through hours and hours of mind-numbing CCTV footage, but still the vain little core of me believes that I can leap over all that stuff and arrive at the truth through the pure brilliance of my insights – and sometimes through my mastery of the mysteries of the English language.

So I don't get into conversation, and I still worry that people have identified as police officers the couple who have, in the last two days, visited me twice. Detective Superintendent James Mitchell and Detective Sergeant Fiona Grant have been as discreet as they know how, asking for me at reception without stating their business, and taking me off to a quiet corner of the grounds for interrogation, but they make an odd couple – she twenty years younger than him – and their clothes, I am afraid, are a dead give-away. Who wears a suit and tie, or in her case dark trousers and a tucked-in shirt, to spend time with a friend in a country hotel at the end of July? My fellow guests are elderly and charming; they are also not stupid.

On their second visit, my interrogators take me off to the same bench, in a rose arbour, overlooking the loch, where they questioned me yesterday. They have a new line of attack, though. Yesterday they must have realised that my putative motive of a long-cherished resentment about our divorce really won't fly. It is a turkey. Not only is there the problem of explaining why this old grudge should drive me to homicide twenty years after the event, when I am now leading a happy and prosperous life, but there is the impossibility of explaining why, after all this time, I should choose to ruin my daughter's wedding day by exacting my revenge. So, nothing daunted, they have turned the argument round: I killed my ex-husband, it seems, because he had ruined our daughter's wedding. Incensed by his flaunting his young mistress at the nuptials and then picking a public fight with her husband, I was driven to an act of madness, and stabbed him in the blossoms of his sins.

They don't put this to me in so many words, naturally. They skirt around, sympathising with the embarrassments of the day, speculating on what my feelings may have been, suggesting that, all in all, I will feel better if I unburden myself to them here and now. They have some evidence, besides my lack of alibi for the crucial fifty minutes, which they trail before me: forensics have found my fingerprints and DNA about Andrew's person. Of course they have: I helped to get him back to the house and put him to bed. *Around his throat area*, they say, as though I had toyed initially with strangling him. *Loosening the lacing on his Jacobite shirt*, I tell them, *making him comfortable, like the forgiving ex-wife that I am*. I refer them to DSu Scott for corroboration, but they exchange a look that I can't quite read and take their leave.

I walk them back to reception in a weedy attempt to maintain the fiction that I have been visited by friends, and on the way back to the lounge I wonder what background checks they have done on me. Has it dawned on them yet that, for me, Glamis castle means, above all else, a powerful man stabbed in his sleep? Has it dawned on them that I, more than any other guest at the wedding, would be certain to know that a man can easily be killed by a stab wound in the eye? They haven't mentioned either of these things, so perhaps they haven't thought of them yet, and perhaps they never will.

Pouring myself a cup of coffee and taking it to a seat by the window, I reflect that I could so easily deflect all this interest in me by telling them that Lavender, the truly, newly, wronged wife, told me at the wedding, not once but twice, that she would like to kill her husband. I shan't tell them because Lavender is not a killer, and I am – contrary to the opinion of many people – a good person, really. Also, they are unlikely to believe me, and anyway the most superficial acquaintance with the classic crime novel tells us that the person who says, *I'd like to kill him* is never the person who *dunnit*.

Chapter Eleven

HIS HOUR UPON THE STAGE

How could it be that she had somehow forgotten that she didn't actually like doing drama? Everyone assumed that she did, because Mum taught it, but Freda really rather hated it. Class drama lessons lower down the school had seemed to her to be somewhere between slightly weird PE (the movement stuff) and the kind of *let's pretend* games that she and her friend Charlie had played at primary school (the improvisation stuff). It was just embarrassing really, and she had been glad to drop it when she made her GCSE choices. She made her contribution to school plays by doing sets and props, and that was enough. She wasn't doing drama or music just to please Mum and Ben. But here she was, already one day in to a week of non-stop drama classes. *WTF!*

When she had woken the previous morning, after her first night in her bedroom at the McCleods' house, her immediate feeling had been a comfortable little tug of pleasure to think that Alex was asleep in the room next door, and she was not in the back of a hire car, heading for Orkney, and then reality had hit her – she was going to have to spend the whole of the coming week *performing*. That was it. That was reality. However sweet Alex was, and however cool Isla seemed to be, the bottom line was that they were all going to be showing off.

She hadn't even known what to wear – and she had little to choose from among the clothes she had packed for trudging round prehistoric sites in the rain. She had a black T-shirt, which seemed an actorly sort of thing, and she was going to put on her new jeans until she considered that they would almost certainly be rolling around on the floor at some point and she wasn't prepared to mess them up. On the other hand, her old jeans were baggy and unflattering. Transfixed by indecision, she had begun to panic, until she spotted the black leggings she had packed for wearing under the old jeans if the burial sites were really freezing. She put them on and surveyed her black self in the mirror. With her hair up in a ponytail, she looked business-like at least – and maybe, she thought as she put on mascara, even something approaching cool.

Driving with Alex into Perth hadn't been quite the dazzling experience she had hoped for because her stomach was knotted up with nerves and she had to concentrate quite hard on not being sick all over Aileen's beautifully clean car. Alex drove in silence for a bit. He seemed very confident, she thought, for someone who had only just passed his test, but he didn't take his eyes off the road to look at her. She wondered if she should be making conversation, but she didn't want to distract him, and anyway she had the full-time job of not throwing up. Eventually he gave her a quick glance.

'Nervous?' he asked.

'Just a bit.'

'The others will be too, if that's any comfort. This is a new course. They'll come from different schools, so they won't all know each other.'

'They are all Scottish, though.'

He laughed. 'So being English gives you rarity value.'

'I'm not very good at showing off,' she said.

'Don't worry. The last thing we'll be asking anyone to do is to show off.'

Reassured, she relaxed, breathed deeply, and wondered what time the lunch break would be. The half slice of toast she had managed at breakfast really hadn't been enough to fuel a morning's work, but Aileen had made really good sandwiches for their lunch.

They were a group of fifteen, with Isla and Alex working with them. Isla was in bright pink – stretchy leggings and a sleeveless T-shirt – and was fizzing with energy. Instead of just sitting round and all saying their names, they had stood in a circle and 'thrown' their names at one another as though they were throwing a ball. Then they threw an imaginary ball to each other, calling out the name of the person they were throwing to. It was actually good fun and quite a laugh, so that by the time they moved on to the dreaded trust exercises she didn't feel as worried as she might have done.

They had done trust exercises in drama at school – she remembered them with horror, especially the one where they were in pairs, and one of you was blindfolded while the other one led you around, all over the upper floor of the Arts building. It wouldn't have been so bad if they had been able to choose their own partners, but she was put in a pair with Hester Bigwood, who hated her, she knew, and was quite capable of leading her to the top of the staircase and encouraging her to plunge down it. She hadn't done that, in fact, but she had led her into the costume cupboard and abandoned her there amongst a host of garments that clung around her like unhappy ghosts.

But here it was different. A nice boy had guided her as carefully as if she had been his old granny, warning her of furniture, steps, uneven paving stones and other people, and then she had returned the compliment. The idea was that you didn't actually lead the other person. You let them go where they wanted to, but you had to anticipate where they were going and look out for hazards. It was all about being aware of one another, as you had to be on stage. As a non-performer, that had never occurred to her: she thought of acting as being each person's individual performance, rather than something you did as a team. If she had thought of it like that, she might have felt better about it.

There was a slightly awkward moment at the lunch break. Aileen hadn't made two separate packs of sandwiches, so when they went out to sit in the little courtyard outside the rehearsal room, she and Alex had to divvy them up. She didn't sit down to eat with him, but deliberately went to sit at another table, but everyone looked at her curiously.

'So, you know Alex?' one of the girls asked. 'How come?'

Freda had rehearsed an answer to this in her head. She had half-expected that they would start the class with a toe-curling session of *Let's all sit round in a circle and introduce ourselves*, but they hadn't – they had just gone into the calling out their names exercise. But most people would have clocked her English accent by now, and she had known that she would have to explain herself.

'My aunt has just got married to his brother,' she said, 'and his parents asked me to stay this week. My parents have taken my little brother to look at Neolithic stuff.'

She kept her tone flat, hoping to shut down further questions, but she allowed herself a small eye roll on the last part, and got a few smiles back. The girl who had asked the question – a very blonde, skinny girl with pale blue eyes and invisible eyebrows – was persistent. *She fancies Alex*, Freda thought – *but then probably all the girls do.*

'But Alex is like still at school, isn't he? His brother must be older.'

Well, doh! Freda thought. *Obviously.*

She said, 'He's just done Highers. And yes, his brother's older.'

'And your aunt...'

71

'Is younger than my mum. Yes.'

She worked hard at not sounding sarcastic, but one of the boys said, 'OK, Alice? Got it sorted now? Interrogation over?' and the girl blushed and swigged her bottle of coke.

Now, today, they were just having a morning session, and then going over to Pitlochry in the minibus to see an adaptation of *Dr Jekyll and Mr Hyde* at the theatre – an open-air performance because the theatre was still closed. In the minibus they talked about plays and productions they had seen, and she definitely scored points for having seen things in London.

On the other hand, she felt like an impressionable tourist as she looked out of the window at the countryside. To the others, she could see, it was just every day. They were absorbed with their phones or listening to music, while she couldn't keep her eyes off the looming hills. Or were they mountains, in fact? She thought of googling, *How high is a mountain?* But since she couldn't possibly estimate how high these were, what was the point? The others would know, of course, but it wouldn't feel cool to ask, so she set her face to impassive as she gazed out, and hoped she looked as though she was having deep thoughts rather than gawping at the scenery.

The theatre, when it came into view, was extraordinary, unlike any theatre she had seen before. She was used to the Aphra Behn in Marlbury, a converted cinema fitted in between the river and the shops, and to the uncomfortably tight squeeze of London theatres, all jammed together. She had been to the National Theatre, and that did have plenty of space, but still it didn't compare to this theatre, which sat up above the loch and stretched luxuriously along its length. It couldn't all be actual theatre, she realised. Some of it would be costume and scenery stores, and workshops and so on. It was frustrating that they wouldn't get inside it. She could see that there were huge windows, which must have fantastic views over the loch to the hills/mountains beyond.

In the car park, they climbed out of the minibus, preparing to walk into the town, where, she was told, there was the best fish and chip shop to be found in Perth and Kinross, but as they headed down towards the bridge across the loch, there – unbelievably – was Granny, sitting on a bench, apparently admiring the view. Freda's first instinct was to fold herself into the middle of her group and see if she could slide past unnoticed. How could she otherwise save herself from the huge embarrassment of being stalked by her grandmother – because she had no doubt that she was here deliberately, checking up on her. How had she found out that she was going to be here? She put her head down and prepared to skulk.

It was no good, of course. Almost immediately she heard her name ringing across the car park, and everyone turned to look at the little woman with wild hair who was waving energetically at her.

'Sorry,' she said. 'My Gran.' And scarlet-faced she pushed her way out of the group and sped across to head her grandmother off before she came any closer.

'What are you doing here?' she said as soon as she got near enough.

Her grandmother sat down and patted the bench beside her. 'Aileen told me you would be here,' she said. 'I hadn't heard from you, so I gave her a ring.'

'I don't need checking up on,' she muttered furiously, sitting down because she didn't want her grandmother back on her feet.

'Your mother will blame me if anything happens to you.'

This, Freda knew, was designed to put her in her place. Just because once she had gone off when Granny was responsible for her – and she had been wrong to do it, she admitted – Granny needn't think that entitled her to interfere in her life whenever she felt like it.

'You're not responsible for me while I'm here,' she said. 'I've got more than enough people looking out for me – even supposing I can't look after myself – Aileen and Duncan, Alex, Isla…'

And even as she said it, here came Mr (*Call me Malcolm*) Ross, who had driven the minibus, chugging over to check up on her. Only he seemed more interested in Granny, slipping on his designer sunglasses, which, she supposed, made him feel sexy. Really, old people ought to get over themselves.

'I just wanted to say how sorry I was to hear about your … about Andrew. I met him at the wedding – had a very interesting talk with him. Such a terrible shock for all of you. And at a wedding too.'

And Granny said, 'Oh, weddings are dangerous things. Think how many of Shakespeare's tragedies start with a wedding or an engagement.'

Malcolm Ross fished his wallet out and handed Freda a note. 'You'll be wanting to get your fish and chips,' he said. 'Can you fetch me a haddock and a small portion of chips? I'll stay here and talk tragedy with your grandmother.'

Freda took the money and started to run down the slope to the road, anxious to catch up with the others, who knew their way to the fish and chip shop. They were already on the bridge.

Apparently seeing her problem, Malcolm Ross called, 'You just take the twitten straight ahead of you on the other side of the bridge, and then follow the road round to the right.'

She need not have worried, actually, because as soon as they were on the bridge the others slowed down, and when she got onto it, she understood why. It was a swinging sort of bridge, like the millennium bridge in London, and as soon as a group of people got onto it walking in step, it swung quite alarmingly. A lively discussion was going on about the merits of taking it at a run, and in the end some of the boys ran in a crazy, drunken sprint, while the rest of them consciously broke their stride. Under other circumstances she might have found it fun, but she was still flustered by her grandmother's arrival, and she felt slightly sick.

She got some odd looks when she gave her double order, and when she muttered, 'The haddock's for Malcolm,' she saw Alice's invisible eyebrows go up, and before she could say something sarcastic about sucking up, she rolled her eyes and added, 'He's dealing with my crazy grandmother, who's turned up out of the blue.'

This got a laugh, and she felt only slightly guilty about the *crazy*.

When they got back, Malcolm and her grandmother were still in conversation. She handed him his bundle and his change, and Granny got up and said she was off. 'I'm coming to the show tonight,' she said. 'I thought it was a subject better seen at night.'

She was probably right. The show was good – just a monologue and brilliantly done – but it probably would have had more atmosphere in the dark. This was the general agreement in the minibus on the way home, before everyone else went back to their phones, and Freda thought about good and evil and what you could do about them.

Chapter Twelve

DAGGERS IN MEN'S SMILES

'*Lady Jane*,' David thought, as Paula Powell drove them through the manicured West Kent countryside. It was an odd thought, triggered by scanning the information on Sir Nicholas Payton which Paula had handed to him as they got into the car. Included was a photo, pulled off the internet, of Cossington Manor, the Paytons' home. A substantial affair on three floors, plus attics, with tiers of fiercely symmetrical windows either side of an assertive, porticoed front door. Scott was no expert on stately homes; contrary to the expectations of TV crime watchers, the chances of a police officer being called out to a crime in one of these were vanishingly small – particularly for an officer in the Met – and Sunday afternoon National Trust/English Heritage visits were not his thing. So the thought, *Lady Jane*, was a spin-off from spending bubble time in recent months with a woman who was in love with Ian McShane.

Gina knew better than to ask him to watch crime dramas in general; she understood that their cavalier inaccuracies and implausibilities were intolerable to him, however good the actors who poured their talent into the preposterous stuff, but *Lovejoy*, she said, was different: the police hardly featured at all, and the dialogue was terribly witty. And so, in the interests of bubble harmony, and in exchange for a couple of good documentaries, he had watched several episodes. It was complete nonsense, filmed in the 1980s in a fantasy rural Suffolk, all thatched cottages, flat caps, tweed-suited toffs, and dim-witted villains, with a peppering of glamorous seductresses with big hair. For Gina, usually so quick off the mark to mock clichés and sentimentality, it had been the Friday night comfort viewing of her youth, when she was a working mother with small children and an unreliable husband, and Ian McShane – all sexy eyes and witty one-liners – was her eye-candy of choice. It had obviously been designed for women viewers – perhaps assuming that men would be at the pub – but there was also the impossibly lovely Lady Jane, played by Phyllis Logan, rich, beautiful, and a jolly good sport, digging Lovejoy out of trouble, and just flirtatious enough for fun. Her stately home, in the absence of her conveniently busy husband, featured prominently in the episodes Scott had watched, and now he couldn't help half expecting the lovely Phyllis to come striding down the drive in her riding boots.

As it was, when they had negotiated the avenue of trees and emerged into a sweep of gravel drive, they were greeted by two Labradors, straight out of central casting, who came charging round the side of the house, followed by a man shouting masterfully but ineffectually at them. He was undoubtedly Major (rtd) Sir Nicholas Payton, and – like the dogs – seemed to have been cast in the role. He was wearing old trousers tucked into boots, an open-necked check shirt of an expensive-looking, heavy material, and a sort of sporting waistcoat that suggested he might be on his way to stalk deer. The clothes were accessorised with sleek, iron-grey hair and a neat military moustache. The only surprising thing about him was his height: he was a small man – tough and wiry but not more than five foot six. A casting director might have hesitated over this, Scott thought, and wondered, as he got out of the car, why this set-up kept making him think of performance, when it was clear that the Paytons were as genuine as you could expect in the world of county gentry – and the man could hardly have grown the moustache in preparation for a police interview, could he?

Their host ushered them round the side of the house to a terrace that ran along the back, and settled them at a weatherworn wooden table outside French doors opening to a rather flowery sitting room. The dogs continued to prance and grumble, and ignored Sir Nicholas's bellowed commands to lie down. A door opened further along the terrace, and a woman stepped out. This was Lady Payton – Scott saw the similarity to Lavender. She was still a pretty woman, blonde and blue-eyed, with Lavender's look of innocence about her.

'Hello!' she called, as if she was delighted to see them, and he could hear the professionalism in her greeting; the years of welcoming strangers to her house – her husband's colleagues, business associates, old army friends, golf buddies, and other assorted jolly good chaps. She shook hands with both of them, smiling nicely at Paula, and offered coffee. Then she clapped briskly at the dogs, said, 'Indoors,' and was instantly obeyed.

Sir Nicholas addressed himself to Scott. 'Beastly business this with my wretched son-in-law,' he said. 'How are you getting on?'

Scott glanced at Paula, then cleared his throat. 'I should explain, Sir Nicholas,' he said. 'I am not in charge of this case. The Angus police are running the investigation, and because a number of the guests at the wedding have returned to Kent, they have asked Detective Inspector Powell here to take some statements at this end. Inspector Powell invited me to come along today simply as a courtesy to you, because she knew that I have some knowledge of the family situation. I've known Andrew Gray's first wife for some time, and I have met your daughter on several occasions. So —'

Sir Nicholas interrupted. 'I would have thought that made you the ideal person to be running the show. You know us – my daughter at any rate.'

'Technically, I am a suspect,' Scott said. 'I was at the wedding – staying in the house where Andrew Gray was killed.'

'Ridiculous,' Sir Nicholas muttered into his moustache.

Scott shrugged. 'There are protocols,' he said.

The word, *protocols,* seemed to appeal to the army man. 'Hmph,' he said, and then turned to Paula Powell. 'So, how can I help you, young lady?' he asked, and Scott held his breath, waiting to see how Paula would respond.

They were saved from a possible explosion by the arrival of Lady Payton, carrying a tray of coffee and a plate of chocolate biscuits. She set the tray down on the table and was about to leave when Paula said, 'Won't you join us, Lady Payton?'

Annabel Payton looked surprised. 'Oh, you have serious things to discuss. I'll just —'

'I'm actually just trying to get an initial picture of where everyone was on the night Andrew Gray was killed, so I will want a statement from you, I'm afraid.'

'From me? But I was here.' She looked at her husband. 'We were both here.'

'That's fine,' Paula said easily, pouring milk into her coffee, 'but we will need a few details, so if you'd like to bring another cup…'

Annabel Payton glanced again at her husband. 'Right,' she said. 'Back in a moment.'

While she was gone, Paula took a sip of coffee and said, 'You referred to your *wretched* son-in-law just now, Sir Nicholas. Did you mean that in the sense of *unfortunate*, or was it a criticism?'

Sir Nicholas gave her one very sharp look and then addressed his coffee cup. 'Never wanted Lavender to marry the blighter – divorced, older, grown-up children – not what I wanted for my daughter. And no money to speak of – had to give them a good whack towards that house. And now –'

'*Nil nisi bonum,* darling!' Annabel Payton sang out as she joined them, carrying a cup of Earl Grey tea. 'Andrew was awfully good to us while we stayed with them during the lockdown last year. And very patient with the boys.'

'All a front,' her husband muttered irritably. 'You were taken in. I never was. Knew it was too good to be true. Turns out he was carrying on with that other woman all along.'

Paula took her opportunity. She said, 'The local police are being very sensitive to your daughter's feelings. They don't want to interview her about her marriage until she has had a chance to get over the shock. It would be very helpful if you can tell us what you understand about how things stood between them – between Lavender and Andrew, I mean.'

Annabel Payton looked at her husband, who sat back in his chair. 'You tell them if you like. You may be able to keep your temper,' he said.

She cleared her throat and looked at Paula. She was a woman who was used to confiding in other women, Scott thought.

'I'm afraid Andrew was not faithful to our daughter,' she said. 'He was having an affair with a colleague at work – quite a serious affair – and Lavender felt that she had no alternative but to sue him for divorce.'

'Fellow was a bounder,' her husband broke in. 'Didn't want a divorce. Wanted to have his cake and eat it – live in my daughter's house and carry on seeing his floozie.'

Bounder? Floozie? Did anyone really use those words any more, Scott wondered. Why did he keep thinking this man was playing a role?

'The house is your daughter's?' he asked.

'In both their names. She insisted on that. Gave them a very substantial deposit as a wedding present. Then the blighter says he'll claim half the value if they divorce, because he's been paying twopence ha'penny a month on the mortgage.'

'Lavender would have liked a clean break, but she was afraid Andrew would get very good lawyers, and she couldn't bear to see him walk away with our family's money,' Annabel Payton explained, now addressing Scott – perhaps because money was something you talked to men about.

'Poor girl doesn't know what to do,' Sir Nicholas said.

'*Didn't* know what to do,' Paula said, looking him straight in the eye. 'It isn't a problem any more, is it?'

'What?' He frowned at her, then drained his coffee cup. 'No, well. All different now, of course. But that doesn't mean…'

'Doesn't mean what?' Paula asked, leaning forward.

Scott could feel her willing Sir Nicholas to look her in the eye, but instead he looked at his wife.

'It doesn't mean my daughter had anything to do with his death,' Annabel Payton said. 'I'm sure you don't think that. Nobody who knows Lavender could possibly think that.'

She looked at Scott as if cueing him to offer a testimonial, but Paula stepped in quickly. 'We don't think anything at the moment. We're still putting a picture together. It's very early days, and what we need to know is where everyone was at the crucial time. You weren't at the wedding, of course, but could you just tell me where you were?'

Annabel Payton looked startled. 'Where *we* were? Why? I mean …'

'Just for completeness, Lady Payton. It is as important to rule people out as to include them among possible suspects. Were you both here last weekend?'

The Paytons looked at one another, and she spoke. 'Yes, we were. We're always here, really. I know we're all supposed to be free to go anywhere, but we aren't rushing to see people – except the family, of course.'

Paula turned to Sir Nicholas. 'So, could you just tell me how you spent your weekend? Anyone you saw, and so on?'

'Alibis you mean. Eh? Well, I spent the Saturday fishing. Out all day'

'And where was that?'

'Here. We have a small fishing lake – over in that direction.' He pointed to a clump of trees in the middle distance.

'Did anyone join you there?'

'What? No. Like to fish in peace. Don't want any chat.'

'And you were there all day?'

'Absolutely. Poor catch but kept at it.'

'And you, Lady Payton?'

'I spent the morning making jam – blackcurrant – and then in the afternoon my daughter Bryony came over for tea with the grandchildren, and in the evening I watched the Prom. A lovely concert – the Birmingham symphony Orchestra with that remarkable young woman with the unpronounceable name conducting.'

'Did you watch that too, Sir Nicholas?' Paula asked.

'Not my thing, classical music, though my wife loves it. Beautiful evening. Preferred to be outside.'

'And Sunday?'

'I went to church, and you went for a ride, didn't you, darling?' She turned to her husband.

'Yes. Went for a long hack across country. Home at tea time.'

'Did you see anyone when you were out riding?'

'Plenty of walkers – that sort of thing. No-one I knew.'

'You didn't stop at a pub for lunch?'

'My dear young lady, I was on horseback. You don't park a horse in a car park, you know.'

'Of course not.' She stood up. 'Do you have a mobile phone, Sir Nicholas?'

'I have. Never use it. Not one of these smart jonnies. Generally switched off.'

'We'd like to have a look at it, if you don't mind.'

'As a matter of fact, I do. Breach of privacy. No call for it.'

Paula picked up her notebook and addressed herself pointedly to Annabel Payton.

'Thank you for your hospitality, Lady Payton. I hope we won't need to bother you again.'

The stress on *you* was clear. She looked at Scott, sending him a wordless message – *Get the phone* – and without saying anything more to Sir Nicholas, she turned and headed briskly for the car. The two men watched her go, while Annabel Payton piled the coffee cups onto a tray and headed for the kitchen. While she was still within earshot, Scott said, 'It really would be better, sir, if you let us have your phone voluntarily. It will be an unpleasant business if DI Powell has to send uniformed officers with a warrant.'

He saw Annabel Payton pause and look round, but she said nothing and went on her way. Sir Nicholas dug in a pocket and pulled out a small Nokia phone, which he tossed onto the table. 'Make what you like of that,' he said. 'Damn thing's always switched off anyway.'

Scott picked it up and turned to leave, but Sir Nicholas, glancing, it seemed, to make sure that his wife was now inside, said, 'Actually, Scott, I wanted to have a quiet word. Take a turn round the lawn here with me?'

Taking him by the elbow, he steered him towards the grass. Paula, Scott thought, wouldn't like this, but he had at least got the phone for her.

'Interests of full disclosure, as they say,' Sir Nicholas said. 'Thought I ought to say my alibi's not quite as watertight as I may have suggested. No lies, you understand, but truth is, I didn't sleep in the house on Saturday night. Spent the day fishing, as I said. Fish weren't biting so I stayed on and decided to bivouac down there. Do that sometimes – back to my service days. Beautiful evening. Nothing like sleeping under the stars. Got a fishing shack down by the lake. Everything I needed in there. Cooked a couple of trout for supper and then bedded down.'

'Did you let your wife know you were camping out?'

'Matter of fact not. Quite late when I decided, and she's one for an early night. Didn't want to disturb her. Wouldn't have worried her. Generally sleep in my dressing room anyway – snoring, you know.'

'But she saw you in the morning?'

'Well, no. Lovely bright morning. Slipped into the kitchen for some iron rations before she was up, and then took my horse out.'

'And you say you didn't see anyone you knew while you were out?'

'Not a soul.'

They had completed their circuit of the lawn and stopped by the house.

'Well, thank you for clarifying that,' Scott said. 'It's always useful to have the complete picture.'

He started to walk away but his host put a hand on his arm. 'Wouldn't want you to think my wife was being untruthful,' he said. 'Thoroughly honourable woman. Just didn't have the full picture.'

'Of course,' Scott said.

In the car, he relayed the conversation to Paula and handed her the phone.

'The devious old bugger,' she said. 'What's he playing at?'

'Undermining his own alibi. I don't know. Unnecessary, of course. We both could see that his story was full of holes. I was surprised you didn't press him more – and her.'

'I'm taking it carefully. He's a former Lord Lieutenant. Friends in high places. If he is our man, I can't have this go off half-cock.'

'You don't really think he's the killer, do you? And this blowing away his alibi is a double bluff?'

'The money's a strong motive, and in his code defending his daughter would feel like a duty.'

'But if he was going to kill Andrew Gray, why go all the way to Scotland to do it, when he lives half an hour's drive away?'

'He'd be far more likely to come under suspicion down here.'

'But if he went all the way to Scotland, he'll have made a plan. This murder was spur of the moment, wasn't it? Using the victim's own dagger? And how could he know that Andrew would get dead drunk and be alone in a house except for two women who weren't paying attention?'

'He'd have known about the dagger if he knew Gray was wearing a kilt. He's been to enough formal dinners, and there's nearly always some geezer flashing his knees in a kilt.'

'You go to a lot of formal dinners, do you?' Scott asked. He had never thought much about Paula's private life, but this was an unexpected feature.

She gave him a sideways glance. 'Since I was made up to DI, the powers that be send me off to represent the force surprisingly often – keen to display their equal opportunities credentials.'

'That must be fun.'

'It's hell. There are only men to talk to, and they try to patronise me or impress me – or both. But back to the dagger. A man like Payton would probably have preferred to use a gun – he's probably got a service revolver, but that's noisy and would be identified by forensics. Using the man's own dagger was a much safer bet.'

'Still, he couldn't have known that the man would be brought back dead drunk.'

'No. He'd have needed an accomplice. How's this for a scenario. He goes off, apparently for a day's fishing, then hops into his four by four and drives up to Glamis. There he parks – no-one except Lavender would recognise his car, and she was in on the plan – and he hides among the trees, waiting for a signal from Lavender. The plan is to wait until everyone is in bed, then when Andrew is asleep, Lavender will let her father in, he will find the dagger, which Lavender will have left on the bedside table for him, and do the deed. It was a pretty professional job, the knife in the eye socket, wasn't it? Then he'd leave, get a few hours' kip in his motor, and drive home – back in time for tea, and Lady Annabel wilfully blind to his absence. Lavender, meanwhile, would sleep in the boys' room or on the sofa, claiming that his snoring had been keeping her awake, and in the morning she would "discover" the body. But it worked out even better than they could have hoped. You brought Andrew back dead drunk, and Lavender was able to summon Dad before the others got back – much safer to do it with fewer people around. Then, of course, she had to raise the alarm as soon as it was time for her to go to bed, which was a bit more dangerous because her father was still in the vicinity, but nobody was immediately looking for an elderly man in a Range Rover.'

'I don't believe Payton would murder a man in his sleep. It would be against his code of honour. And Lavender? You haven't met Lavender. I can't imagine her conspiring to murder her children's father while they were sleeping practically next door.'

She shrugged. 'The Scottish police are soon going to have to stop handling her with kid gloves. She can only play the weeping widow for so long. Have they looked at her phone, do you know?'

'I don't. What about Payton's? He wouldn't have handed it over if there was anything incriminating on it.'

'It won't have anything,' she said dismissively. 'Objecting to handing it over was just a ploy. There'll be another one.'

'Oh come on, Paula, you've seen what he's like. Do you honestly think that he or Lavender would know how to get hold of an unregistered phone?'

'Pagers would be all they'd need.'

'I don't buy it.'

'Well, I'm not wedded to it, but the local force haven't come up with any better suspects. How are you doing with the London suspects?'

'I'm seeing the Staffords tomorrow – Andrew's woman and her husband – and planning to talk to some of his other colleagues, get their take on Stafford as a killer, though he seems to have been seen by others throughout the crucial time period.'

'Unless his wife is covering for him?'

'If he killed her lover?'

'Guilt?'

'Mm.'

They were silent for a while, and then he said, 'I don't think Payton is the killer, but there is something about him I don't believe in. What did you think about his language?'

'His language?'

'Yes, you know – *fella's a bounder, floozie,* and so on.'

'That's just how they talk, isn't it, that lot?'

'Well do they, really? Fifty years ago, maybe, but when have you heard anyone use words like that recently? Do the chaps you meet at the dinners they send you to talk like that?'

She considered. 'They do on TV.'

'Exactly. It's like he's playing a part.'

She shot him a look. 'I did the research on the family myself,' she said. 'He's definitely kosher.'

Scott laughed. 'I'm not sure that's a word he'd want to have applied to himself,' he said.

'Why?' She looked puzzled, and then said, 'Oh, I see.'

And Scott could hear Gina's voice in his ear: *People are so careless about the way they use metaphors. They never think about what they actually mean.*

He needed to talk to her.

Chapter Thirteen

SOME WORDS UPON THAT BUSINESS

I am sitting on a strategically placed rustic bench in the hotel garden, and I may appear to the casual eye to be enjoying the view of the loch in a mindless sort of way, but actually my mind is on evil. Jekyll and Hyde have been in my head since yesterday's performance, which was surprisingly powerful, given the limitations of a one-man show and the open-air staging, and I have found myself scanning the faces of my fellow guests for intimations of the black and deep desires that may lurk behind their social smiles.

'*There's no art to find the mind's construction in the face,*' I say out loud, continuing my policy of challenging our bad luck by courting it, and then, more appositely since it is Lavender I am thinking of, I add, '*Look like the innocent flower, but be the serpent under it,*' because, you see, I really am wondering about our fragrant Lavender.

The police have been entirely convinced by her helpless little woman performance, and they have let her slip away into the protective arms of her brother-in-law. I can quite see how that would be. After all, I have spent years feeling guilty about her because I thought she was no match for Andrew's untamed egotism. Only now I see, when I think about it, that when things threaten to be intolerable, Lavender finds a way to deal with them. When her obnoxious little boys were running rings round her, she bounced Andrew into paying a very expensive supernanny to come and sort them out, and when lockdown isolation with the boys and Andrew threatened to overwhelm her, she installed her parents in the spare room to force Andrew into a semblance of a co-operative husband and father. That is her technique – she uses her genuine helplessness to enlist support. I have to admire it because it is a skill I entirely lack; nobody has ever so much as hoisted a bag onto a luggage rack for me.

So, faced with the worst crisis of her life, what would she do? She blubbed all over me, of course, but I wasn't the Galahad she needed. Suddenly I see her *I want to kill him* as on a par with *I want to put in a new bathroom.* She will have got a man in. Her father? Her brother? They weren't on the spot, though, whereas there was someone who was presumably as pissed off with Andrew as she was. Henry Stafford, the cuckolded husband: I can see the two men, scarlet with drink and fury, tugging and jabbing ineptly at each other while the dancers reeled round the marquee. Suppose Henry and Lavender had talked earlier, drawn by their mutual humiliation, and exchanged phone numbers. When we brought Andrew back to her in a state of alcoholic collapse, and then, as she thought, left her alone in the house with him, what would have been easier for her than to phone Henry Stafford and offer to let him into the house, where he would find his enemy at his mercy?

I am roused from these dark thoughts by my own phone ringing. I see David's name, and when I answer, there are, as usual, no preliminaries.

'A language question,' he says.

I am stunned. Here I have been, feeling utterly unwanted – David ignoring me, the local police quite uninterested in my insights and allocating me firmly to the suspects box, my daughters not bothering with so much as a postcard, not a single man in the hotel showing me the slightest attention, and Freda obviously desperate to avoid me. I have been alone and palely loitering here for three days, and now here is David, actually asking for my opinion – on a language question.

'Do you know Lavender's parents?' he asks.

'I've met her father once. At one of Nico's birthday parties. Ellie invited Arthur, and for some reason it was his grandfather who brought him.'

'Did you talk to him?'

'Briefly. Why?'

'Anything you noticed about his language – idiolect it's called, isn't it?'

'Very good! No. As I say, if was just a brief exchange. I do remember thinking that he was brighter than I expected, though.'

'Really? Why?'

'Well, you know what Lavender's like.'

'What made you think he was brighter?'

'We were standing in the hall while a horde of seven-year-old boys marauded around us, and I said, "*I don't know what they'll do to the enemy but by God they frighten me.*" I suppose it was the military connection that made me think of it, but he looked at me rather pityingly, and told me there was no evidence that Wellington ever said that, any more than he had the "*By God sir, I've lost my leg; By God sir, so you have*" exchange with Lord Paget. He said it quite nicely, but I felt a bit of an idiot.'

'Which doesn't happen often.'

'No.'

'So nothing special about his language? No old buffer *dontcha know* stuff?'

'Not that I remember. Why?'

'Because Paula and I interviewed him this morning, and he was full of it. And there was something about it that made me feel he was playing a part, but I can't work out why.'

'What does Paula think?'

'She's not much interested in language.'

'Is he a suspect?'

'He has a motive.'

'The divorce and the money?'

'You know about that?'

'Lavender told me. Aren't-We-Grand Hall would go under the hammer, and Andrew was threatening to sweep up the profits.'

He wants to kill him, I can hear Lavender saying, but I keep quiet.

'Well,' I say, 'if he realises that he could be a suspect, he might just be trying to look too stupid to be the murderer.'

'Yes, I thought of that.'

'Or too old-school honourable to murder a man in his sleep.'

'I thought of that too.'

I am annoyed. 'Well then, you don't need me, do you?' I snap.

'I thought you might come up with something more sophisticated. The thing is – and this really is in confidence, you realise that? Because—'

'I am like a Trappist nun up here. You're the first person I've spoken to for days, apart from ordering my meals, and I'm not about to reveal classified information to the waiters, am I?'

'All right. The thing is, he gave us an alibi and then trashed it.'

'What do you mean?'

'You don't need the details, but he told us he had been at home all the time, and his wife backed him up, and then he took me to one side and pointed out long periods of time were actually unaccounted for.'

'Enough time to travel to Scotland and back?'

'Just about.'

'And Lady P was lying?'

'Not exactly. Making assumptions.'

'At what point did he tell you this?'

'At the end. When Paula had gone back to the car.'

'Did Paula talk to him about Lavender in the interview?'

'Yes. Why?'

'Then my guess is that he could see that you have a strong case against Lavender – motive and opportunity – and maybe he's beginning to think she might have done it – and he really is an old-fashioned, honourable chap, and sees it as his duty to protect his daughter. He's ready to take the blame himself, if need be, so he started by thinking he needed to give you his alibi and then realised that it might be better if it wasn't watertight.'

'And the old buffer language?'

'Perhaps that wasn't for your benefit. Perhaps he was making himself the person he felt he needed to be – wrapping himself in the old certainties about defending his womenfolk, and putting his own life on the line.'

'You really think that's possible?'

'I think we all have a picture of our better selves somewhere, and every now and then we have a go at being Mr Hyde. And there's a lexical element to that?'

'*Lexical*?'

'Vocabulary.'

'Thank you.'

He rings off, and I sit looking at my phone. 'Yes, I'm having a lovely holiday, thank you for asking,' I mutter, but I am not really cross. I am feeling rather pleased with myself.

Chapter Fourteen

CONSIDER IT NOT SO DEEPLY

The evenings, which she had been a bit worried about, had actually been fine – an unrushed supper in the conservatory, with news exchanged about the day's activities, and then a film on TV or a game of Monopoly. She felt a bit awkward about the game because she felt sure that it was to entertain her, and wasn't what they would normally have done – in fact, when Alex went to get it out of a cupboard in the sitting room, she could see that it was stored with the Christmas decorations – but everyone made a good show of enjoying it and said they should do it more often. They were really terribly nice people.

And then the weird thing happened. On the Wednesday evening, Alex said he was going to meet some of his friends at the pub, and when he had gone Aileen said, 'I've a task to do which you might like to help me with, Freda, if you've nothing else in mind,' and she took Freda upstairs to the room which must once have been Jon's, and was currently full of stuff.

'Jon's and Marianne's,' Aileen said. 'Things they haven't moved into their house. It can all wait, but tonight's job is these boards.'

She pointed to where, stacked against a wall, stood the big

photo boards that had been on display at the wedding, with pictures of Jon and Auntie Annie from babyhood to now.

'I need to sort these out. Some of them are theirs, some came from your granny, and some are ours. They mined our photo albums for them, and I want to retrieve them and put them back where they belong. They are all marked on the back – my idea to avoid confusion later – so we can put them into three piles – mine, Gina's, and a joint one for Jon and Marianne, which they can fight over if they want to.'

It was a lovely job, getting a chance to see properly the photos she had only glimpsed at the wedding, because there was always a crowd around them. She particularly liked the childhood pictures. Jon, she noticed, was always smiling, all freckles and curly red hair and gappy teeth, while Auntie Annie was quite often scowling. Mum would be smiling to order, but Annie was the grumpy little sister beside her.

Then she saw one where Annie was smiling broadly. She was just a toddler, and she was sitting on her own on the bonnet of a car. Mum wasn't in the picture, but there was a bit of someone else – probably Granny – just on the edge. Grandpa must have taken the picture, she thought. She put it onto Granny's pile, and then picked it up again and showed it to Aileen.

'She'll be glad to have this one, won't she?' she said. 'Grandpa must have taken it. He always loved his cars.'

As soon as she had said it, she felt stupid – it sounded as though she meant that he loved his cars but not his daughters – and she opened her mouth to explain, but realised that Aileen was looking at the photo with a kind of horror on her face.

'Are you —' Freda started to ask, and Aileen looked at her as though she wasn't quite seeing her. Then she shook her head and smiled.

'I'm sorry,' she said. 'It just gave me a shock – the number plate, you see.'

She held out the photo, and Freda looked at it. The number plate on the car was clearly visible, but she couldn't see anything wrong with it.

'The number plate?' she asked, feeling stupid, but Aileen shook her head again.

'It really doesn't matter,' she said. 'Just me being silly. It's a lovely photo.'

They carried on their sorting in silence, Freda feeling she couldn't start a new topic of conversation, but after a few minutes Aileen put down the bundle of photos she was holding and said, 'I should explain. It's not fair of me to behave like that and then not explain. You know half the story anyway, don't you? About what happened to Lucy, Jon's mother?'

'Alex told me. I didn't think...'

'It's not a secret, of course, though Jon doesn't like to make a big thing of it. No, the thing is that when the accident happened there were people who saw it, and one of them remembered – or thought they remembered – the first two letters of the car that hit Lucy.'

'And those were the letters? TN?'

'They were, and I remember because when I first knew Duncan he was always looking out for those letters, wherever we were.'

'I don't know anything about number plates,' Freda said. 'Do the letters, like, mean anything?'

'They show the place where the car was registered. TN's not a Scottish registration.'

'So where?'

'The South of England. Maidstone.'

Maidstone? Freda's stomach plunged. She looked at Aileen and she remembered her face turned towards Grandpa as they sat round the table the evening before the wedding, and she could see him being charming and telling her about the time he had spent in Perth. Grandpa's car with its Maidstone number plate – had Aileen made that connection? Was that the reason for the horror on her face? Had Grandpa said when he was in Perth? She couldn't remember. Aileen was still talking about Duncan's pursuit of car numbers, but Freda knew she had to get away, and she had to make a phone call.

Chapter Fifteen

APPROACH THE CHAMBER

'Have you ordered a search, boss?' DS Rula Bartosz asked. 'I thought this was going to be a nice, quiet interview with our victim's Other Woman.'

Scott surveyed the marked police van sitting outside Andrew Gray's chambers and quickened his pace across the square towards the building.

'Nothing to do with me,' he said. 'Who the hell's blundered in here?'

The van looked ostentatiously out of place against the symmetry of the surrounding buildings, cool and elegant with their rows of gleaming windows, glossy front doors and polished brass plates. Even without the van, though, a sense of unease about the building in front of them was palpable – a low hum of discreet disturbance oozing from the open front door. They walked in, and were met immediately by a large, balding man, who pushed open a door marked *Clerks' Office*, cast a glance at their proffered warrant cards, appeared unimpressed, and said, 'Upstairs on the right.'

'What?'

'First door on the right. Your chaps are in there. That's where most of the damage was done, as far as we could see.'

'Right.' Scott glanced at Rula Bartosz, who gave him a *What the hell?* look in return. 'We'll go up then,' he said.

As they climbed the stairs, she muttered, 'What d'you think's going on, boss?'

'No idea,' he murmured, 'but we won't let them know that.'

Interviewing Bernice Stafford about the night of Andrew Gray's murder was clearly going to have to wait for the moment because, as they looked into the room to the right at the top of the stairs, he saw two SOCOs at work, methodically taking the place apart. What kind of foul-up had brought them in to trample all over his case? Because whatever was going on here, it was his case all right: it hadn't escaped him that a discreet card on the door of the room read *Andrew Gray QC*.

As he hesitated on the landing, Rula surprised him by taking charge. 'Gary!' she called. 'That is you under there, isn't it? This is D/Su Scott. He needs to talk to you. Come out here.'

The man addressed as Gary came out of the room, peeling off his mask to reveal a cheerful, freckled face. 'Morning, sir,' he said. 'DC Gary Donoghue. This is a bit low level for a D/Su, isn't it, if you don't mind me saying? I thought DI Clough was …'

'DI Clough called you in?'

'Yes. Eight o'clock this morning.'

Scott knew DI Ian Clough slightly – a young DI, pushy and ambitious, he thought.

'Well, it looks like DI Clough and I need to have a conversation. We're here on a murder inquiry, DC Donoghue. So no, not too low level.'

The man's smile faded. 'Did she die, then? I knew they'd taken her to hospital, and there's a fair bit of blood in there, but she was able to ring in an emergency call, so I thought…'

'Who?' Scott asked sharply. 'Who do you mean by *she*?'

'The cleaner. Surprised intruders and got clobbered for her pains. The paramedics had taken her away by the time we got here. So, this is a murder inquiry now?'

'Don't get excited, Gary,' Rula Bartosz said. 'Our murder happened last week.'

'So why...?'

'The victim was the man who worked in this office – the guy with his name on the door.'

'So, you think...'

Scott stepped in briskly. 'Too early for speculation. We'll let you get back to work. Any evidence of what the intruders were after?'

'It's not clear. They tried the safe, but I guess it was too upmarket for them. There was no money in there, anyway. Only papers. And it looks like they tried to hack into the pc. They'd switched it on, anyway. We'll take it away with us for the lab to look at. Otherwise, it looks like info they were after – drawers open, files all over the place.'

'What about the other offices?'

'Don't seem to have been touched. The other lawyers were let in briefly to look round and they all seemed to think no-one had been in there. They've been sent home now. I don't know if DI Clough will want us to –'

'I'll be talking to DI Clough,' Scott said. 'Thanks.'

As they went back downstairs, Scott said, 'We'll find out where Bernice Stafford is. If she's still in the vicinity, we may as well talk to her. Otherwise, we'll put her on hold and go back to HQ, and I'll have the conversation with Ian Clough.'

'He's not going to like it – having his case taken away from him.'

'I'll keep him involved. Andrew Gray's murder is a high-profile case. If I offer him a foothold there, I think he'll come quietly.'

The clerk – Jim Donaldson, as he now introduced himself – was hovering in the lobby and seemed to have re-calibrated his attitude. Addressing Scott as 'Detective Superintendent', he asked if there was anything at all he could do to *expedite the inquiry*. When Scott asked where he could find Bernice Stafford, Donaldson made no pretence of being surprised – he was presumably well acquainted with the personal lives of the members of chambers – and told him she was likely to be out in The Walks.'

'The Walks?' Scott asked.

'The gardens, sir. They took their laptops out there to work until they can get back into their offices.'

'How big are these walks?' Rula Bartosz asked.

'About six acres, I believe. I have a map. I keep them for new members. Helps them to—'

Rula interrupted. 'That won't be necessary. We can call Mrs Stafford.' She looked at Scott. 'We have her mobile number.'

'Good,' he said. 'Thank you, Mr Donaldson. We'll take it from here.'

As they were leaving, Donaldson called out, 'There's no admittance to the gardens for the public until noon, I'm afraid.'

'We are not the public,' Rula called back, and then, more quietly, 'Don't you just hate places like this? So bloody exclusive, so entitled. Makes me want to go and pull up a plant or two.'

Scott looked at her and wondered what it said about him that he couldn't help liking stroppy women. Rula, daughter of Polish immigrants, was quietly ambitious. He liked working with her in interviews, where she was an ideal combination of warm empathy and killer precision. She had hidden her stroppiness from him until she was confident that he didn't mind it.

'Make that call,' he said. 'I wouldn't mind talking to her out in the gardens, if we can pinpoint a meeting place. It's a nice morning and there'll be no call for masks. Unless this break-in is a piece of deliberate misdirection, it suggests that it was Andrew Gray's professional life, not his personal failings, that got him killed.'

Rula walked a few metres away and was soon talking animatedly.

'Got her!' she said, as she came back towards him. 'She's in the top garden by the main gate in Theobald's Road. It's a short walk from here, she says. I couldn't hear that well, but I thought she said she'd meet us by the *stealy* – which makes no sense.'

'Yes, it does. A stele is a monument – like a standing stone, usually with an inscription on it.'

Rula looked at him. 'How do you know that?'

'I'm interested in archaeology. They were all over the place in the ancient world.'

'I'm not that interested in the past,' she said. 'The future, me.'

They found the stele – small and rather disappointingly discreet – but no sign of Bernice Stafford. While Rula scanned the manicured lawns and glossy shrubs of the garden for her, Scott stopped to read the stele's inscriptions. Both were quotes from Francis Bacon, philosopher and statesman. The lower one, exhorting men to leave the future to divine providence, wasn't particularly helpful, Scott thought, but he liked the upper one:

If a man shall begin in certainties he shall end in doubts but if he will be content to begin with doubts he shall end in certainties.

Not a bad piece of advice for a detective, he thought. He would have pointed it out to Rula, but she wouldn't like *a man,* he thought – and Bacon had penned the advice with men only in mind, of course, in spite of having been a minister to an astute and clever queen.

Looking up, he saw Bernice Stafford approaching, negotiating the expanse of grass in her high heels. She looked very different from her wedding guest persona – dark-suited now, with the red hair drawn back austerely, its flames subdued to a muted auburn. She pointed to a nearby bench, and there was a moment of awkwardness before Rula spread her jacket on the ground and sat on it, leaving Scott and Bernice to sit at either end of the bench, angled towards one another.

She spoke first. 'This rather alters things, doesn't it? The break-in?'

'You think so? We don't know enough about the break-in to make a judgement about that.'

'We know Andrew's office was targeted – no-one else's was touched. You don't think that's significant?'

He looked into her face – sharp, alert, and slightly amused – and thought that it was as well to remember that she was not just Andrew Gray's mistress, nor the dazed woman he had watched being interviewed in the hours after Gray's death. Today, she was in professional mode – composed and challenging – and she had rather remarkable pale green eyes, which he was finding disconcerting.

He found himself taking refuge in officialese. 'We have it in mind, of course, that Mr Gray may have been targeted as a result of his legal work – that is a part of our inquiry, and if you have any insights about that we'll be glad to hear them, but I'd like to start by confirming a few points about the night of the murder – now you have had time to reflect.'

Her mouth – impeccably lipsticked – twisted ironically. 'Don't the police say that catching witnesses while they are still in shock gets the best results?'

Ignoring that, he said, 'The fight. What was that about exactly?'

'Me. It was about me.'

'But you had been together all day – you and your colleagues. What triggered a fight then?'

'Andrew asked me to dance, and Henry took exception.'

'How did you feel about that?'

'Deeply embarrassed. If it had been a proper fight, I might not have minded, but they were just messing one another's clothes up.'

'Your husband knew you were having an affair?'

'I assumed he did. We never discussed it, but I didn't try very hard to keep it from him, so I thought he must know.'

'Lavender Gray knew about the affair, and she wanted a divorce. Is that what you wanted?'

'It wasn't what Andrew wanted. He was a having and eating man – eating his cake at home and having it with me. They produce men like that at our public schools.'

'If you thought your husband knew about the two of you, were you surprised that he agreed to go to the wedding?'

'I assumed that he wanted to keep an eye on me.'

'And he didn't like what he saw?'

'Evidently.'

'After we took Mr Gray away, what exactly did you and your husband do then?'

'Henry went outside, and I followed him. He was quite drunk, and I didn't want him making another scene.'

'How long were you out there?'

'Not long. I called the number of a taxi firm that I'd been given, and they said it would be fifteen minutes. They arranged to pick us up from the car park, so we walked down there.'

'Past the house where the Gray family was staying.'

'Yes, but I can assure you that Henry was with me the whole time – he didn't nip in and stab Andrew. My husband can be a complete prick, but he's not a murderer. He hasn't got the guts.'

'Where were you staying?'

'In a B&B. There didn't seem to be any actual hotels in the vicinity. We were out in the wilds somewhere.'

Scott looked at Rula, who was uncharacteristically quiet, and raised an eyebrow. She gave a minimal shake of her head. He turned back to Bernice Stafford.

'So, let's move on to the possibility that the murder and the break-in are in some way related to Andrew Gray's work. Do you have a particular case in mind?'

'Not at all. Andrew specialised in upsetting rich and powerful people – anyone from ethnic cleansers to corrupt officials creaming off foreign aid. The possibilities are endless. When he was killed, I thought revenge was the motive – he's done a few cases involving Russians, and we know how they like to mop up their enemies – but the break-in suggests that someone was trying to derail a case, doesn't it? Someone looking for evidence with a view to destroying it?'

'It's too early to say. We don't have all the results from our search yet.'

'But someone was looking for something, weren't they? I only got a glance in as I was on my way to my office, but I could see his files were all over the place.'

'So, if we're looking for a current case, that narrows the field,' he said. 'You must have discussed his work with him. Can you suggest which case it might be?'

Surprisingly, she laughed. 'I'm the scarlet woman, Mr Scott. My assignations with Andrew were strictly in that capacity. Pillow talk didn't cover prosecutions at The Hague, I'm afraid!'

Infuriatingly he found himself blushing. 'You were fellow members of chambers,' he said stiffly. 'Do you never have meetings? Aren't you aware of one another's cases?'

She looked at him with the tail end of her laughter still in her eyes, then seemed to take pity on him. 'Of course, we are aware when someone has a big case on the go. My guess – with no evidence to back it up – is a Saudi princess.'

'Really?'

'I don't mean that she did any of it herself, you understand. But her husband's a billionaire, so there'd be no problem hiring staff to do it.'

'What has she done?'

'People trafficking, false imprisonment, domestic slavery, assault, GBH… She came to police attention when a young woman escaped from her Kensington mansion and walked, barefoot and bleeding, into a nearby Danish restaurant. It was a good choice – Danes take a dim view of that sort of thing – and the police eventually screwed themselves up to prosecute for assault – the case waiting in a very long queue. They found several other women working at the house. They were clearly terrified and showed signs of abuse, but all denied that they were being held against their will, so initially the police wouldn't touch the other charges – lack of evidence, lack of resources, lack of balls. But Andrew was ready to prosecute for people trafficking and false imprisonment, and convinced the police to add the more serious charges. And now they've taken the monster princess's passport away.'

'Do you have a name for the princess?'

'Adita something. I don't remember the surname. If our intruders didn't find it, there'll be a file in Andrew's office.'

'And on his desktop?'

'Yes.'

'Well, thank you, Mrs Stafford.'

'I think you might as well start calling me Bernice. I'm sure we'll be meeting again, won't we?' She stood up. 'Do you have any idea when we might be allowed back into our offices?'

'None at all, I'm afraid.'

She gave him the twisted smile again. 'You're too important to be concerned with such trivialities?'

'Something like that.'

He and Rula Bartosz walked back in silence for a while, but as she was about to unlock the car she said, 'She played that well, didn't she? Led you very nicely where she wanted you to go. Lawyer's tactics.'

'Led me. I don't know what—'

'From *There must be a connection between the murder and the break-in* to *It must be about his work* to *And here's a nice juicy case he was working on, all laid out for you.*'

'I asked her what he was working on.'

'You did. And she was very willing to oblige. So, is that where we're going with this now? Looking for a hired killer? Quite likely an Arab?'

'It depends on what comes out of the search of Gray's office.'

Rula opened her door and slid into the driver's seat. As she manoeuvred the car out onto the road, she said, 'It's very convenient for her, the break-in, isn't it? Good timing.'

'What are you getting at?'

'Well, you'd arranged to interview her – and her husband – later on today, so you were obviously still interested in them as suspects. Only now, here's a turn-up. It seems Andrew Gray's murder was nothing to do with his messy personal life after all. *Thank you, Mr and Mrs Stafford, you're free to go.*'

'What are you saying, Rula?'

'I'm saying I wonder how the intruders got in. I wonder if a key was involved.'

'Oh, come on!'

'She wouldn't have done it herself. A grateful ex-defendant could have done it for her.'

'And all this would be to protect her husband – the *complete prick* – because he's the killer?'

'What about protecting herself?'

'Because she gave him an alibi? The local police have checked out the time they got into their taxi, and her story adds up.'

'But on their way to pick up their taxi they walked past the house where Gray was asleep.'

'And what was she doing while he went in for the kill – never mind the problem of a locked door?'

'I don't know about locked doors, but I'm thinking maybe she was the one who went in.'

'And killed him? Why? He was her lover.'

'Yes, he was, and he wanted it to stay that way. What he didn't want was to be her husband. That's pretty humiliating, you know. He wanted to carry on his nice comfortable life in his country house with his posh wife and his boys, and expected her to be available for extramarital bonking whenever he felt like it. Wouldn't make a woman feel great. You weren't looking at her hands when she said he wanted to have his cake and eat it – I don't blame you – she's got a very pretty face, hasn't she?'

'What was the matter with her hands?'

'They were curled up into tight little fists. She wasn't as relaxed as she wanted to seem. And that line about those kinds of men learning their entitlement in their public schools – that and the *having his cake* stuff – once a woman starts comparing her man with Boris, I'd say the relationship was in trouble.'

'I can see that. But kill him? Why not just walk away?'

She was silent for a minute, negotiating the traffic, then she said, 'Supposing she misread her invitation to the wedding? Supposing she thought that he had invited her so that he could present her to the family, make her official – and he'd invited her husband so he could see it too. And then she got there and found it wasn't like that at all. He was there, surrounded by family and his pretty young wife, and she and Henry were just 'work colleagues', invited to make up the numbers. Her explanation of how the fight started was pretty lame, wasn't it? That Henry objected to Andrew asking her to dance? It wasn't as though it was smoochy dancing – it's all just hopping about, isn't it, Scottish dancing?'

'And your explanation is…?'

'Maybe she asked Andrew to dance. Wanted him at least to step out onto the dance floor with her. And he turned her down. Said it wouldn't look right. If he was as drunk as you say, he might have put it quite crudely.'

'And her husband hit him? Wouldn't he have been glad to see them fall out?'

'Not necessarily – not if he was drunk as well. You should see the Bartosz family when it gets together and everyone's been on the vodka. People'll take offence at anything. Maybe Henry felt this was his moment. If Andrew had disrespected Bernice, he could show himself to be the perfect gentleman, defending his wife.'

'It's a stretch,' he said. 'And what happened then?'

'She's furious. She's been made a spectacle. She's been drinking too. All her resentment at the way she's been treated as just his bit on the side wells up in her. I had a look at her background – not posh. A London comp and then university – not Oxbridge. My guess is she's got a lot of confidence in her own ability, but she's insecure in other ways – socially. Did you notice how perfectly groomed she was this morning? I'm sure you did. She's just lost her lover under traumatic circumstances, but there she was, perfectly groomed, recent manicure and all. She needs to feel good about herself, and the way Gray behaves at the wedding makes her feel rubbish. So, she watches him being carried off to bed and she hates him. She wonders how she's come to turn her life upside down for this crappy man. Then a few minutes later she and Henry are walking past the house – the *family* house, where he's tucked up all smugly. She knows the rest of the family are still at the party – maybe she hasn't realised that Lavender is at the house. Henry hardly knows what's going on – she said he fell asleep as soon as they were in the taxi. She sends him off to the taxi and slips into the house.'

'Via a locked door?'

'Well, I'm sorry, boss, but are you absolutely sure that door locked behind you when you left? Could it have been on the latch?

He said nothing. He was sure. He had slammed it behind him and checked that it was properly closed. He remembered because he had thought at the time about what Gina had just said: *You have a pathologically overdeveloped sense of duty, do you know that?*

Rula pulled to a halt at traffic lights and looked at him.

'Just saying,' she said.

Chapter Sixteen

THAT TEARS SHALL DROWN THE WIND

'So the dates fit,' Freda says, and she sounds utterly tragic.

I know something is wrong when my phone rings at eight o'clock in the morning. Eight o'clock is the time you ring when you have been awake for hours, worrying about something, and have decided that this is the earliest time that you can make the call you need to make without creating a drama out of it. But it is a drama, however Freda tries to disguise it as a casual enquiry. I don't know how she is getting on in the drama classes, but she is a terrible actress in everyday life. Her enquiry is about when her grandfather was in Perth, working with the SNP on ideas for human rights legislation.

'I happened to hear him talking to Aileen about it the other evening, and I just wondered when that was,' she says.

Yes, right, you just wondered, Freda, and that's why you're so wound up you can hardly speak.

It so happens that I am able to answer her with no trouble. I remember it well: it was September 1994, Annie was three, Ellie had started school, and I had just gone back to full-time teaching. A bit of hands-on parenting from their father would not have come amiss, but instead he opted to go and spend six weeks in Scotland, talking to the SNP about possible human rights legislation that a putative Scottish parliament might pass in the event of the government caving in to demands for a devolution referendum, and the results going the SNP's way. It was another four years before I actually ejected Andrew from my life, but it was in the autumn of 1994, as I battled with feral teenagers by day and stroppy infants by night, that the iron entered my soul. It really did – I could taste it like blood in my mouth.

So, 'September and October 1994,' I tell Freda, and it is not the answer she is hoping for – hence the tragic tone.

'You're sure that was the date?' she asks.

'I am. Is there a problem? You don't sound happy about it.'

'No, it's fine,' she says. 'I was only wondering. Just something Aileen ...' I hear her take a breath. 'Granny, I need to tell you something, but I can't do it on the phone. Could you possibly come over here, do you think? I need your advice.'

Strengthen the sinews, summon up the blood. I can feel it happening – feel my heart rate going up, sense the adrenaline surge. When was the last time anyone – anyone at all – asked me to tell them what they should do?

'Today?' I ask.

'Can you?'

'I can.'

'That would be brill. We could meet at lunch time. One o'clock, when we have our break?'

'Excellent. Where?'

'There's a pizza place near the theatre.'

'I'll be there. Have your phone on in case I can't find you.'

I look up times of trains on my phone. They are few and far between, Pitlochry being something of an outpost, and qualifying for a station only because of the theatre being here, I guess. There is a train scheduled to get into Perth at 12.55, but I dare not go for that one. There is every chance that the train will be late, and then I have to find my way to the restaurant, by which time half of Freda's lunch break will be over. And I don't want to leave her sitting there on her own, prey to any passing sex maniac. The previous train, though, gets in two hours earlier, condemning me to two hours' wandering in an unfamiliar – and not, I think, particularly exciting – city, prey to unwise purchases and overdosing on millionaire's shortbread. I enquire at reception about taxis. A taxi will cost money but will also save me from spending it. Economical, really. And the driver they find for me is the husband of one of the hotel's housekeepers – a Bulgarian, named Ivan, who has just set up his own one-man taxi service and is delighted to be hired for a longish ride, so I can feel philanthropic as well.

I arrive at the restaurant before Freda and sit sipping fizzy water and scanning the street outside. I have been running through possible reasons for Freda's concern about the date of Andrew's sojourn in Perth, and I really can't come up with anything sensible. If we were in a TV soap it would turn out that Andrew was Jon's father – the result of a short-lived affair, relaxation from wrestling with the complexities of competing freedoms in the world of human rights. That would make for a tear-jerking drama, of course: *Annie and Jon are brother and sister! Who is going to tell them? They must part! The nation weeps!* As it is, it can't possibly be the case, and not only because I am sure that Jon's mother was a devoted young wife, even if Andrew was not a devoted husband. The dates don't fit: in autumn 1994, Jon was five years old. In fact, that must be around the time that his mother died. A car accident of some sort – I have never heard the details, but there was a drunk driver, I think.

Freda arrives. She shows no evidence of what was probably a sleepless night, because she is only just fifteen and is elastic, proof against the thousand natural shocks that

113

flesh is heir to. She just looks like someone who has had an energetic morning – flushed and slightly sweaty. She plonks herself down opposite me and says, 'I'm starving. Can we order and then talk?'

A waiter has been keeping an eye on my table since I arrived and said I was waiting for my granddaughter. He now sashays across. He thinks he knows the score – Grandma will be up for treats – so he starts to regale us with the delights of the specials and the enticements of the mocktails, and is sulky when we order a coke and a fizzy water, two pizzas *ai funghi,* and a green salad to share, rejecting suggestions of focaccia, olives, or more exciting salads.

'I think he may put us on the back burner,' I say, as we watch him stomp off. 'Time to start talking.'

Freda picks up the cloth shoulder bag that she has dumped on the floor, and takes out a photograph, which she pushes across to me. I recognise it: earlier this summer, Annie asked me to send the family photo albums to her, so that she could pick out pictures for the display boards at the wedding, and I am pretty sure that this one made the cut. I look at it now. Annie – aged two, I would say – is perched on the bonnet of a cream-coloured car, wearing a pale green summer dress and a huge grin. She is grinning at her father, who will have been taking the photo, though whether it was his daughter or his car that he was interested in it would be hard to say. I think I remember that car, although Andrew changed them so often it was hard to keep up. He liked to buy British, and I think it was a Jaguar – and now I look more closely I can see the big cat face just below Annie's feet. He loved it, and it was very much his car. His family scarcely travelled in it – I generally drove the girls around in my very old Fiat. (Oh yes, I was a driver once upon a time; it was just when I ejected Andrew that I renounced him and all his works.)

114

I look at Freda. 'It's Auntie Annie, sitting on Grandpa's new car.'

'Yes,' she says. 'Look at the number plate.'

'What am I looking for?' I ask. 'Is it supposed to be some sort of code?'

'No! It's a number plate! You know Jon's mum was killed when a car crashed into hers? It was a hit and run. The other driver was speeding, and he drove off. But there was a witness, and they remembered part of the number – the first two letters. Aileen says they were TN.'

'There must be loads of cars with TN in their number. I'm sure I've seen them around.'

'Yes! Because it's a Kent number – for cars registered in Maidstone! I googled it last night.'

I stare at her. It is no good pretending that I don't know where her fears have taken her. I am right behind her. Now I'm in a different drama. This isn't a soap, with its arbitrary plot twists tossed in whenever the viewing figures start to slump. I am wading deep into tragedy here, with its roots in human frailty, and all its terrible inevitability. Eugene O'Neill, I think. Andrew, in the exhilaration of his expert's status, his expensive car, his freedom from his tiresome family, speeding down the unfamiliar Scottish roads, feeling immortal. Then the crash, the panic, the vision of a career destroyed, the flight. And that is just Act One. Last weekend, we saw Act Three: the bereaved husband sees the evidence – a random photograph among many – and he knows the truth. He has seen his wife's murderer led away, drunk and at his mercy; he knows the dagger is in his sock; if he is seen in the house he can explain it away – he is family after all. The justice he has wanted all these years is his.

Pull yourself together. This is real life. Be a grandmother, for heaven's sake.

'Darling,' I say, 'I know where you're going with this, but let's be logical,' I say. 'Let's just suppose that it was Grandpa who caused that accident – and that's a big suppose because the only evidence is a bit of a registration number, and the witness could have misremembered that anyway – and let's suppose that one of the McCleods saw the car in that photo, do any of them really seem like people who would grab a knife and stab someone to death in revenge for something that happened nearly thirty years ago?'

'Aileen said that Duncan went on looking for that car number for years – even after he had married her.'

'All the same, wouldn't he have gone to the police if he really thought that photo was evidence? Wouldn't he have wanted to get it checked out? You know the kind of man he is.'

She stares back, tears spilling out of her eyes. 'I've thought about that – of course I have – most of the night. If he'd put the police onto it, and they somehow found proof, Jon would have had to know that his father-in-law had killed his mother. That would have been terrible – it might have made Jon and Auntie Annie split up – so he might have decided just to do it himself – to be the hand of justice.'

'Without any more evidence? Without giving Grandpa a chance to defend himself?'

'Maybe he did give him a chance. He could have talked to him at the wedding, couldn't he? There was that whole afternoon when we don't know what they were doing.' She stops, and then adds, 'And then there's Jon.'

'What?'

'Jon. She was his mother, after all. If his father was always looking for that car number, Jon would have known it too. And he was in the house that night. No problem about how to get in – all that stuff about keys.'

As it happens, I have a bit of a theory about keys and access which I'm thinking of running past David, but I'm saying nothing about that for the moment.

'Freda!' I say. 'Jon? On his wedding day? Creeping down from the bridal suite and then going back to Auntie Annie and saying, *Oh by the way, I've just stabbed your dad in the eye because he killed my mum. You don't mind, do you?*'

She puts her head down so I can't see her face. I don't know if she is going to laugh or cry, but we are interrupted by our waiter with our pizzas.

'Excellent timing,' I tell him, smiling graciously.

Freda looks at her plate.

'Eat up,' I say, as the waiter disappears. 'Life has been full of shocks in the last few days, and you've had a sleepless night and a morning of physical theatre. You are definitely hypoglycaemic, I would say. Get some solid carbs into you and you'll see things differently.'

She pushes her plate away. 'That's right,' she says. 'I am five years old, and this is a magic pizza that is going to make everything all right.'

'That's not so far from the truth. It won't change the objective facts, but it will change the weather in your head. Brain chemistry.'

'You're talking nonsense,' she says, but she does pick up her knife and fork and cut a large slice.

I chomp my way through my pizza without tasting it much. I think I am going to have to talk to David about the car number. I don't believe for a moment that Duncan or Jon is a killer, but I do think Andrew just might have been. It would be better to leave well alone, I know, because Andrew is dead, and stirring things up can only cause trouble, but I need David to tell me that.

When we have finished, and mollified our waiter somewhat with an order of salted caramel ice cream for Freda, I walk to her theatre with her and look for my taxi. Ivan has waited for me. During the forty-five-minute taxi ride here from Pitlochry, we bonded sufficiently for him to offer to stay and take his lunch break here, and drive me back at minimal extra cost. Now he has texted me to say that he is parked round the corner from the theatre, which turns out not to look much like a theatre at all when Freda leads me to it. It is a large hut, really, with a tin roof and no fly tower. It has some production posters bravely displayed on its façade, though, and Freda presents it proudly.

'It's a real community theatre,' she says. 'Grass roots. No touring productions with TV celebs.'

She has bought into the scruffy ethos of this place, and she is quoting someone – Alex? Isla? Malcolm Ross?

'Great,' I say. 'Enjoy yourself.' And looking round quickly to check that there are no teenage observers, I give her a quick hug. 'Don't worry. You're not living with a murderer. Relax and enjoy yourself.'

Then I get into Ivan's car and worry all the way home, because I know I saw something in that road next to the theatre that disturbed me, but I'm damned if I can pin down what it was.

Chapter Seventeen

MY BOSOM FRANCHIS'D
AND ALLEGIANCE CLEAR

If it weren't for the possibility of being seen, Freda felt she could have skipped into the theatre. The relief of having told someone – no, not someone, actually, but Granny specifically. You never wanted to tell Granny things, because she had such a way of taking over, but on the other hand what you wanted sometimes was exactly that – you just wanted someone to say *Leave this to me*, and then you could just dump the whole thing and make it theirs. And Granny had taken it. First, she had looked with clear eyes at Duncan and Jon and made Freda see immediately that they couldn't possibly have been the murderers – if it hadn't been for Jekyll and Hyde, Freda would have seen that for herself – and then she had taken charge of the stuff about Grandpa and the car accident, and what, if anything, she was going to do about it. She guessed that she would tell David and leave it with him. And he would most likely decide not to investigate, wouldn't he? Because it was a long time ago, and Grandpa was dead now anyway.

So now she could commit herself to enjoying the rest of this week, and it was going to be especially good because she had got out of the acting bit! The others were doing another week and doing a performance at the end of it, but Freda would be long gone by then, so she had offered to create a set. She couldn't do much because the performance space was in the round, and anyway the show was going to be a *devised piece*, which meant that they were making it up as they went along, and kept changing their minds. They did seem settled though on a chess theme – the characters were chess pieces in some way, and thought they controlled their own moves within the rules but were actually at the mercy of *The Great Hand*. Freda thought there surely had to be two hands, but she had been told that she was being *too literal*, so what did she know? Anyway, the chess board seemed a safe starting point for her set. She couldn't paint the stage floor because the others were rehearsing there, but she had been offered some small stage blocks, which she was planning to paint in a distorted checkerboard pattern, starting that afternoon. There was no space backstage so she would have to take them outside, where grit would blow into the paint, but if the blocks looked a bit distressed that was a good thing, she thought. Actually, this was going to be fun.

Chapter Eighteen

CONFUSION NOW HATH MADE HIS MASTERPIECE

'What did you say?'

'Nothing.'

'I don't think it was nothing, David.'

'You know what I said.'

'I know what I think you said but—'

'I said, *These bloody women*. All right?'

There was a silence. Scott doodled on the pad in front of him. Then Gina's voice came again, dangerously reasonable.

'Would you like to explain? Get it off your chest?'

'Police Scotland seem to have lost interest. They've let Lavender off the hook – she's back in Kent with her parents – leaving just you in the frame as far as they're concerned – and they're admitting they don't have any evidence except your DNA on Andrew, and we've told them you helped to put him to bed. So it's on the back burner for them, whereas I, who was supposed just to be lending a hand with interviews down south, am besieged by people offering me suspects and theories.'

'People?'

'Women, as it happens. I can take it from Paula and Rula – it's their job and I got them involved – but then Bernice Stafford comes at me with her theory – and she's supposed to be a suspect – and now here's Freda with her red herring, or *Finnan haddie* or whatever, implicating a pair of perfectly decent doctors in some sort of revenge drama, not to mention accusing her grandfather of murder.'

'It was unfortunate that they're showing *Dr Jekyll and Mr Hyde* at the theatre, but I think she's over that now. I just told you about Andrew and the car number because … well, I don't know why, really. I think it's possible that he was driving that car. The dates fit, and he came back from Perth very suddenly and was in an odd mood. But you couldn't find the evidence now, and he can't be prosecuted anyway.'

'So, the point of this phone call is what, exactly?'

'I told Freda I would deal with her worries, and I felt I had to do something.'

'Like pass them on to me?'

'Yes.'

'Thanks.'

There was a silence, and then he said, 'And don't tell me that you don't have a suspect in mind too?'

'As a matter of fact, I do.'

'Amaze me.'

'I have a side bet on Lavender.'

'I thought you two were getting on rather well these days.'

'We are. But that's because she has realised that I probably wasn't the wife from hell that Andrew had described, and I've realised that she isn't altogether Mrs Sweetiepie. She's a survivor. When her back's against the wall she'll find a way out – installing her parents in the house during lockdown so that Andrew was forced into playing the perfect husband and father, for instance. I'm convinced, by the way, that his affair with Bernice was revenge for that – or his reward to himself for three months of domestic servitude, at least. But that's by the by. The point is, she's got a ruthless streak and Andrew had her cornered.'

'Paula's money is on her too.'

'Well, there's a turn-up. The first time Paula and I have agreed on anything – except you, of course. Is she still carrying a torch?'

'That's a fantasy of yours and it's bollocks. Anyway, Paula thinks Lavender and her father were in it together.'

'So, she feels the same as I do, that Lavender is capable of planning it but probably didn't put the knife in herself. I had Henry Stafford in the frame as the accomplice.'

'How come?'

'They were the wronged partners in the affair. Suppose they got together earlier in the day and agreed to make common cause – not murder necessarily but just to work together to get what they wanted out of the mess. Then Henry picks the fight with Andrew – something has really riled him – and he sees his enemy being half-carried off to bed and follows, because he's not finished. He hangs around outside the house, sees Lavender come to the door, sees you leave, and gets Lavender to let him in. Phones her, probably, because I think I would have heard the doorbell. He's not bothered about me because he assumes I hate Andrew anyway. He's very drunk, of course. I don't suppose he is planning to kill him at that point – just return some of his own humiliation – but Lavender isn't drunk, and she hands him the dagger.'

'It's a nice story. The only problem being that there is absolutely no evidence, and Bernice Stafford says she was with her husband the whole time, until their taxi arrived.'

'So maybe it was just Lavender then. I don't suppose she's squeamish. She was probably taken hunting as soon as she could stay on a horse, and got blooded, as they say. A knife in the eye might be nothing to her, though even Lady Macbeth found she couldn't wield the dagger herself. That was because the king looked like her father, though, which you couldn't say of Andrew and Nicholas Payton, but Lavender obviously adores her father, so…'

'Gina, you're wittering, and I must go. I have your information about the car number, and I'll put it in the system. The accident is a very cold case now, and it's not ours, but we'll see what kind of follow-up there was on tracing the car. In these cases, where there will have been damage to the driver's vehicle, we usually put out a call to garages to report on cars brought in for repair jobs. There might be something, but you know —'

'I do. What would be the point?'

'Exactly. So, enjoy the rest of your week and —'

'Hey!'

'What?'

'You can't dangle the other suspects in front of me and then ring off without telling me who they are. Who else do *these bloody women* suspect?'

'I really don't —'

'Briefly and succinctly. I won't ask supplementary questions. Come on.'

'All right. Rula thinks Bernice could have done it – a complex psychological thing you would probably like, about her being the one who was humiliated that day, because she expected her invitation to mean that she was being presented to the family as Andrew's official partner, but it didn't work out like that – he behaved to her as if she was just another work colleague.'

'But why would —'

'No supplementaries. Then Bernice's theory. What you don't know is that there's been a break-in at their chambers – specifically into Andrew's office – nowhere else touched. So, Bernice thinks it's too much of a coincidence and that Andrew was murdered because of a case he was working on. She's offering a Saudi princess, who he was prosecuting for people trafficking, domestic slavery and other things. She has broken bail and disappeared from her London home. She has plenty of money to hire a killer and deter anyone else from taking the case.'

'I think I read about the case. Adita something. She sounds vile.'

'Bahader. Adita Bahader. I wasn't inclined to take Bernice's idea seriously, but there's a file on Andrew's work PC – the only one that's password protected – and its name is just AB. They're trying to get into it in the lab.'

'Well, if they're trying passwords, tell them not to bother with the names of his wife and children. I can guarantee they won't feature.'

'I'll be sure to pass that on. Now, is there anything else I can help you with? Or can I get back to ridding our great capital of crime?'

'Can I just sum up?'

'Go on.'

'Paula thinks Sir Nicholas did it, aided by Lavender, and I think Lavender did it, possibly with the help of Henry; Rula thinks Bernice did it, and Bernice thinks it was a Saudi princess; Freda thought one of the McCleods did it, but she's over that now, and the police up here think I did it. Correct?'

'Correct. And nobody has any real evidence, and I haven't the authority to put anyone else onto a case which is not the Met's anyway.'

'You know what you should do? You should get each of us to investigate someone else's suspect. I don't mind starting with the Saudi princess – there'll be plenty of stuff in the public domain. I'll let you know if I come up with anything, and you let me know if you get into that file. Talk soon. Bye.'

Exit in pursuit of a bright idea, Scott thought, as he put his phone down and sat back in his chair. Well, she couldn't do any harm pursuing the Adita Bahader case, could she? She would just look up past copies of the Guardian on line. That was all she could do while she was up in Scotland. When she got back to London, he would have to put the frighteners on her to stop her from trying to talk to Adita Bahader's friends and neighbours. He quailed at the image of Gina turning up on the doorsteps of Kensington mansions with implausible stories designed to get her into the house. These people were unimaginably rich, therefore powerful, therefore dangerous. Would he be able to convince her? Perhaps, he thought, she would be onto something new by then.

He reached out for the pad he had been doodling on, pulled it towards him and looked at what he had written while they had been talking:

Paula – Sir N (+ Lavender)
Gina – Lavender (? + Henry S)
Rula – Bernice
Bernice – Adita Bahader
(Freda – Duncan or Jon McCleod)
DI Mitchell – Gina

He considered the list for a moment, then idly drew a line to link Gina's name with Adita Bahader. *Get each of us to investigate someone else's suspect.* That was daft, of course, but not completely stupid. He traced lines from Paula to Bernice, and another from Rula to Sir Nicholas and Lavender. That might actually work. They were all slippery characters, Lavender, her father, and Bernice; a second interview with a newcomer with a fresh approach could well unsettle them. Paula would do well with Bernice Stafford, one professional woman to another; she might well get under her guard and get more from her than he had managed. And Rula. He smiled as he imagined Rula with Sir Nicholas. She wasn't anything like as prickly as Paula; getting to where she was now from her struggling immigrant background had been a lot tougher than Paula's career, with her good degree and secure, middle-class family. Rula had learnt how to pick her battles and she wouldn't turn a hair if she was called *my dear young lady*. She would flirt with him, in fact, and get right behind his defences. She could have a go at Lavender too, while she was down in Kent. Rula's knack of being all warm sympathy one moment and sliding the stiletto in the next would catch Lavender off guard after her easy ride with the Scottish police.

Well, that could work, and he would get them onto it, but that was the limit as far as Gina's ideas were concerned. He looked again at his list. If he could get the Angus police to find themselves a suspect other than Gina he would, but he had no evidence against anyone else to offer them at the moment. He wasn't letting Freda anywhere near the investigation after the near disaster of last summer in The Lakes, and Bernice's place was among the suspects, however skilfully she had angled herself otherwise. There was no way he would let her get on the inside.

Chapter Nineteen

THE PERFECTEST SPY O' TH' TIME

I have found myself the perfect cover for contacting Bernice Stafford. My offer to research Adita Bahader for David was quite genuine; I remember the story from back before lockdowns and I would like to know more – and it is not beyond possibility that she paid someone to dispose of Andrew. However, since it was Bernice who suggested this angle, it would be perfectly natural for me to ring her to talk about it, and then I can see if we can find common ground. There is something I think she could do which would put my mind at rest, and which I can't do myself – certainly not from up here, and probably not at all, since I don't have the hair and the legs and the bosom. But she does.

So, I look the story up online and find, as I expected, that Adita Bahader is a nasty piece of work. Mind you, it looks as though she has been pretty badly treated herself. She was not born a princess, but married into the royal family and then failed to produce offspring. Sent to London ostensibly for someone in Harley Street to sort her out, she seems to have been put under luxury house arrest in her husband's Kensington mansion and forbidden to come home, while her husband enjoys domestic life in Saudi with his other wives, all busily popping out babies. Not much fun for her, I know

– lonely and humiliating – but no excuse for staffing her house with trafficked women, and starving, overworking, and beating them. One of them managed to escape only because she had become so emaciated that she was able to get through a tiny pantry window. Once outside, she had the sense not to ring any doorbells, but stumbled, barefoot, into a Danish restaurant, where the staff appear to have behaved in exactly the low-key, practical way that makes me wish I could be a Scandinavian. They found her a sweater and a pair of shoes, fed her a bowl of soup, called the police, and absolutely refused to talk to reporters about what had happened. It was diners in the restaurant who rushed out to tell all and sundry about the exciting accompaniment to their smørrebrød, meatballs, and pork with parsley sauce. The restaurant is called *Hjem*, by the way – *Home* – which feels ironic, doesn't it?

I can't work out, from the reports I can find, what exactly the police did, but they obviously made a mess of things, charging her with something minor and releasing her on a million-pound bail, which she casually jumped, thus thwarting Andrew, wearing the white hat, in taking her on in court. She may be out of the country, with the prince's connivance to avoid family embarrassment. I don't imagine life will be very comfortable for her, wherever she ends up, but it will probably be better than Holloway. If she has got away, I don't really understand why she would have needed to order a hit on Andrew. Simple revenge, perhaps.

I find a fulsome profile of Andrew, relating to the proposed prosecution, in the *Indie*, and I scan it queasily since it verges on the idolatrous. *Fearless, principled, and relentless in pursuit of justice*, we are told, and why should anyone care that he was no pleasure to live with? Which takes me to Bernice Stafford.

The thing is, I really need to know whether there is any likelihood that Andrew was responsible for that car accident.

Something happened to bring his little adventure in Perth to an abrupt end. At the time I half suspected that it was a woman, and decided that I was too busy to worry about it since he seemed to be running away from her anyway. Now I have a different picture, and I think Roddy Carmichael might have the answer. David said that with these hit and run crimes they put out a call to all garages, asking them to report on bodywork repairs done, in the days following the accident, to relevant vehicles, but Roddy would have done the repairs, no questions asked and certainly no sneaking to the police, because good old Roddy was an old school chum of Andrew's and would never sneak to a prefect about a prank in the dorm. Roddy runs an upmarket garage in West Kent, exclusively for clients with cars expensive enough to be worth his time. I haven't seen him since Andrew and I parted, but I have checked online and found the website for Top Motors, complete with a grinning photo of Roddy, a bit greyer, but otherwise unchanged. He dresses as though he is about to jump into his spitfire and head out over the Channel – sheepskin jacket, boots, and a Leslie Howard moustache – and twenty years ago he regarded any attractive young woman as a personal challenge. I don't imagine that has changed, and as I obviously don't fit that bill any more, I am proposing to enrol a woman who does.

It is no trouble to find the phone number for Andrew's chambers, to announce myself as Andrew's wife, and to get put through to Bernice's office. She sounds briskly professional, if apprehensive, when she answers, and I feel conscious of being perched on the bed in my hotel room, in holiday attire, as I imagine her dark-suited and seated at her desk.

'This is Bernice Stafford. How can I help you, Mrs Gray?'

Her voice is unexpected – lower and more carefully modulated than the clothes and hair at the wedding led me to expect.

'Don't worry,' I say. 'I'm not the current Mrs Gray. I'm Gina. Andrew may have mentioned me? Or perhaps not?'

'Well, I saw you at the wedding, of course.'

'Yes. Mother of the Bride, avoiding speaking to Father of the Bride."

'Tricky etiquette, isn't it? Even worse being Mistress of Father of the Bride.'

'I can imagine.'

'So, how can I help you? Do you want to warn me off going to the funeral?'

This disconcerts me. I haven't even thought about a funeral. I have a sudden vision of Lavender, Bernice and me sitting together in a front pew, and I nearly laugh, but stop myself because she at least is actually grieving for him, I suppose.

'That's not my business,' I say. 'I guess Lavender and Andrew's brother will be organising things. I imagine both of us will be pretty *non gratae,* won't we?'

'So, what is it you want?'

She has that *I have things to do* tone, so I speed up.

'It's a professional matter, actually, though relating to Andrew. I gather you've suggested that his murder might be connected to his prosecution of Adita Bahader?'

'Who told … oh, of course, Superintendent Scott is your partner, isn't he?'

'It's not a term I like.'

'So what do you like?'

'I'm trying *paramour* at the moment.'

That makes her laugh, and I think I could really like this woman.

She says, 'It was just a suggestion – the Bahader case. You'll have heard about the break-in at our chambers, and the raid on Andrew's office. Unless that's deliberate deflection, it suggests that his death might be connected with his work, doesn't it? And your detective asked me to suggest a possible case.'

'And I've volunteered to find out more about the case. His remit is limited – he's just supposed to be following up on a few of the guests down south, to help out the Angus police – so he has limited resources. I've found out what I can online, but I can't find out exactly where things stand as far as an imminent prosecution goes. She's disappeared, is that right?'

'Yes. Jumped bail and failed to appear at the scheduled court hearing where Andrew was lined up for a prosecution on charges of people trafficking, false imprisonment and ABH.'

'Do we assume that she has left the country?'

'I'm not sure. She's had to surrender her passport but she's got the resources to get hold of another one. Her problem would be that her husband doesn't want her back, so he would ensure that she wasn't allowed back into Saudi. Or if she did get back in there's a good chance he would disappear her – an embarrassment and inconvenience to be disposed of.'

'So would she have gone somewhere else?'

'Her husband could cut off the money supply, and I doubt she would feel safe in another Arab country. The prince has a long reach. The UK is probably the safest place for her to be.'

'So where do you think she is?'

'Not far from her Kensington home is my guess. I wouldn't be surprised if she's actually hiding out in the depths of her vast house, with the staff too scared to give her away. But she doesn't want to stay in hiding forever, and maybe she thought that without Andrew on her case the prosecution would be dropped, and she could come out of her burrow.'

'So, someone needs to stake out the house, really.'

'I guess. I hope you're not thinking of doing that yourself. Andrew mentioned your amateur sleuthing – he was rather impressed, actually – but she's a dangerous woman.'

'I'm in Scotland, so no chance.' And then I spot the perfect segue into the real objective of this conversation.

'Talking of which,' I say, 'there is another investigation I would be pursuing if I were down south – and if I were young and attractive.'

'Really?'

I'm sure I can hear her looking at her watch.

'Something that's emerged about Andrew, and I think you and I would both like to know the truth about—'

She breaks in. 'If it's about another woman, I'm really not interested.'

'It's not. It's about dangerous driving.'

'What? Well, you can forget that. Driving over the limit? Andrew would never have risked his career like that. He didn't drink at all when he was going to drive.'

'What about speeding?'

'Never. He loved his cars, but I noticed he never went over the speed limit – even in places where everyone does it.'

'Maybe that's because of an experience he had in the past.'

'Maybe it's because he valued his career.'

'I'm going to tell you a story,' I say, and then I tell her: 'Andrew's bunking off to Perth in 1993 to talk about human rights legislation for a putative Scottish parliament, the hit and run accident that killed Lucy McCleod in September 1993, the partial car number, Maidstone registration, remembered by a witness, the photograph at the wedding, the car, the date. And Top Motors.'

'And on top of all that,' I say, 'Andrew came home suddenly, unexpectedly and in an odd state – nervous, agitated, not like himself.'

There is a long pause, and then Bernice asks, 'Is that it?'

'Pretty much.'

I don't say anything about Freda's revenge suspicions because I'm dismissing them, and I don't want to muddy the waters.

She says nothing.

'What would you say if it was a police case? As a lawyer?'
I ask.

'Prosecution or defence?'

'Either.'

'Actually, it would be the same for both. Not enough evidence. If I were defending, I would give the jury some stats about how many cars with English registration plates cross the border into Scotland every day, I would emphasise that two letters constitute hardly more than a quarter of a car number, I would point up the defendant's unblemished driving record and I would get his vengeful ex-wife into the witness box and demolish her alleged recollection that he had been *in an odd state* when he returned from Scotland. I would put the defendant himself in the box, too, of course, where he would impress them with his good sense and probity. And frankly, Gina, I am pretty pissed off to think that you can believe that Andrew could ever have killed a woman and run away.'

'He was at the beginning of his career,' I say, 'and he had everything to lose.'

'So he was careful. As I say, he never —'

'He wasn't so careful when he was young,' I break in. 'I knew him, remember. He could put his foot down sometimes – I didn't like him driving the children anywhere.'

'There's only your word for that.'

'And my word doesn't count because I'm an ex-wife?'

She says nothing.

'I don't want him to have done it,' I say eventually. 'If it were ever proved, it would make a hell of a mess in the family for a start. But I can't just forget it. And now you'll find you can't either, I bet you.'

'Well thanks for that, but I think I'll manage. I have no idea what you think I can do about this, but my answer is *no*, whatever it is. You have all kinds of stored-up resentment against Andrew – and some of it may be justified for all I know – but I loved him, and I'm grieving for him, though I may be the only one who is. You're a cold-hearted pair, you and Lavender, but if you can't grieve you can at least leave his reputation alone.'

And with that she slams down her phone.

Damn, damn, damn.

I pushed her too hard, and now I've lost her. I throw my phone onto the bed and go to look out of my window. What to do? It's no good my trying to talk to Roddy Carmichael. He fancied me once, but that was a very long time ago, and I'm quite sure he saw Andrew as the wronged party when I threw him out. Bernice was my only hope. I gaze across the loch at the hills beyond and decide that a really punishing walk is what I deserve. I find my walking boots, stuff water, tissues, sun cream and phone into a shoulder bag, don sunglasses and a floppy hat, pick up my key, and leave the room. I am heading downstairs when my phone rings and I wrestle it out of my bag, still on the move.

'All right,' she says. 'You knew I wouldn't be able to leave it alone, didn't you?'

She is back! I pump the air, but keep my voice cool.

'So, would you like the address of the garage?' I ask.

'I've got it. Top Motors, you said? Near Sevenoaks?'

'That's right. Can you take your car in for some fine tuning? Say Andrew recommended—'

'I know what to do, I don't need coaching.'

'Right. One thing though. He's a car snob. Top Motors means what it says. Is your car, you know…?'

'It's a year-old Range Rover. I don't think he'll turn his nose up.'

'A Range Rover,' I say. 'That must be convenient in London.'

'We have dogs,' she says, and then, 'Let's be clear, I'm doing this with the aim of proving Andrew's innocence.

I'm on a hiding to nothing trying to prove a negative but I'll give it a damned good try. I don't think you want him to be innocent. We're not on the same side here.'

'But you'll let me know how you get on?'

'Probably,' she says.

Chapter Twenty

LOOK LIKE THE INNOCENT FLOWER

Freda peeled off the last strip of masking tape from the box she had been painting and surveyed the effect critically. It looked all right, she thought. It had taken some time to work out the best way to get the edges of her checkerboard squares clean and straight, but she was there now. Working outside in the yard had its advantages and drawbacks. She liked being outside and not having to breathe in the paint fumes all the time – and people walked by and said encouraging things, which was nice. Even Malcolm had stopped to say how lucky they were to have *someone with a good eye on the team*. On the other hand, the dust and grit did get into the wet paint, and yesterday there had been a sudden shower, which had her frantically dragging newly painted boxes under cover. On the whole, though, she was enjoying herself – and it beat posing and performing any day.

Her phone rang. Not Lisa or Mia, nor Mum, because they had their own ringtones. She wiped her hands on a rag and stood up to fish her phone out of her jeans pocket. She didn't recognise the number.

'Hello,' she said cautiously.

'Freda darling!'

Lavender's voice was instantly recognisable.

'Oh hello, Auntie Lavender,' she said. 'I didn't know you had my number.'

'You gave it to me ages ago – that time when... the dog... you know?'

'Oh. Yes.'

There was a pause. What did she want?

'The thing is, darling, I'm in a bit of a pickle, and I wondered if you could help me.'

She wanted to say *No, no, no, I can't. For all I know you're a murderer. Leave me alone.* Instead, she said, 'You do know I'm in Scotland, don't you?'

'Yes, I do, darling, and so is your granny. That's the point really.'

Freda was pacing the small courtyard, and realised that she was actually grinding her teeth.

'Why?' she asked, and she didn't care if it sounded rude.

'I said something silly to your granny – on the day when... on the day of the wedding – and I'm afraid she might have taken it seriously – might even have told the police...'

'Have you asked her?' Freda felt for a moment as though she was the adult here.

'Well, no...' Lavender twittered. 'You see, Granny and I are in a tricky situation – being the two prime suspects for Grandpa's death, being alone in the house with him at the crucial time. Of course, neither of us did it – I mean how could we? We're not that sort of people, are we? But I did say this silly thing, because I was so upset, and you know how you say things you don't mean when you're upset? And if the police have been being beastly to Granny, I'm afraid she might have told them about it.'

'What did you say?' *Let's get this straight*, she thought, *and stop piddling about.*

'I said I wanted to kill him.'

'Kill Grandpa?'

'Yes.'

'Blimey!'

'Yes.' Lavender gave a nervous little giggle. 'So stupid – just letting rip. Of course I didn't mean it.'

'And you think Granny's told the police?'

'I don't know!' she wailed. 'But if she has, I thought you could talk to her, and get her to talk to David. Say she's not sure that was what I said. Or that it was just a joke. Or… I don't know… but something…'

This was ridiculous, Freda thought. You couldn't take back something like that.

'Why do I have to do it? Why can't you ask her?' she said.

'Because that would be tampering with the evidence – interfering with a witness – that sort of thing.'

'And if I ask her for you, it's not?'

'Not if you do it really subtly, darling, as if it's your idea.'

'I don't think it's the kind of thing you can do subtly,' she said.

'But you're such a clever girl – and so grown up.'

Rage suddenly seized Freda – a great rush of it that made her feel hot and shaky.

'Granny's a suspect, Lavender,' she hissed, because she didn't seem to have enough breath to speak normally, 'and I'm not going to ask her to do anything that might make things worse for her. And I can't believe that you've asked me to.'

And then she closed her phone, stuffed it in her pocket, and continued to pace up and down the little courtyard.

What made adults think they could do this? Screw up big time and then expect someone else to sort out their mess – even if that someone was a child? Because that was what she was, wasn't she – legally? And in any other situation adults were only too keen to point that out to her – that she was *still a child* – that she was too young to understand, to make choices, to go where she liked and do what she liked. But Lavender thought it was quite all right to put all this responsibility on her. Well, she wasn't bloody doing it, that was for sure. Did Lavender think she was stupid? Why would she do anything to get Lavender off the hook when that would put Granny more firmly on the hook, as far as the police were concerned?

She stopped pacing and sat down on one of the boxes that were waiting to be painted. She would bet, in fact, that Granny hadn't told the police what Lavender had said. She was too honourable for that, and she would know when someone meant what they were saying and when they were just mouthing off. And if she had told them, then they would have asked Lavender about it, wouldn't they, because it would be evidence against her? Even if they were taken in by her poor little widow act, they couldn't just ignore that, could they?

She got up and picked up her paintbrush. Granny might not have told them, but somebody should, she thought, dipping deep into the black paint. If Lavender was stupid enough to say she wanted to kill her husband, then she could take the consequences. Somewhere on her phone she had a number she could call, and as soon as she had finished this box, she was going to call it.

Chapter Twenty-One

BUT BE THE SERPENT UNDER IT

He was in a senior staff meeting when his phone, set to silent, gave the urgent little spasm that signalled a thwarted incoming call. He should have ignored it, of course, but the useful business was done, and he – like most of his colleagues, he judged – was beginning to get restless. The Deputy Assistant Commissioner was all very well, but she didn't know how to wrap up a meeting. Surreptitiously taking out the phone, he glanced at the caller ID, and his heart lurched. FREDA, it read, and that could only mean an emergency. He stood up and edged towards the door. The Deputy ACC looked up and Scott waggled his phone apologetically. 'So sorry,' he said, 'this is urgent, I'm afraid,' and made his escape.

'Freda?' he said, as soon as he was out of the room. 'What is it? What's happened.'

There was a moment's silence, in which his heart rate accelerated, and then her voice came, sounding very young and rather distant.

'I'm sorry to bother you, David. You sound very busy.'

'It's fine, Freda. What is it? Are you all right?'

'Yes, I'm all right.'

'Is Gi – is your granny all right? Has something happened to her?'

'She's all right, I think.'

'So, what is it?' He was slowing down now, approaching his office, and beginning to feel ridiculous for his moment of panic.

'What it is,' she said, 'is did Granny ever tell you, or the other police, that Lavender told her she wanted to kill Grandpa?'

'She what?' He was juggling a file of papers and his phone while unlocking his office door.

'On the day of the wedding, Lavender told Granny that she wanted to kill Grandpa – because of that woman, you know, and all that.'

'And your granny told you that?'

'No. Lavender told me.'

'Lavender? Why?'

He went over to stand by his window and leant his head against the cool glass. What was she talking about?

'She rang me just now, and said that she had told Granny she wanted to kill Grandpa, and now she was afraid that Granny might have told the police and – would you believe – she wanted me to talk to Granny, and get her to talk to you, and somehow say that Lavender hadn't said that after all.'

And now Scott could see what had happened. Rula had been in Kent that morning, interviewing Lavender and her parents. Where the Angus police had allowed Lavender to flutter away, Rula had not. Rula had rattled her cage, and now she was scared. And Gina was right that Lavender had ruthless instincts. She could see that whatever Gina did – tell the police at this late stage of her threat to kill, or try to take back what she had told them – either would put more suspicion on her, and the more Gina was suspected, the safer Lavender would be.

He felt one of his infrequent but powerful surges of affection – maybe love – for Gina. She would not have told the Angus police about Lavender's threat, for a multitude of reasons: because Lavender had spoken to her as a friend, because she was sure she didn't mean it, because it would be beneath her dignity to save herself from suspicion by diverting it to someone else, and – probably most importantly – because she lived a lot of her life vicariously through literature and she would have been only too conscious that the suspect who has uttered threats against the murder victim never turns out to be the killer, but she couldn't trust the police to know this.

He laughed, and heard Freda say, 'David?'

He said, 'Thank you for telling me, Freda. I think I know why Lavender's worried. Say nothing to Granny. I'm pretty sure she hasn't said anything, because—'

'Because she's too honourable,' she broke in. 'That's what I thought too.'

'Exactly. Leave it with me. You did the right thing. How's the course going?'

'Brilliantly. I'm doing scenery and I'm covered in paint.'

'Pig in clover?'

'That's me!'

After she rang off, Scott settled with difficulty to the pile of reports which, as he kept reminding himself, represented his real job. The break-in at Andrew Gray's office had given him a legitimate angle on the murder case from the Met's point of view, but it was still technically a case for the Angus police, and he ought to be pushing it back to them. Instead, he was sitting at his desk, distracted, waiting to hear the outcome of Rula Bartosz's trip down into Kent to interview the Payton family.

He did not have long to wait. A tap on the door heralded the entrance of Rula, looking quite unlike her usual self – in costume, in fact, for a particular role. She was a strikingly pretty woman – slim and dark, with high cheekbones and clear hazel eyes – but she usually dressed down, wearing no obvious makeup, pulling her thick curls into a tight bunch at the nape of her neck, and dressing in her own uniform of dark jacket and trousers and flat shoes. Today, though, she was dressed in clothes which he thought she must surely have borrowed, unless she had a wardrobe for a non-work life that he had never guessed at. She was wearing a sleeveless, longish, pink and white patterned dress, and high-heeled sandals. Her hair was loose on her shoulders, and she was wearing a pink lipstick that made her look very young.

'Excellent outfit,' he said. 'I hope Sir Nicholas appreciated it.'

She laughed and swished her skirt. 'I felt like I was under cover,' she said, 'and I can't wait to get these shoes off. I borrowed them from my sister, and they're too small.'

She was very pleased with herself, he saw, still on a post-performance high, in spite of the two-hour drive back. She needed food, tea, and a change of clothes, he thought, before he would get a sensible report from her. And, if he was honest, he needed her to look more like her usual self.

'If you've got other clothes with you, do you want to change and get something to eat before we debrief?' he said.

Even as the words came out, he could hear how repressive he sounded, how old, how dull, how unresponsive to her high spirits, and he saw the excitement drain from her face.

'I just wanted to let you know that I was back,' she said flatly. 'What time would you like me to come back? Or I can submit a written report, if you would rather.'

Knowing he had to rescue this, he said,' Why don't we meet down in the canteen in fifteen minutes? This morning's trip was above and beyond the call, so I'll buy you lunch, and you can give me the lowdown.'

'Right,' she said, 'Thank you.'

He found her in the canteen twenty minutes later, in navy trousers and a dark green shirt, her hair tamed by an elastic band. She gave him a smile, which he took as a token of forgiveness, and turned back to her negotiation with a woman who was swabbing down the empty tables. It was the post-lunchtime lull, and the remains of the hot dishes on offer had been cleared away. As he approached, he heard the woman say, 'Seeing as it's you, Rula, and you've been all the way down to Kent and back, I'll get them to rustle you up a ploughman's. What d'you want to drink with that?'

'A pot of tea, please, Rosa.'

The woman turned a baleful eye on Scott. 'I suppose you're the one sent her down to Kent,' she said. 'D'you want a drink?'

'Coffee, please. Black.'

'Who's paying?'

'I am,' he said, and followed her obediently to a till.

As she put the drinks on a tray, she said, 'She's a treasure, that girl. You mind you look after her.' And there was a strong implication that she knew people who would sort him out if he didn't.

As he carried the drinks to the table by a window, where Rula was sitting, he reflected that of course she would know the canteen staff by name, and yes, she was a treasure.

He set the drinks down and they both looked out over the murky stretch of Thames in view below. As Rula poured her tea and added milk and – surprisingly – sugar, he sought around for a topic to occupy them until her food arrived and they could start the debrief.

'Were your drives all right?' he asked.

'No problem driving down – I started early. More traffic coming back, but I was never actually static, which isn't bad for the M25. It was a pity I had to take the motorway, really. It must be nice countryside – the Garden of England and all that.'

'It is. What did you think of the Paytons' pile?'

'Proper stately home, isn't it? I half expected to be asked for my ticket.'

145

'Quite a bit of land, too – fishing lake and all.'

'I know. I was taken there.'

'You were? Who—'

He broke off as Rula's ploughman's arrived, deposited by Rosa with another warning glance at Scott.

'You eat for a bit,' he said. 'I've got a couple of text messages to send, and then we can talk.'

She dived into her ploughman's with enthusiasm, while he started texts both to Gina and to Freda, but gave up on them as inadequate for the complexities involved. Then Rula, swallowing a chunk of bread, said, 'Shall I start?'

'Go ahead.'

'Well, I saw Sir Nick first, and I'm glad you warned me. He did call me *my dear young lady*, and at one point he congratulated me on how well I had done, *considering my background*. I'm not at all sure what he thought he knew about my background, but perhaps he just meant having a funny foreign name. Anyway, I played up. I smiled nicely and told him you had sent me *just to note down a few details* – actually interviewing him as a suspect being well above my pay grade. In no time, he was like my kind old uncle, and walking me off to the fishing lake to show me where he camped on the night of the murder. Not a good idea in my sister's sandals, but I kept smiling, and soon he was telling me that he thought he had *given the wrong impression* when he was talking to you, and you might have thought that he didn't really have an alibi for that night. It was true that he had cooked supper and camped by the lake on the Saturday night, and then gone off for a long ride on his horse on the Sunday morning, but he had *just remembered* that he had called in at the house on the Sunday morning before he went for his ride, and had left a note for his wife on the kitchen table. I asked him why he hadn't phoned or texted, but he said he didn't like mobiles and kept his switched off. Very handy.'

'It seems to be true,' Scott said. 'They found virtually nothing on his phone in the lab. Did you check with Lady P about the note?'

'Yes!' She laughed. 'Poor woman. She didn't know what she was supposed to say, I think, so she said, *Well, yes, there might have been a note – or perhaps that was another day – no, she thought it was that day, and if that was what her husband said then it must have been.*'

'But she hadn't kept it?'

'No. But Sir Nick *just remembered* something else. He had taken his car – a big four by four, by the way – to the garage for servicing the week before, and they had made a note of the mileage. He got me to look at his milometer, and unless he or the garage had fiddled it, that car hadn't done a trip to Scotland and back since it went in for servicing.'

'Is it his only car?'

'Yes. Lady P has one, but she used it on the Sunday morning to give someone a lift to church.'

'Did you get the name of the garage?'

'Yes. It was too far away for me to go there right away. He takes the cars there because the owner is – was – a friend of his *wretched son-in-law*, apparently. It's called *Top Motors*.'

Scott's brain tingled. A garage belonging to a friend of Andrew's, a car damaged in a hit and run incident. He would have to talk to Gina.

'So, the question is, why didn't he come up with the alibis right away?' he said. 'Do you think he actually wanted to have suspicion fall on him, because he wanted to protect his daughter?'

'It's possible. And now he thinks she's not a suspect, so he's trying to row back. And poor old Lady P doesn't know what she's supposed to say.'

'Not on message?'

'Not quite.'

'What about Lavender?' he asked. 'Did you talk to her?'

'I did. She's a piece of work, isn't she?' She swallowed a chunk of cheese and went on. 'She took me for a walk, too. What is it with these people? Am I too much of a peasant to be allowed into their house?'

'Paula and I were kept outside too. I took it as a COVID thing.'

'Well, maybe. Her excuse was getting away from the kids. They were in the kitchen, though, and Lady P seemed to have them under control. Anyway, she took me off to the rose garden, and we sat on a bench that left green smears on my nice dress.'

'Lavender will have appreciated the nice dress.'

'I guess so. It felt like we were a couple of Jane Austen girls, sitting there in our flowery dresses. She started off defensive – saying she'd been interviewed up in Scotland and they were quite satisfied with her answers, but I only had to give her a little nudge – saying it was lovely at her parents' house but she must be keen to get back home – and she was off, chatting away, telling me what a bastard her husband had been, planning to sell the house and screw her father out of his money, and all about her plans. She's sending the boys off to boarding school, apparently, and starting a riding school at her home – a joint enterprise with a friend. A male friend.'

'She's been thinking she's in the clear, hasn't she, to be talking that indiscreetly? Only now she may be regretting it. Do you think she could have killed him?'

'I think she's probably always got what she wanted. Spoilt rotten, I would say, and outraged at her husband not giving her what she wanted. I should think she was quite capable of sticking a knife into him. Not necessarily planned, but when she saw the opportunity, she wouldn't hesitate.'

'And what about Sir Nicholas? Paula Powell thinks they could have been in it together – she let him in, and he did the deed.'

She took a long swig of tea and then said, 'I don't know. It's possible, but he seemed to me like a decent man. He was a soldier, so I suppose he may have killed people, but I'm not sure he would kill a man in his sleep.'

'Yes, that's what I thought. And so did Gina.'

She looked up sharply from pouring herself more tea. 'You've been discussing the case with Gina?'

'Well, I – she knows the people involved, of course, so she has a useful ...' He broke off, feeling a flush of embarrassment rising in his face.

'But she's a suspect, isn't she?'

'Only theoretically.'

'Theoretically?'

'She had opportunity – she was in the house – but no motive.'

'Have the Angus police excluded her from their inquiry?'

'They haven't interviewed her again.'

'That's not the same thing, is it?'

He rallied. 'There's no shortage of suspects with real motives – Lavender and her father, Bernice or Henry Stafford, not to mention any number of people with a grudge against him as a result of his legal work. Gina comes very low on anyone's list.'

He thought she was going to argue, but instead she started rummaging in the briefcase she had with her.

'That reminds me,' she said. 'When I checked back at my desk just now, I found this.' She handed over a printed sheet. 'It's a list of the contents of the safe in Andrew Gray's office. The intruder tried to break into the safe – he could just have been after money, of course, but I thought it was worth seeing what else he might have been looking for. The bundle of press cuttings is the interesting item. Why would you keep that in a safe? And you'll see – the case they relate to was one of yours.'

Chapter Twenty-Two

WOULD YOU HEAR IT FROM OUR LIPS?

Bernice has sent me an email with a startling attachment. She not only went to see Roddy Carmichael at Top Motors, but she made a covert recording of their conversation on her phone – *to shut you up,* her email says, *and make it clear that this is the end of it. Listen to it, draw your own conclusions, and then don't contact me again.* I half expect her to have me issued with a restraining order, but I can't help liking her punchiness. In spite of her ownership of a Range Rover, I do feel that she is a woman after my own heart.

Anyway, here is the recording. I have played it through, and really the dialogue is better than many afternoon dramas on Radio 4 – so much so that I am going to present it to you here in script form, with the addition of sound cues where necessary, and a little scene setting. Of course, I have never written a radio script, so this is my amateur version, but it will give you an idea.

Scene: Mid-morning in late summer. A garage. Birdsong and an engine turning. A man (RODDY) is humming.
(Sound of a 4x4 arriving and stopping. Car door slams.)

RODDY *(50s, public school, professional charmer with*

RAF moustache) Well, this morning just got sunnier! Good morning, madam. How can I help you?

BERNICE (*Late thirties professional, red hair, dressed for effect)* I'd like someone to give this beast a service and a general tune-up. Can you do that for me?

RODDY: Certainly can. I'm Roddy. Proprietor of this place. *A poor thing but mine own.*

BERNICE: Bernice Stafford.

RODDY: Great pleasure to meet you, Bernice. Won't shake hands – engine grease and COVID, take your pick – but delighted you've chosen our humble establishment. Any particular problems with the motor?

BERNICE: She's running pretty well, but she was a bit sluggish in the mornings last winter.

RODDY: Weren't we all, my dear? I certainly need a shot of caffeine in the starter on a cold morning. Talking of which, can I offer you a coffee? We have a mean machine out at the back.

BERNICE: That sounds tempting. Breakfast coffee was some time ago.

RODDY: Have you come far?

BERNICE: *(laughing)* Isn't that what the Queen says to everyone?

RODDY: *(very camp)* Well that's the first time anyone has mistaken me for a queen, duckie!

BERNICE: *(more laughter)* Andrew said you were a hoot.

RODDY: Andrew?

BERNICE: Andrew Gray. He recommended you to me.

RODDY: *(crestfallen)* Dear old Drew. What a tragedy that was. Couldn't believe it. Haven't got over it. So, you're a friend of his?

BERNICE: A good friend, yes.

RODDY: Wait a minute – not just a friend. Woman like you – don't mind my saying – Drew wouldn't have been just a friend.

BERNICE: We were close.

RODDY: *(hint of a leer)* I'll bet you were. My condolences. Really. Jolly tough for you. Let me get you that coffee.

(Footsteps disappearing, then voices at a distance.)

RODDY: Quite a chichi little spot we've got round here. Set up by my assistant for al fresco entertaining. *(calls)* Suse! Can we get a couple of coffees out here? What will you have, Bernice? The machine does anything except a G&T.

BERNICE: Espresso would be lovely. Black.

RODDY: Make it a double?

BERNICE: Why not?

RODDY: *(calling)* Suse darling, two double espressos – and anything delicious you've got to eat.

(Sounds of scraping of chairs and settling down.)

RODDY: So, you were Drew's – what should I call you? What's the PC word these days?

BERNICE: I'm not sure there is one. Someone the other day suggested *paramour*. A bit OTT, but...

RODDY: No, I rather like it. It has style.

BERNICE: Actually, you must know the woman who came up with it – she's Andrew's ex-wife.

RODDY: Gina? My god! Terrifying woman. Never liked me. Saw right through me.

BERNICE: Really? And what did she find?

RODDY: Oh, mass of insecurities, you know, shy, self-effacing...

BERNICE: *(well into her stride now)* Of course!

(clink of mugs on tray)

152

RODDY: Suse darling, you're a star. Millionaire shortbread. Yum.

(*Sound of retreating footsteps.*)

RODDY: So, Bernice, you haven't come here for tlc on your motor, have you? You want to talk about our mutual friend, Andrew Gray QC.

BERNICE: You're not just a pretty face, are you?

RODDY: Ha! What do you want to know? If he ever talked about you? Was he a good bloke? Would he have been faithful to you? What is it you think I know? Help yourself to one of those mouthfuls of cholesterol and tell Uncle Roddy.

BERNICE: Just the coffee's fine, thanks. It's very good, by the way.

RODDY: Suse has her uses.

BERNICE: Cards on the table, I want to know about something that happened twenty-eight years ago. It's—

RODDY: Sorry! Stopping you right there. Terrible memory. Too much of the Glenmorangie over the years. Can't help, I'm afraid.

BERNICE: But this would have involved the garage. You must keep records, don't you?

RODDY: Had a nasty fire a few years back. Destroyed all the paperwork. Very unfortunate – just before the VAT chap was due for a visit, too. Shouldn't say that, should I? Talking to a lawyer.

BERNICE: I didn't say I was a lawyer. So, did Andrew talk about me?

RODDY: Might have mentioned you. Chap likes to let his friends know when he's got a clever redhead on his arm – or anywhere else.

BERNICE: Did he ever bring a car to you for repairs after an accident?

RODDY: Well, we all get the odd scratch or dent. Very impatient parker, Drew was – slammed into a space and rushed off. We did a bit of bodywork for his motors over the years.

BERNICE: This was more than dents and scratches. A collision.

RODDY: A prang? Noooo.

BERNICE: No prangs?

RODDY: No dope. Code of the Old Abbots. My lips are sealed.

BERNICE: So there was an accident, but you're not going to tell me about it because Andrew asked you to keep it quiet?

(Sound of chair scraping on patio – Roddy is getting up.)

RODDY: Whoa! No lawyers' tricks with me, Ms Stafford. I'm saying if there had been an accident, I wouldn't tell you about it. Final answer. Been a pleasure to meet Drew's *inamorata*, but now must get on. Cars won't sell themselves.

BERNICE: Or repair themselves.

RODDY: Let me see you out.

(Confused sounds of footsteps, car doors opening and closing, engine starting up, car on the move.)

Silence

BERNICE *(not playacting now)* Well, there you are, Gina. Speaking as a lawyer, I can tell you that this is evidence that would never have stood up in court – and Roddy Carmichael would have stuck to his *memory shot to pieces* let-out. Speaking as the only person who is grieving for him, I can tell you that I'm not prepared to believe that he killed anyone, and I will not talk about this again. Final answer.

The recording finishes and I swear I can hear a very final click even though mobiles don't click.

So, what am I supposed to think now? Twenty-eight years is a long time, and if Roddy did repairs, no questions asked, for Andrew, he has probably done them for other people and makes a point of forgetting about them. And it may be true that his brain is pickled and his memory shot, so the fact that he clammed up may not mean anything. That's what Bernice has decided to believe – but she loved him. I don't know why I had to feel guilty when she said that she was the only person who was grieving for him – after all, I divorced him to get him out of my life. Is it my fault that his family aren't grief-stricken? Well, possibly. Slightly. The girls, anyway. I suppose the drip, drip of my rancour over the years may have had something to do with it, but I take no responsibility for Lavender and the boys. And Freda had her own reasons for distrusting him – an incident of a dog in a night.

Still, none of this makes him guilty of killing anyone, and I can't really see the point of pursuing things any further. It is impossible to prove that Andrew wasn't the driver of the car that killed Lucy McCleod, and proving that he was would just cause distress all round – for the McCleods, for Annie, for Freda. *Cui bono*? I ask myself, and I am answered by silence.

Chapter Twenty-Three

SUCH PROPHETIC GREETING

As Scott drove through the Kent countryside, he wondered whether this trip was a complete waste of time. When Rula had presented him with Sir Nicolas's new alibi of the mileage on his car, vouched for by a garage owner with connections to Andrew, it had seemed a line worth pursuing. He had intended to talk to Gina first, to see what she knew about Andrew's friend, Roddy Carmichael, but then Rula had casually dropped her bombshell – the bundle of press cuttings. *The case they relate to was one of yours,* she had said, and of course it was – the same case that had taken Gina to the Lakes last summer to try to make good some of the fallout from it. It was actually two cases – a child pornography ring and a murdered girl – but Andrew Gray had collected all the press coverage about both of them. Why? Why, unless he had somehow been involved? He certainly hadn't been involved as a lawyer, so how else? And why had these cuttings warranted special treatment – secreted in his safe? He would have to tell Gina, but there seemed only one possible reason for Andrew's keeping this hidden cache, and he thought it would devastate her. It was one thing to complain about her ex-husband as arrogant, selfish and neglectful, quite another to confront this new possibility.

So, he hadn't spoken to Gina before setting out on this trip to see Roddy Carmichael, which meant that he had no background information about him, and anyway checking out Sir Nicholas's alibi was looking less promising now the contents of that safe had come to light. Wasn't it more likely that the motive for Andrew Gray's murder lay in his past? Wasn't it the case, in fact, that his own motive for getting into his car this morning and driving off into Kent was mainly that it allowed him to delay talking to Gina?

He was approaching Sevenoaks now and was following the satnav, diverted from the town along a meandering road so narrow there was barely passing room. Just as he was informed that his destination was a hundred yards away, a gleaming, dark green Range Rover came speeding towards him, passing so close that it clipped his wing mirror. As he wrenched at the wheel, he had a view of the driver through her open window – red hair, a summer dress, a challenging smile. He watched in his mirror as she raced away, and she raised her arm in a wave. Apology or taunt? And what was Bernice Stafford doing here? She must have been at the garage – it was too much of a coincidence for her to have been anywhere else. What had she been looking for?

He drove into the garage forecourt and waited while a middle-aged man with expensive clothes and a proprietorial air advanced to greet him, calibrating his professional smile to suit Scott's just about acceptable two-year-old Prius.

'Morning, Squire,' said Roddy Carmichael, and Scott's immediate thought was that Gina must have loathed this man, this old friend of Andrew's. Entitled, pleased with himself and – Gina would have thought – stupid, though Scott was reserving judgement on that.

He wound down his window. 'Morning,' he said. 'Mr Carmichael?'

'Guilty, your honour! Trouble with the motor or looking for a new one?'

'Neither.'

He displayed his warrant card, and Roddy Carmichael peered at it as though he ought to be wearing glasses.

'From the Met?' he asked. 'And a detective superintendent? Honoured, I'm sure, but what brings a top chap from the Met to our neck of the woods? No international criminals hiding behind my petrol pumps, officer. Scout's honour.'

Scott got out of his car. 'I'm conducting a murder inquiry,' he said. You knew Andrew Gray, I believe?'

'Ah, poor old Drew, yes. Known him forever. Since we were spotty youths. But you can't think—'

'Routine inquiries,' Scott said. 'Checking alibis.'

A glint came into Roddy Carmichael's eye. 'A detective superintendent checking alibis?' he said. 'I should cocoa, if you'll pardon the expression.'

'I happened to be in the area,' Scott said repressively. 'I'd like to take a look at your records.'

Roddy Carmichael sketched a salute. 'Right you are, officer,' he said. 'All in order, I assure you. Wouldn't try to dodge the VAT man, you know.'

'Shall we go inside?' Scott said.

He was led round to the back of the building, and into a room that seemed to combine kitchen and office. A woman in her forties, Scott guessed, with long, fading blonde hair and a harassed expression, was sitting at a computer, and looked up at them with the anxious, eager expression of a well-trained dog.

'Suse darling,' said Carmichael, 'the men in blue have caught up with you, and this very senior policeman wants to look at your records. So, keep your knickers on but show the nice man anything else he asks for.'

You didn't have to be Gina to find this man unbearable. Scott turned to the woman, who had jumped to her feet and was pushing a nervous hand through her hair.

'David Scott,' he said. 'And you are Ms…?

'Susannah Bowden,' she said. 'How can I help?' and her accent was good enough for *Downton Abbey*, Scott thought.

'If you have things to do, Mr Carmichael,' he said, 'we can have a chat later. I'm sure Ms Bowden can give me the information I need here.'

Roddy Carmichael looked only too pleased to be dismissed. When he had gone, Susannah Bowden said, 'Can I get you some coffee? We have an excellent machine.'

'Thank you. Yes.' Coffee would be welcome, and making it, he thought, would help to steady her.

When he had been given an espresso and she had some kind of herbal tea, she sat back at her computer, adopted an air of professional competence, performed a few mouse clicks, and said, 'Our system isn't the newest in the world, I'm afraid, but I should be able to find you what you're looking for, Detective Superintendent.'

A state-of-the-art coffee machine and an old computer – that sounded about right for this place.

'You keep detailed records of the services you carry out?' he asked.

'Oh yes. I use those to set up the invoices.'

'Does Mr Carmichael do the work himself, or does he employ mechanics?'

'Roddy does them sometimes, if it's an interesting car, or it's for a friend, but Paul is our mechanic. He's not in this morning. He's taken his wife to an antenatal appointment.'

'And when they do a routine service, they record the mileage on the clock?'

'Oh yes. We recommend a service every 10,000 miles, so I keep a record of our clients' average mileage so that we can remind them when a service is due.'

'Very efficient.'

She blushed. 'It was my idea, actually.'

'That's easy, then. The service I'm interested in was a couple of weeks ago. Sir Nicholas Payton.'

'Oh, yes.' She stopped. 'That's Lavender's father. Her husband ...'

'Has been murdered, yes. Which is why we have to check up on everyone who knew him.'

'Oh, but Sir Nicholas—' she protested, and then stopped. 'Sorry. You don't want my...'

She turned back to her screen and started tapping keys. 'There we are,' she said, and angled the screen towards him.

'Perfect,' he said. And it was. According to the mileage he had seen on the car's clock a few days before, the car had done barely more than fifty miles since it was serviced.

'What is Sir Nicholas's average mileage like?' he asked.

She smiled. 'Oh, very low. He doesn't go anywhere much. Lady Payton is always nipping about, but not Sir Nicholas. I get the feeling he doesn't much like driving really. He'd rather be on his horse.'

'Thank you,' he said. 'You've been very helpful.' He wanted to add that Roddy Carmichael was lucky to have her, and he hoped he appreciated her, but he knew it would sound patronising. 'Thank you for the excellent coffee,' he said.

Back on the forecourt he found Carmichael circling his car. Had he been kicking the tyres?

He looked up as he heard Scott approaching, and asked, 'How do you find it, honestly? Aside – you know – from the green signalling?'

'Green signalling?'

'Yes – *look how concerned I am about the planet, blah, blah, blah.*'

Scott ignored the challenge. 'Well,' he said, 'it's silent at low speeds, of course – useful in my work if stealth is called for.'

Carmichael looked at him, unable to work out whether

this was a joke or not, Scott thought. He kept his face impassive. Then he unlocked his car and moved round to the driver's side.

'I've got the information I needed. Ms Bowden was most efficient.'

'Oh, good old Suse, yes,' Carmichael said. 'Is that it, then?' His relief was undisguised.

'For the moment.' He opened his door. 'That was Bernice Stafford who passed me on my way in, wasn't it?' he said casually, as he got in. 'Is she a regular customer of yours?'

Carmichael's eyes darted momentarily to the building behind him, to the office where the efficient Suse kept the records. He was wondering what answer would get rid of him most quickly, Scott thought.

He opted for what was probably at least partly true. 'Not, actually,' he said. 'Nice motor, though. Said Drew had recommended me, but nothing wrong with the car. Just wanted to talk to a friend of poor old Drew's, I think.'

'Well, I'm sure you were a great comfort,' Scott said, and drove away.

Retracing his drive, he considered what Bernice might have been up to. It was possible that she had actually wanted to talk to someone else who might be mourning Andrew but Gina's crazy suggestion that he should get all the women with theories about the murder to investigate one another's suspects was niggling away at him. Had she set this up? Could she? Would she? If Bernice was making her own inquiries, who was her suspect? And what did she think Roddy Carmichael knew? Bernice, as she needed reminding, was a suspect herself – and fairly high up on the list if Rula's scenario of humiliation at the wedding stood up. He had asked Paula to interview her, but she hadn't reported back yet. He pressed speed dial.

'Hello, Boss.'

'Not your boss, DI Powell. Just helping out.'

'Except you seem to have taken over the case.'

'And I thought no-one had noticed.'

'Maybe not north of the border. How can I help you?'

'I was wondering if you had had a chance to talk to Bernice Stafford.'

'I tried this morning. Rang her chambers and was told she was working from home. Rang her home and got no reply.'

'That's because she was in Sevenoaks, doing her own bit of investigating.'

'And you know that how?'

'Because I was there too.'

'So, I am well behind the curve here, aren't I? And you still tell me you haven't taken over this case?'

Scott could hear that she was deciding whether to be annoyed or not.

'Sorry,' he said. 'I should have reported back. I sent Rula Bartosz to follow up on our interview with Sir Nicholas. She prettied up and got him off guard – also, she thinks he feels that Lavender is off the suspects list now, so he's not so keen on presenting himself as a suspect. He's *suddenly remembered* a crucial bit of alibi – he had his car serviced just before the murder and the garage has a note of his mileage. Unless he's managed to fix the clock, he'd hardly driven anywhere between then and when we checked his car.'

'He doesn't look as though fixing is one of his skills.'

'Well, he knows a man who could. I'm pretty sure Roddy Carmichael would be willing, but his assistant said that Sir Nicholas hardly did much mileage at all. Roddy's not the brightest bulb in the box but even he would surely have been suspicious about a journey of over a thousand miles that Payton wanted disappeared – especially when it coincided with the murder of the man's son-in-law – someone he was ready to bad-mouth at any opportunity.'

'OK. But why was Bernice Stafford at the garage? What was that about?'

'He says she wanted to weep on his shoulder – was looking for someone who cared that Andrew was dead.'

'Possible, I suppose.'

'Mm. Maybe. I've got a niggling feeling that it was something else. I'm afraid I can see Gina's fingerprints on this.'

'*Gina's*? Why?'

'It's a long story. Freda has a hunch about a revenge scenario, and—'

'*Freda*? Who's she?'

'Gina's granddaughter.' He felt ridiculous.

'And since when have we been recruiting children to CID?'

'Well, she's fifteen, in fact, but—'

'Are you serious about this?'

Was he serious? And how much did he need to tell Paula?

'Well,' he said, 'revenge is always a possible motive for murder, and we have had it in mind that he was killed because of something that he had done in his professional life. Freda thought she had unearthed something way back in his private life – a fatal car accident.'

'A fatal car accident that Freda knows about but we don't? How does that work, exactly?'

He could hear that her irritation was about to escalate into outrage, and he couldn't afford to lose her.

'It's nonsense, of course,' he said firmly. 'There's no evidence for it – just a fifteen-year-old getting over-imaginative. She had issues with her grandfather. And then she wound Gina up and—'

'And Mrs Gray has gone off on one of her solo missions.'

'Not only that, but I think she may have taken Bernice with her.'

'She thinks this garage guy – Gray's old pal – covered up for him, and that's why we don't have a record of it, and she's sent Bernice off to honey trap the guy.'

'Exactly. You were always fast, Paula.'

'And Gina was always crazy.'

He let that go. 'It's a red herring,' he said. 'I'll deal with it. But if you could see Bernice asap, I would still like your take on her as a possible killer. Don't mention the garage expedition – it's not relevant to her motivation for a murder a week ago.'

'Except, if she really loved Andrew Gray, why would she go digging for dirt about his past? If that was what she was doing this morning, couldn't it be because she wanted to find some extra justification for killing him?'

'Maybe. I'll talk to Gina, you talk to Bernice, and we'll debrief. There's some other stuff to tell you too. Bizarrely, an old Marlbury case of ours has cropped up again, with a link to Andrew Gray. I don't know what I think about it yet, but it may be a game-changer.'

'You'll keep me in the loop?'

'Of course.'

As he drove on, he thought Paula had every right to be pissed off at the idea that not just Gina but Freda was chipping in with her opinions. How had he justified that to Paula? *Freda had issues with her grandfather.* It was pretty weak stuff. And then a realisation hit him – hit him so hard that he felt the car swerve and he struggled for a moment to control it. Freda's issues with Andrew had started – what? – four or five years ago? He had been dealing with a high profile murder case in Bloomsbury at the time, the victim the niece of a senior Indian diplomat, so he hadn't really been paying attention to the daily dramas of the Gray family, but he remembered that Nico had been in hospital and Freda had been staying with Andrew and Lavender in Kent, and there had been a panic because she had run away. She had made her way to London, to Gina, and things were smoothed over, but he had noticed how she and Andrew had avoided each other at the McCleods' on the evening before the wedding. There was a story he had been told at the time about Andrew getting rid of the family dog, but that didn't seem enough to warrant the discomfort between him and Freda five years later. Now he knew that Andrew Gray had secreted in his office safe a bundle of press cuttings about the busting of a paedophile porn ring in Marlbury and a cluster of successful prosecutions. There had been no suggestion at the time that Andrew had been in any way involved, but why would he follow the cases otherwise? Scott had known that they hadn't nailed all the clients of the porn peddlers, who had claimed that the deals had been rigorously anonymous, and had given no names even when offered the possibility of reduced sentences.

If Andrew had been involved, what did that say about his relationship with Freda?

Chapter Twenty-Four

SUCH WELCOME
AND UNWELCOME NEWS

I have almost done my time here. The local police seem to have lost interest in me, Freda has had no need of me, cushioned as she has been by the kind attentions of the McCleods, and Ellie and Ben will be here tomorrow evening, ready to carry her off down south on the sleeper. I am flying down to London from Edinburgh on Sunday. I have had more than enough solitary thinking time – I haven't enough to occupy me on an eight-hour train journey.

I did speak to Freda this morning. Having decided that I might as well take Bernice's view that Andrew was innocent because not proved guilty, I wanted to put her mind at rest, so I rang to tell her that 'investigations' had found no evidence of her grandfather's involvement in the car accident. Considering the state she was in when she broached her suspicions to me, I thought she would be hugely relieved, but she hardly seemed to be interested. I recognised the obsession that any kind of performance generates. She could talk of nothing but the play: Alex's role in helping with direction, and her blessed painted boxes, which will, in her mind, make or break the show. She is thoroughly disgruntled about being taken off home before she has a chance to see the performance, and she can't understand why I am not willing to stay on to see it myself . We were mostly at cross purposes, and I came off the phone feeling jangled and unappreciated.

I decided to take a walk round the loch to restore my temper and work up an appetite for lunch. In the interests of calm contemplation, I didn't take my phone with me, and now, returning to my room after lunch, I find I have two missed calls from David.

What does he want? In my experience, if David rings me when he is in the middle of a case, the likelihood is that he wants to berate me for interference, and if that's what he wants now, then I am not in the mood to hear it. I shall not ring him back immediately.

This resolution lasts for seventeen minutes. Then I call. Oddly, he sounds flustered at my calling.

'Oh, Gina, hi,' he says, which is not his usual style. *What do you want, Gina?* is the norm.

'You called me,' I say. 'Twice.'

'Yes.'

I wait. 'I was out for a walk,' I say, 'without my phone.'

'Yes.'

I wait again, then ask, 'Did you have something to tell me, or did you want to upbraid me? It must be one or the other.'

He rallies. 'Both, actually,' he says, 'but the upbraiding can wait. I have something to tell you, and I'm afraid you're not going to like it.'

'Fire away,' I say.

'You're really not going to like it.'

'Oh for God's sake, spit it out,' I say, but I sit down, just in case not liking it is an understatement, because a voice in my head is telling me that what he has to spit out is that they have evidence linking Andrew to Lucy McCleod's death.

'Rula has been through the contents of the safe in Andrew's office. Nothing much there, but there was a packet of press cuttings.'

He pauses.

I say, 'Right. And...?'

'They all relate to an old case.'

'Which is the hit-and-run accident that killed Lucy McCleod?'

'What? No! No, not that at all. Marina Carson. The murder of Marina Carson, and the associated crimes.'

My first reaction is simply giddy relief. Then I say, 'Marina Carson again? What can her death possibly have to do with Andrew?'

He doesn't answer right away. Then he says, 'That's what we have to think about.'

'What's there in the cuttings?' I ask.

'Everything. Local papers and national press. The murder trial and the trial of the dealers in child pornography. There's even an account of the attack on you. *LECTURER BLUDGEONED IN ABBEY CLOISTERS.*'

'And I thought he didn't care!' I say. 'Well, he is a lawyer, and it was a high-profile case right on his doorstep. I suppose it caught his interest.'

'Enough to keep all the cuttings and secrete them in a safe, when all other documents in his office are out in files on shelves?'

'Perhaps he stuck them in the safe for some reason and forgot about them.'

'Or perhaps he had a personal involvement.'

'He can't have done. He doesn't do those kinds of cases. And you would have known at the time if he had been on the case.'

'I don't mean involved in that way,' he says.

'Then I think you'd better say what you do mean and stop fartarsing around,' I snap.

'OK. We know we didn't catch all the men involved in the child pornography ring. The three men and the boy who were charged and convicted refused to give us any other names. They claimed that everyone used aliases. We didn't believe them, but they held out, even when they were offered the chance of reduced sentences. They held out because they were jolly good chaps and pillars of the community, and so were the others involved. It was an old boy network, and Marlbury Abbey school was at its heart – Andrew's old school. I am suggesting that the only plausible explanation for Andrew's obsessive and secretive interest in the case was that he knew the people involved intimately – and was involved himself.'

I am not exactly conscious of opening my mouth to speak, but I obviously do, because I find I am shouting, 'No, no, no no…' and I don't seem to be able to stop. It's the equivalent of sticking my fingers in my ears and shouting, *'Can't hear you',* I know, but there it is. I keep going until I run out of breath.

Eventually, David says, 'It's a lot to take in. When you're calmer, think about it. If he was involved and got away with it, that could be a motive for his murder. A parent of one of the abused children – even one of the young people themselves. It was twelve years ago – they'll be adults now. These things fester. We'll need to talk again to Annie's school friends who were at the wedding. We interviewed them quite briefly early on – we saw no reason then why they should be suspects.'

'And there's no reason now.' I find my voice again, but it is a croak. 'If any of them had reason to feel murderous towards Andrew, why wait till now?'

'From the start, we've thought that the murder may not have been premeditated, but opportunistic, using Andrew's own dagger. Maybe seeing him lording it at the wedding – and he did lord it – father of the bride, with his loving daughters and his little boys – was enough to enrage someone.'

'It's balls, David. Total balls. I was married to him for ten years. I am not stupid. I would have known. And he certainly didn't have an unhealthy interest in his daughters – they mostly just irritated him.'

'And Freda?'

'Freda? You know he and Freda barely speak to each other.'

'And why is that?'

'You know why. The business with the dog. When Freda was staying with him and Lavender. He tried to get rid of the family dog, and Freda caught him out.'

'Freda was only ten, but she ran away from their house and caught a train to London on her own. I never really understood why she did that. It was an extreme thing to do.'

'It was because of the dog.'

'No, it wasn't. You and she only worked out what Andrew had done with the dog after she came to you in London. Didn't you?'

'So, what are you saying?'

'I'm saying Freda must have had another reason why she ran away from Andrew.'

'He shouted at her. She said he shouted at her.'

'We're going to have to talk to her, I'm afraid.'

'You can't.'

'We must.'

'Let me.'

'This is a murder investigation. She has to be interviewed by a police officer. Not me – I'm too close. I'll send Rula and a WPC to talk to her as soon as she's back down south – which is Sunday, right? We know how to do these things, Gina.'

'All right,' I say, meekly, because I have every intention of talking to her before they do.

'Good,' he says, and seems to feel that our conversation is finished.

I want to go on denying everything, except that an appalling thought has come into my head.

'You know that encrypted file on Andrew's computer?' I say. 'The one titled AB? Have your nerds got it open yet?'

'They haven't. We didn't see it as a priority.'

'Because you thought AB meant Adita Bahader, and you'd moved her down the suspects list. But I think it may not be to do with her. If Andrew was protecting the same secrets in his safe and on his computer, then AB refers to the heart of that porn ring. Think about it, David. Get that file opened, whatever it takes, and then, please God, tell me I'm wrong.'

Chapter Twenty-Five

HE WANTS THE NATURAL TOUCH

Freda sat looking at the phone in her hand. It felt hot, as though it was as embarrassed as she was about the conversation she had just had. Quite honestly, she thought her grandmother was going off her trolley. First, she had rung this morning to tell her – as though it was a great revelation – that Grandpa hadn't been the other driver in the accident that had killed Jon's mother. She'd talked as though this was going to be a huge relief to Freda, when she could have told her that she was so over worrying about that – that it had just been a weird, late-night brain blip that had made her come up with a *McCleods take revenge* theory about Grandpa's death, when anyone could see that no-one in the McCleod family could possibly be a murderer. She had tried to make the conversation as brief as possible – she was on a deadline for her set painting apart from anything else – but Granny had wanted to make a big emotional thing of it, and it had taken ages to talk her down. And now, this afternoon, she had been back again.

It had taken a moment or two to work out what she was on about. She started talking about the time Freda had run away from Grandpa's and Lavender's house and caught a train to London. That was five years ago, for heaven's sake, and she hadn't been able to understand what Granny was on about. And then she got it. There were the buzz words, familiar from Mrs Webster's PSHE classes at school. *Personal, Social, Health and Economic Education* they were supposed to be, but they were nearly always about sex, in fact. Or rather about not having sex, if possible, and if you had to have it, avoiding the worst of the personal, social, health and economic consequences. Mrs Webster was particularly keen on *recognising inappropriate behaviour,* on *talking to someone about any behaviour that makes you feel uncomfortable,* and on *resisting being pressurised.* They had all noticed that her neck went very red when she's said those things, and Freda imagined her grandmother's doing the same as she tiptoed round with, *I just wondered if Grandpa might have...* and *You would have told me if... wouldn't you?* She knew that she herself had been mean, because she had pretended not to know what Granny was on about, so that she had to go on floundering around. Eventually, Granny had asked, 'Did Grandpa ever do anything like cuddling you in a way that you didn't like?' and Freda had just laughed.

'Granny,' she said, 'I don't think Grandpa ever cuddled me in his life. I don't think he ever touched me, actually. He usually ignored me, and that didn't make me uncomfortable – it made me sad.'

And then, because she really couldn't deal with Granny getting all emotional about that, and anyway she had to get on with her painting, she said, 'Sorry – have to go – things to do,' and rang off. And that was why she was sitting here now with a hot phone in her hand, feeling bad because Granny was fussing out of love, and she had been mean to her.

Resolutely, she tapped in a message:

Sorry if I was snotty just now. Understand you had to ask. Am a bit stressed finishing my set painting before Mum and Ben arrive tomorrow and drag me off home. ☹

Love you. F xxx

Then she put her phone in her pocket and went back to her painting.

Chapter Twenty-Six

WE STILL HAVE JUDGEMENT HERE

Scott was running along the Embankment, and wondering exactly why he was doing it. Early on a Saturday morning was a good time to run here – no office workers on their way in, and tourists still enjoying their full English breakfasts – but why do it at all? It wasn't as though he expected ever to run after a suspect again – he had people to do that for him – so why do it? Pounding along, he considered whether there was any sense in which he was enjoying this. Was there physical pleasure somewhere in the pain? Did he feel virtuous, cleansed, smug? When his phone rang and he pulled it out of his pocket and saw that the caller was Paula, the relief he felt in having an excuse to stop gave him his answer. He hated the whole bloody business, and he didn't feel any satisfaction at the end of it – only the mild pleasure of knowing that he wouldn't have to do it for another week.

Leaning against nearby railings, he controlled his breathing and then said, 'Paula?'

'Are you at the gym?' she asked.

'Running,' he said. 'Saturday morning penance.'

'I won't ask for what sins. I just thought you might like feedback on my talk with Bernice Stafford.'

'You got hold of her?'

'Yes. Visited her in her detached executive property in Tenterden.'

'And?'

'I don't think she's our killer. Of course, she's a barrister, so she could just have been putting on a very plausible performance, but I don't think so. Rula's wrong about her being humiliated at the wedding. She didn't expect Andrew to make any kind of announcement – she knew he wanted to keep the status quo, and she was happy with that. She didn't want to leave her husband – she wanted what she calls *a grown-up arrangement*, and she hoped that by her being at the wedding – with her husband – they were putting out a message that this was how things were going to be. She was furious with her husband for blowing it by losing his temper and starting the fight, but he wasn't the one who got killed, was he?'

'No. And we still haven't ruled him out.'

'But you said you had a lead on a link to an old Marlbury case?'

'Yes. You remember the murder of Marina Carson? Thirteen-year-old, pushed down the stairs at her home.'

'Yes. It turned out to be about an indecent images ring. We broke it up and roped in the perpetrators. Congratulations all round.'

'We may not have got all of them. It looks like Andrew Gray may have been involved too. We found stuff in his office safe.'

'Paedophile porn?'

'No, no. Cuttings of all the press coverage of the case – accounts of the trials and so on.'

'You don't think he was just taking an interest? Local case, Gina involved?'

'Why keep the stuff in his safe? There was nothing else of that sort in there.'

'Right. So you're thinking the killer might be one of the children who were filmed? Grown up now, and wanting revenge? Looking for closure?'

'Something like that.'

'Do you have the names of the children involved?'

'Some of them.'

'It'll need delicate handling if you're going to interview them.'

'It will.'

'Well, good luck.'

'Most of the kids were local. They may still be living in Kent.'

'You want us to get involved?'

'Maybe.'

'Well, thank you. That's just what I need.'

'We're trying to get a computer file opened. I told the IT guys yesterday not to go home till they'd got it. It may have the answer.'

'You wish.'

His phone was not yet back in his pocket when it rang again and Rula spoke, as if summoned by the wish.

'Boss,' she said. 'They've got it.'

'The file?'

'Yup.'

'And?'

'You were right about what AB meant. It's what you thought. Are you coming in?'

'Can't you hear me running?'

As he jogged back towards the station, he was almost oblivious to his surroundings, conjuring up instead Marlbury's Aphra Behn theatre, a tarted-up cinema crouched by a scruffy stretch of river. Here, a predatory pair had dreamt up the grimly simple plan of luring wannabe child stars to 'auditions', ferrying them up the river in plain sight, with the ignorant connivance of their ambitious parents, and in a decaying country house had used them as models for soft porn DVDs. As a process it was horribly plausible. The children would have been told that they should be prepared to do 'difficult' or 'embarrassing' things if they wanted to be actors, and the need for confidentiality impressed on them. It was, he thought, the same technique that was used on the young athletes by their trainers to justify and hide the abuse that had come to light only recently, the victims still scarred in their adult lives.

So how had Andrew Gray been involved? The men involved were his type – socially confident, entitled, public school types. One of them was a housemaster at his old school. Had Andrew given them advice on how to keep on the windy side of the law? Had he dealt with gagging any suspicious parents who threatened to make a fuss? Had he simply been a customer?

It was only as he went in through the plate glass doors of the station that he considered how inappropriately he was dressed – the thought triggered by something hastily suppressed on the face of the desk sergeant, possibly. He was in jogging pants, a sweaty T-shirt and grubby trainers that had never had a designer logo; he had not shaved and was not sure that he had even cleaned his teeth. Also, he needed coffee.

He headed for the washroom, where he splashed his face and sluiced his chest and arms with water and ran wet hands through his hair, glad that at least his T-shirt was black and not showing obvious patches of sweat, though there was nothing he could do about its smell. He yearned for coffee. It was against his Gina-imbued principles to send Rula to the canteen for a coffee, but she might offer.

He found Rula at her desk, going through the contents of the file, printing pages off and making notes. The lad, Martin, from IT, whom he had more or less locked in his lab last night, with orders to get the file open by morning, was lounging at a desk nearby, looking slightly febrile, nursing a cup of coffee and spinning his chair in a way that put the coffee at risk and made Scott feel queasy.

'Well done, Martin,' he said. 'How did you crack it?'

'Went through those press cuttings, looking for names. Finally got it.'

'What was it?'

Martin stopped spinning, grabbed a sheet of paper, wrote, and handed the sheet to Scott. He looked at it and then started to laugh.

Rula looked away from her screen. 'Why is it funny?'

Scott shook his head. 'Only funny to me,' he said.

He picked up the sheaf of printouts from Rula's desk and looked around for somewhere to sit. Martin hauled himself to his feet.

'I guess I can go home,' he said.

'Thanks again, Martin,' Scott said. 'Good work.'

He watched as the young man ambled to the door, taking the aroma of his coffee with him.

'Martin,' he said. 'Could you get me a coffee from the canteen before you go?'

The look he got back was one of pure astonishment – as though no-one had ever asked such a thing of him before.

'What? And bring it back here?' he asked.

'Yes.'

As Martin stood, apparently stunned, Rula started to get to her feet. 'I'll go,' she said.

'No, you're busy. I'm sure Martin won't mind going.' And then, knowing that he would find nothing but his door key in the pockets of his joggers, he added, 'But if you could lend me the money, I'd be very grateful.'

Ten minutes later, he was settled with coffee and one of the doughnuts that Rula had added to the order, and was ready for whatever he was going to find there. A preliminary scan told him that what he had was a dossier that traced the histories of the three men and one boy who had been prosecuted for running the paedophile pornography ring in Marlbury. In effect, it took over where the press cuttings left off. If he had to guess why the dossier had been given such a high level of security, he would say that it was because of the dubious legality of the way some of the information had been obtained. The outcomes of the trials were in the public domain, of course, but there were confidential reports on the men's time in detention, and detailed accounts of their post-prison lives, which could only have been acquired by questionable means. Andrew Gray had probably used his position as a QC to blag the prison records, Scott thought, and other material looked as though private detectives had been involved. And that meant money. Andrew had spent time and money on this, had possibly risked his professional reputation. Why? Scott decided to leave that question for the moment and concentrate on what was here.

He started with the two men who worked at the Aphra Behn theatre and had dreamed up the nasty little enterprise: Neil Cunningham and Alexander Driver. Both had been sentenced to eight years for the production, possession, and distribution of indecent images of children. They had each served four years, in different prisons, and then been released on licence. Both had been model prisoners, and seemed not to have had too hard a time, in spite of the *paedo* taint they came in with. Scott tried to remember who the public figure was who had said that he really hadn't found prison too hard after spending five years at Eton. A politician. Jonathan Aitken, perhaps? Anyway, these two ex-public schoolboys seemed to have taken it in their stride and made themselves useful. Cunningham had helped other prisoners with literacy, and Driver had organised his fellow inmates into amateur shows in the open prison where he spent his last year. After his release, he had put together an acting company which went into prisons, giving entertainment and, in some cases, involving the inmates in their shows. Cunningham had spent his period on licence living almost as a recluse on his parents' farm in Sussex, and then had gone abroad, initially to Spain. As far as Andrew's PDs knew, he had not returned to the UK.

After these two, Scott turned to Edmund Carson and Marcus Bright. The first had been a sixth form student at Marlbury Abbey school at the time of his offences, and the other had been head of sixth form at the school. Bright, who was given a four-year term for ABH (his attack on Gina), had not adapted as well to prison life as the others had done. The *paedo* label stuck to him. The carefully neutral language of his prison report did not disguise physical attacks of a pretty brutal kind. He had spent time in the prison hospital, recovering from injuries and suffering from stomach complaints and high blood pressure. He was now teaching in a language school in the Midlands, run by an old schoolfriend.

Edmund Carson, on charges of possessing and distributing indecent images, had put on a performance in the witness box worthy of his actress mother, and his very expensive defence barrister convinced the jury and the judge that his involvement in the business had been peripheral, and had made much of the multiple tragedies in his life – his stepsister's death, his stepfather's suicide, his mother's breakdown. His real father (who had presumably paid the barrister's fees) had come back into his life, and, as a celebrated film designer, was in a position to give the boy a start in the film business. The judge had given him a suspended sentence, and he had taken off for Hollywood. Scott remembered thinking that the boy was a psychopath, but perhaps it wouldn't be noticed there.

As he read it through, the dossier seemed to be further evidence of Andrew Gray's obsessive interest in the fates of this criminal group. What explanation was there, other than that Gray himself had somehow been involved – as a customer, if nothing else? The money and time spent on acquiring this information he put down either to anxiety that one of these men might yet inform on him, or to guilt about their fates, when he himself had escaped – a need to reassure himself that things had not turned out too disastrously for them in the end. Then he came to the letters at the end of the file, and his view changed. These, he saw, were copies of letters sent by Andrew – sent officially from the chambers of Andrew Gray QC – to employers, to local government officials, to Social Services, even to the US embassy. At first glance, Scott thought these would be Andrew's contributions to helping the men's rehabilitation – testimonials from an influential source, but as he started to read, he saw that they were nothing of the kind. They were, in fact, the opposite.

With a small surge of excitement, he saw that what he had here was as strong a motive for murder as he could have hoped to find. Far from helping these men, Gray wanted them isolated and excluded. It could have been pure vindictiveness, but Scott thought not. The tone of the letters suggested that Andrew simply did not believe that it was safe for these men to be out in the world. So, for every place any of them had lived in since their release, there was a letter from him to the relevant police force, asking for reassurance that they had been entered on the sex offenders register, and where no reply had been received, there was a follow-up letter, reminding the local authority of its statutory obligations and the possibility of legal action. If the local authorities were slow to respond, there were judiciously threatening follow-up letters.

The resulting replies yielded the following information:

Neil Cunningham failed to register when living on his parents' farm in Sussex, and a quick check on dates showed that it was after a third letter from Andrew to West Sussex social services that Cunningham had left the UK, heading for Spain, and then who knew where?

Edmund Carson had been on the register while he was at Art College, but Andrew had additionally written to the principal of the college, alerting him to Carson's status as a sex offender, and asking for guarantees that his course would not involve teaching placements with children, or any other contact with young people. He had received a surprisingly emollient reply, giving assurances that all students in the college were over eighteen and that the course required no interaction with children, adding that it was their policy never to employ child models in life drawing classes. There was a less emollient reply from Justin Chaput, Carson's birth father, to a letter demanding similar guarantees for Carson's contacts on film sets. Chaput wrote back tersely that he believed he could be trusted to make appropriate judgements regarding his own son's work and social contacts. A letter to the US embassy, questioning whether all the facts of Edmund Chaput's criminal conviction under the name of Carson had been revealed in his visa application, produced assurances that a 'very robust scrutiny' was applied to all visa applications, and had been applied in Mr Carson's case.

Alex Driver, it seemed, had played by the book. Hackney social services, after prompting, had replied that he had been on the register since his release from an open prison, and a letter from Gray to the director of HM Prison Service, warning that Driver's drama workshops should be confined to adult prisons and not extend to young offenders, was answered with a brief assurance that Mr Driver had made a full disclosure of his personal history and was making a valuable contribution to the work of the service.

Marcus Bright, having served a one-year sentence for possession of indecent images running concurrently with his sentence for ABH, was now off the register, but Gray had written to the director of the language school where he taught, and had been reassured, in a breezy letter from the director, that the school was strictly adults only, specialising in business English. Scott felt a momentary twinge of pity for Bright, with his good Oxford degree and his ambitions of a public school headship, but then he remembered seeing Gina in bed, her head swathed in bandages, and reminded himself that Bright could have killed her, and the past twelve years of his own life would have been unimaginably different.

Shaking the thought off, he shuffled through to the very back of the dossier, where he found photographs. Here again, he thought, a PD had been employed. There were the arrest mugshots of each of them – Driver blank-faced, Cunningham with one eyelid drooping, as if almost in a wink, Bright pale and sweaty, and Edmund Carson attempting a sneer. There was a graduation photo for Carson, a picture of him with a student group at an exhibition of their work, and a flash-lit glossy of him at a Hollywood party, sleek and smiling, with his arm round a sun-bronzed blonde. For Bright there were just a couple of shots taken from the language school website – an individual shot of *Mr Marcus Bright MA (Oxon)*, and a group photo of the staff, arranged on some steps, smiling encouragingly. Bright looked pasty and overweight; his hair needed cutting and the suit he wore was cheap and too tight. While adversity had made Bright fatter, it had slimmed Alex Driver down to wiry fitness, bordering on the stringy gauntness of the obsessive exerciser. The photos of him were taken from the website of his theatre company, *Inside Out*, and showed him shaven headed, wearing tight black trousers and a vest top, in action, coaxing groups of prison inmates into drama and mime. Of Neil Cunningham there was only one picture aside from the original mugshot. It was a blurred snippet from a local newspaper and showed him with an older couple, *Mr and Mrs Gerald Cunningham of Barley Farm and their son Neil,* attending the West Sussex County Show, at which *'The Cunningham family carried off the Best in Show award for their breed of rare sheep'.* Not much could be seen of Neil, who was partly hidden by his beaming parents, but he was recognisable as the man Scott had arrested and questioned twelve years before. Older and greyer, of course, but weren't they all? The absence of any further photos suggested that Gray's employment of PDs did not extend to pursuing Neil Cunningham around Europe – or the world.

Scott looked through all the photos once more, and then sat back in his chair, deflated. Had any of those men been at the wedding? He didn't think so.

Chapter Twenty-Seven

HERE ABJURE THESE
TAINTS AND BLAMES

I am as edgy as hell. I have tried to walk off my unease by marching round the loch, but it was no good, and now I am pacing my hotel room, muttering to myself in a way that has deterred the chambermaid from knocking at the door. In an attempt to get myself under control, I make a mental list, and then an actual list, of the separate anxieties that are combining to tip me into lunacy.

1. Ben may crash the car on the drive down from Orkney
2. It looks as though I was married for ten years to a man who has abused children
3. We still don't know who killed him, so I am not off the hook, and the discovery of 2) above could be seen as a motive
4. I was clumsy with Freda yesterday and feel stupid despite her forgiving text
5. There is nothing I can do about any of these things

So, when my phone rings and I see that it is David calling, I can only assume that he has more bad news.

'What is it now?' I snap.

'Something I thought you'd like to hear, but if you'd rather I—'

'Oh, spit it out. Nothing can make me feel worse.'

'What's happened?'

'Oh, nothing. Just, everyone I love is in a death machine, hurtling down the highlands, the father of my children turns out to be a paedophile, the Scottish police think I murdered him, and my granddaughter thinks I'm an idiot. Nothing to worry about at all.'

'Well, I can't do anything about the first and the last, but I have news about Andrew that changes things – including the suspicions of the local force, I predict.'

'Go on then. Talk.'

And he does. It turns out I was right about what AB meant on that file, and it turns out to be what David calls a dossier, which he itemises to me in dizzying detail.

When he finally stops, I say, 'So you're telling me Andrew was a one-man vigilante, hounding the Marlbury porn-mongers?'

'I think he probably saw himself as the man in the white hat, driving the bad guys out of town.'

'That's how he always saw his work, I'm sure. But why this case? There are cases like this all the time – and much worse. Why fixate on these guys?'

'I don't know, but there is the Abbey School connection. I have picked up from your diatribes about him over the years that he was a devoted Old Boy.'

'Abbot.'

'What?'

'Old Abbots, they call themselves.'

'Exactly. And he loved being one of those, so when this scandal broke, he must have been mortified by the Abbey connection – two of the accused were old boys, one was a teacher there, and one was a pupil. You can see from the press cuttings he collected that the papers made quite a lot of that.'

'I suppose.'

'And then there's you, of course.'

'Me?'

'He kept the press report in the local paper about your being mugged in the Abbey cloisters. The paper didn't make a connection with the porn case, or the murder of Marina Carson, but Andrew was sharp enough to make the connection. He knew you, after all.'

'You're not saying this vigilante campaign of his was all about revenge for my being bonked on the head?'

There is silence at his end. He is trying to make up his mind whether to tell me something. I am slightly scared.

'David?'

'Yes. Do you remember saying that the techies shouldn't bother with family names when they were trying for the password on that file? Andrew would never think of using them, you said.'

'Well, he wouldn't.'

'Do you want to know what the password was?'

'Tell me.'

'Write this down.'

'Hold on.'

I scrabble for the tiny pad beside the phone, and the even tinier pencil. 'OK. Tell me.'

He dictates, and I write – sloppily, because I have the phone in one hand and the little pad skids about.

'Upper case V, one, r, nine, one, n, one, at symbol.'

I write it down: V1r91n1@. I blink at it, put the phone down, and write it out again more neatly. I can't deny what it says.

I say, 'This is a wind-up, isn't it, David? Come on, tell me what it really is.'

'That's what it is, Mrs Virginia Gray. And the guys got it because of your inspiration about AB standing for Aphra Behn. It took them back to the press cuttings to look for clues, and would you believe, in the account of the attack on Mrs Virginia Gray, someone had circled the name in red ink. They tried a few versions, and presto!'

'This is bonkers,' I say. 'This feels like Andrew playing a trick on me from the grave. I'm going to ring off and raid the minibar.'

'It's ten o'clock in the morning,' he says.

'I don't care.'

Chapter Twenty-Eight

AN ABSOLUTE TRUST

Freda sat on one of her boxes, munching a ham and tomato sandwich. Aileen was an excellent sandwich maker: the fillings had been different each time in the course of the week, and all delicious. This was not the case in her own home. Mum was a slapdash maker, and Freda had often found half the filling sitting in the bottom of her lunch box. Since she had started making her own packed lunches, she had found out how problematic sandwiches were, and Mum now bought bags of rolls with the supermarket shop, and stored them in the freezer. They were easier, but you had to remember to get one out every evening to thaw. She hadn't expected to be eating a sandwich lunch today, but Malcolm had texted at midday to say that he could meet her for a *get-in* (technical term to be remembered) at two o'clock, when they could move her boxes onto the stage, and she could see what they looked like. Alex had a band practice, so he had dropped her off early, and she was killing time until Malcolm arrived. If they had finished before Alex's rehearsal broke up, she had arranged to meet him in the café along the road. *A table for two – I'm meeting someone,* she imagined saying to a waitress, and then later Alex would come in, looking good, and a bit tousled after his rehearsal, and she would feel very mature. She sighed as she felt again the treacherous edge of reluctance at the idea of going home, back to being a child.

And bang on cue, a text message came in on her phone from her mother – the third today so far: *Just stopping for lunch at motorway services with view of hills. Eta still 4.30 xxx* She looked at it. There were going to be more of these – Mum reporting on their progress every hour on the hour, and then there would be Granny ringing, all anxious, wanting to know if she had any news, and it was going to be embarrassing, with Malcolm thinking she wasn't independent of her family. She switched the phone to silent and put it away in her jacket pocket.

Malcolm should be here any minute. Getting up, she climbed onto the box she had been sitting on and stretched up on her toes, just able to see the side road where he would park his flash car. Well, *flash* was the wrong word for it, because it wasn't a fast racer; it was old-fashioned looking in an expensive way – *vintage*, she supposed. It had a characteristic sound, as well. Perched on her box, she watched and listened. When he had parked, he might go round to the front and come in through the theatre, but it was more likely that he would come straight here to the yard, along the back alley, the *twitten*, as he would call it. She thought about that for a moment, then jumped down and headed for the back gate.

Chapter Twenty-Nine

WHAT ARE THESE FACES?

Scott stood at his office window, gazing unseeingly at the thickening Saturday traffic below. The answer to this case was feeling tantalisingly close now, and he had expected – hoped – that Gina would be eager to talk through the new possibilities, rather than having a fit of the vapours and diving for the minibar. Now, at last, there was a solid motive for the murder. One of the main problems so far had been that nothing they had turned up felt strong enough to drive a decent, conventional member of the non-criminal classes to homicide. Yes, Andrew's personal life was slightly tangled, with opportunities for resentment and even rage, but murder? Scott had thought not and considered Andrew's professional life a more likely breeding ground – the stakes higher and the potential suspects drawn from a world of high crime. The trouble with that was that, if they were out for revenge, there seemed no convincing reason why they should choose to exact it at a wedding in Scotland. The break-in at Andrew's office showed that they knew where he worked, and no doubt they knew where he lived, so why not attack there? With the new suspects, though, the venue made sense: none of these men could afford to be seen in Marlbury, where they could be recognised. And the motive was powerful: Andrew Gray was pursuing them relentlessly, determined that they should carry the consequences of their crimes with them, denying them a fresh start or a clean slate. What his motivation had been it was hard to know, but that was not the point.

He considered the four of them. Edmund Carson and Neil Cunningham were apparently out of the country, but Rula had now been on to the Border Agency with a request for an urgent check on their possible re-entry in recent weeks. Of the other two, Marcus Bright was his prime suspect. Alex Driver seemed, in the parlance, to have *turned his life round,* wanted to *make a difference,* and had, quite possibly, *found God.* The people he worked with knew about his background – Andrew's interference posed little threat to him. For Marcus Bright, though, things had not gone well. The shabby suit he was wearing in his photo suggested either that he was spending all his pay on drink (the puffy face inclined that way) or that the 'friend' who had taken him on at his language school was not paying him generously. Why would he need to? And Bright was capable of violence, of course. He had hit Gina hard enough to kill her – only a tough head and a Russian fur hat had saved her. He had a clear enough motive, but method and opportunity were more difficult. How did he know about the wedding? Or that he would have the opportunity to get Andrew alone? And if he was planning to kill him, wouldn't he have taken his own weapon? Scott had some answers: he had checked back copies of the Marlbury Herald on ine and found, as he thought he would, an article with a beaming photograph of Andrew and Annie, and the headline, *LOCAL BARRISTER'S DAUGHTER TO WED IN GLAMIS CASTLE.* If Bright was in the habit of keeping track of life in Marlbury, there it was. And it was possible that murder had not been in his mind. Had he possibly gone up to Glamis to talk to Andrew, hoping to catch him in a generous mood and plead with him to leave him alone? If Andrew had rebuffed him, then there was a good reason for rage. Seeing him incapable with drink, he could have followed them to the house, where Scott reluctantly admitted he and Gina could have left the door on the latch when they hauled Andrew inside and up the stairs. Could Bright have been at the wedding unnoticed? It wouldn't have been that difficult. Guests were not asked to show their invitations, after all. If they turned up looking like wedding guests (Bright would have had to hire a better suit) then they were welcomed in, and then it was easy to get lost in the mêlée.

Reflecting on his reasoning, Scott thought that if an eager DS had brought him this scenario, he would have picked a dozen holes in it, and sent her/him packing. It wasn't great, but it was all he had for the moment, and if Marcus Bright had a cast iron alibi for that weekend, then he had nothing.

At the sound of a knock at his door, he turned from the window. Rula put her head round, and then came in.

'The Border Agency are onto checking Carson and Cunningham,' she said. 'I did my best to push the urgency – possible killers et cetera – but *It's the weekend, Only a skeleton staff, Many other requests* de-da-de-da. I got these, though.' She waved a sheet of paper. 'Addresses and phone numbers for Driver and Bright. One in Hackney, one in Leicester. I wondered if you wanted to catch Alex Driver before he goes out to do his Saturday shopping.'

Scott considered this. He was as restless for action as Rula was. 'I'd rather talk to Marcus Bright,' he said. 'Call Driver and tell him we'll want to talk to him later – you can say it's in connection with Andrew Gray's death – put the wind up him a bit. In the meantime, what would you say to a trip to sunny Leicester?'

Chapter Thirty

THE MIND'S CONSTRUCTION
IN THE FACE

I don't of course raid the minibar – not really. I am a far more conventional woman than I pretend to be, or would like to be. I make myself a cup of tea and I tip a modest slurp from a brandy miniature into it. It's a drink my mother recommended for period pains when I was young, I remember. You would have thought that as a doctor she would have come up with something more pharmaceutical, but this was her prescription, and it is very comforting anyway.

While I am sitting, sipping it, a text comes in from David with attachments and the message, *Any of these at the wedding?* It occurs to me that, ironically, David might for once have wanted to talk over his new information with me, and I had flaked out. I open the attachments and find that they are photos. Edmund Carson, all grown up at a showbiz party, I recognise immediately, and Marcus Bright, podgy and dissatisfied, is still the man I knew. The other two I saw only once or twice in the aftermath of Marina Carson's death, but I can see which one is Alex Driver – skinny and still pleased with himself. So the other, snapped at some sort of open-air tweedy occasion, must be Neil Cunningham, but the picture is blurred, and anyway I don't remember him clearly. I am no help. *Ring no bells. Sorry*, I type, and rummage for a biscuit to eat with my tea.

The truth is that I am not really focused on Andrew's possible killer at this moment; it is the password that is obsessing me. Virginia? Really? David, I can tell, is convinced that it is evidence that Andrew still loved me in some twisted way; I am convinced that it is not. I heard one of those Valentine's Day programmes on the radio once, where people rang in with *Love is…* contributions. As I remember it, the contributors were all women, which says something in itself, and what they offered was not transcendent happiness, nor the sense of being utterly at one with another person, nor even the sense that you could not go on living without your beloved. What they offered were everyday acts of unselfishness, from taking the children out early on a weekend morning so you can sleep in, to clearing up the cat sick or eating the crusty ends of the loaf so you don't have to. If that is what love is, then my husband never loved me – not even to the extent of offering tea or comfort when I was newly pregnant and puking with our first child. And I'll bet he didn't do it for Lavender either. He just wasn't that sort of man. And perhaps I'm not the right kind of woman for those sorts of attentions anyway. One woman on the radio said her boyfriend showed his love by putting the toothpaste on her toothbrush every morning – I would have shouted at him to keep his grubby hands off my toothbrush. And to be honest, I didn't do much of that sort of thing for Andrew, either, except in the very early days. I did those things for my girls, of course – that was where my love went.

Andrew did not love me, and was certainly not sentimental about me. That password comes from somewhere else, and I have a very distant, dawning feeling of where that was – and an infuriating conviction that it is somehow important.

The brandy and tea have lulled me a bit, but I can't sit around here. I get up and go out for another trudge round the loch, pushing myself to go faster, inviting disastrous stumbles and broken bones. When I get back to the hotel, I don't want to go inside, so I sit on an ornamental bench and look out over the water, unfocusing my eyes, trying to switch off my brain. And then it comes to me – the picture I have been groping for. I am at the wedding, glass in hand, talking to Andrew's former PA, Jeanette, and her silent husband – Derek? No, Dennis. Jeanette is saying what a kind man Andrew was – how kind he had been to her when they had had *family troubles*. And I remember now that one day, back in my newly-divorced era, when I was enlisting Jeanette's help in getting Andrew to sign a form that required both our signatures, she had looked at the form and said something like, '*Oh, your full name is Virginia. That's our daughter's name – but we call her Ginny.*' I was too preoccupied with my own affairs to ask or care about Ginny, but Andrew had asked, and had been kind. And in my state of preternatural understanding at this moment, I know that it is that Virginia's name that is the password, because Andrew's pursuit of the Marlbury porn-brokers was on her behalf – because she had been one of their victims, and that had been Jeanette's *family trouble.*

That's not all, though, because Jeanette, Dennis and I are not the only people in my picture of that scene at the wedding. As I view it in my mind, the couple are standing facing me, and over their shoulders I can see Andrew. I remember that he was there, unseen by them, and I remember that I felt a little stir of satisfaction that he had been given an accolade and hadn't heard it. He was busy playing the host, talking animatedly to a man who would have looked like a Velasquez grandee if it hadn't been for his dark glasses.

Oh God! I know who the man is. I couldn't see it then because of the shades, but I sat next to that man a few days later, sat rather closer than I would have liked in these distancing times, sharing a bench outside the theatre. He was wearing shades then, too – I remember him putting them on as he came across the car park, and thinking it was a bit of an affectation on a dull day. But when you look at someone close to, from the side, you see quite a lot of their eyes, even if they are wearing dark glasses, unless they are real wraparounds. I saw the drooping eyelid – the almost wink that gave his face an ironic touch in his police mugshot, and which he hides behind dark glasses whenever he can.

For a moment I am simply pleased with myself, elated by my own cleverness, and then a great tide of nausea comes over me. Freda. I fumble with my phone, and it takes me several tries to call up Freda's latest text, received just as I came in from my walk:

Malcolm is helping me to set my boxes up this afternoon so I shall get a chance to see them on stage! Yay! xx

I look at the time. One-twenty. There is time. I ring her. There is no reply. I send a text that is all capitals and exclamation marks. I ring again. There is still no reply. *This afternoon.* That means after two o'clock, doesn't it? There is still time. I run inside.

At the reception desk, I request a taxi immediately for a trip into Perth. 'Ivan took me last time,' I say. 'He was very good.'

The receptionist looks at me doubtfully; however well I think I am concealing it, she can spot incipient panic, and that is not the sort of thing they want in this nice hotel on a sunny August Saturday afternoon. She moves slowly to find the number, seems to wait forever before the phone is answered, and then embarks on lengthy social preliminaries, enquiring about the health and well-being of each member of his family in turn before getting round to asking Ivan if he could possibly drive a lady into Perth. Ivan's answer is lengthy, punctuated by *yes, yes* and *I see* and *of course, yes, you would,* from the receptionist. I start to despair.

'Tell him I'll pay double,' I hiss, 'because it's last minute.'

She looks as though she might refuse to pass on such a foolish message, but she does, in a tone of deep disapproval. The response at the other end is short.

'I'll tell her,' she says, and puts the phone down. 'Ten minutes,' she says to me, and turns away. I slink upstairs, convinced that I have, at the very least, taken a man away from his child's birthday party.

He looks quite cheerful, though, when I come back downstairs to find him waiting. 'To the theatre again?' he asks.

'As fast as you can go,' I say.

As I sit back in the car, I am assaulted by a powerful whiff of déja vu – as you may be too, Dear Reader, if you have taken an interest in earlier crises in my life. Almost exactly two years ago, I was in this same situation – sitting in the back of a taxi in a state of sweaty terror, sick with the conviction that Freda was in the hands of a killer. That time, we had hundreds of miles to go; this time, at least it is only a forty-minute drive. That time, I had a knife with me – only a fruit knife, admittedly; this time, all I have is a pair of fold-up scissors that live in the untidy depths of my handbag. That time, I was driven by Gary, who turned out to be a hero; this time I am not sure that I can expect heroism from Ivan.

I think about calling the police, but what can I say? '*I think Malcolm Ross may not be who he says he is, and he is spending the afternoon with my granddaughter*'? Remembering the hopeless police response I got when Freda actually disappeared, I can't see that working. *Malcolm Ross*! Why didn't I see that it had to be a false name? A man calls himself after two characters from *Macbeth* and I don't notice? Such stupidity. I sit with my phone in my hand, and though I can't see how he can do anything from hundreds of miles away down in London, I ring David.

'Where are you?' he asks. 'You sound as though you're driving.'

'I'm in a taxi. Where are you?'

'In Leicester. We've been interviewing Marcus Bright.'

'You've got the wrong man.'

'Yes, we think that now, but we couldn't know that until we—'

I glance at the COVID shield that divides me from Ivan, and I am not sure that it muffles sound. I lower my voice.

'Malcolm Ross,' I hiss, 'is Neil Cunningham.'

There is a moment's silence. 'Who's Malcolm Ross?' he asks.

'Neil Cunningham, I told you.'

'No, I mean, I don't know a Malcolm Ross. Where has he come from?'

'Two characters in *Macbeth*. Malcolm is the pri—'

'Gina!'

'Sorry. I forgot you probably didn't meet him at the wedding. Distinguished looking. White hair and beard. He's the director of the little theatre in Perth – he came over with the kids who did the performance.'

'I thought there was a young woman with them.'

'There was. Isla. But he was there too – he drove the minibus.'

'And why do you think he's Cunningham?'

'The drooping eyelid. You can see it plainly in his police mugshot, and it's there in that fuzzy news photo as well, if you look carefully. He wore dark glasses at the wedding, and when I met him here at the theatre, but I caught a side view, and that eyelid definitely drooped.'

'If that's all—'

'I've got a gut feeling. I felt there was something creepy about him. All that facial hair, for a start. And the name, of course.'

'I'll bet there are loads of Scots called Malcolm Ross.'

'Exactly. It won't have been that difficult for him to find a dead Malcolm Ross, whose identity he could steal when he was applying for a theatre job just a few miles from Glamis Castle. Just the kind of private joke he'll have enjoyed.'

'Even if you're right – and I'm not convinced – he can't have killed Andrew. If he drove the minibus, then he left with the kids before Andrew was killed. We saw them, didn't we, as we were getting Andrew back to the house? They were on their way to the minibus. The local police interviewed them briefly and ruled them out.'

'I've got a theory developing about that, but it's not the important thing at the moment. The real thing is that he's a predatory paedophile, and he and Freda are supposed to be meeting any time now to do something with some scenery she's been painting. How convincing does that sound to you? The director of a theatre giving up his Saturday afternoon to hump scenery about so a girl can see it on stage before her parents take her off home? He's got to be a saint, or else a devil – and I know what I think.'

I hear David draw breath.

'And don't tell me Freda's too old to be prey for a paedophile – he may not be that fussy – and anyway he may be out for revenge – on Andrew for hounding him; and on me. He knew I helped to root out their porn ring, and he knows I'm here.'

He says nothing for a moment, and then he asks, 'Why are you in a taxi?'

'Why do you think? I'm on my way to Perth to stop him.'

'And how are you going to do that?'

'Well, I don't know, do I? I'm sure the police here won't help if I call them – I was hoping you could put some pressure on them.'

'I've got nothing to push with – a drooping eyelid, a Shakespearian name.'

'Well don't bother then,' I snap. 'Forget it. I'll deal with it.'

I click off and look into Ivan's mirror. He looks back at me, and it is clear to me that he has heard everything, understood enough of it, and wishes he had stayed at home. I am not letting him off, though. When we have parked in the side road by the theatre, I order him to stay put, as I shall need him for the return journey, assuring him that I won't be long, although I have no idea whether that is true.

I know there must be a back route into the theatre yard at the back, and I find the alleyway easily. It is easy to find my way into the yard, too, because the gate is wide open. I look around. Freda's blocks are scattered around, but she is not there. I think this is reassuring. If Cunningham/Ross was going to assault her, wouldn't he have lured her inside? I have tried her phone several times in the car, but still have had no answer. Has she not arrived yet? Is she in Aileen's car, driven by Alex, loud music on the radio, the phone inaudible? I try the door that leads into the green room at the back of the theatre, but it is locked. I suppose I have just to sit and wait.

I survey the stage blocks, which are nicely painted, and sit down on one, about to get my phone out and ring Freda again, and then I see it. At my feet is Freda's favourite denim jacket. I pick it up and find her phone in the pocket. She must be here. She goes nowhere without her phone. Stupidly, I stare round the yard as though she must be here, hiding as though this were a game. I stand up and shout her name, and it echoes back to me from the walls of the yard.

Well, the police have got to listen to me now. I go back to Ivan in his car. He can drive me to the police station, and I'll march in and demand that they help – batter down the doors to the theatre, track the man down to his home, put up road blocks, do something…

I get into Ivan's car, and I am just about to tell him to get the police station on his satnav when I hear a car start up – a car that has been parked further down the road, and which I recognise. I saw it the last time I was here, and I knew then that I had seen it before. Why am I so stupid about cars? Disastrously stupid. It is one of those distinctive, vintage-looking, sporty, handmade cars that last a lifetime, and which I saw several times twelve years ago, when it sat in the car park of the Aphra Behn theatre, in a space with *Director* marked on it. If I had thought about it when I saw it here three days ago, everything would be different, and Freda would be safe. I could beat myself senseless against the car window, but instead I shout, 'Follow that car,' and if that is a cliché in Polish, Ivan shows no sign of being amused.

Chapter Thirty-One

SOME DANGER DOTH
APPROACH YOU NEARLY

On a side street in the centre of Leicester, David Scott and Rula Bartosz emerged from a once-elegant nineteenth century house, now much in need of care and attention. The exterior had clearly been heavily air brushed for the images on the website of the King's School of English (the illustrious name barely justified by King Street being the name of the road). They stood on the pavement and looked at one another.

'If he hadn't nearly killed Gina, I could almost feel sorry for him,' Scott said.

'If Andrew Gray was stopping him from getting a job anywhere else, that certainly gave Bright a motive for getting rid of him,' Rula said.

'Except they work him so hard there, he's got a rock-solid alibi. No weekends off for our Mr Bright. Saturday is *cultural pursuits* day, and he was conducting a group of Japanese flight attendants round the cathedral and the Richard III museum, and on Sunday morning he was off to the airport in the minibus to pick up a new group of students. I think we can rule out the possibility that he drove hell for leather to the highlands and committed a murder in between times.'

'So, back to Alex Driver then?'

'It looks like it. Shall we find a pub for a sandwich first?'

'I was hoping you would say that.'

And then his phone rang. He pulled it out and looked at the caller ID. Pointing to a pub that was visible out on the main road, he said to Rula, *'Gina. Sorry,'* and watched her head off towards the pub before answering the call. It was noisy at the other end.

'Where are you?' he asked. 'You sound as though you're driving.'

'I'm in a taxi,' she said, and then she was off, talking, fast and furiously, and he was racing to catch up with her: someone called Malcolm Ross – false identity – drooping eyelid – stuff about Macbeth – Freda in danger, and Gina dashing off in a taxi to confront a possible killer. And the thing was, he believed her, every word. How the hell he was going to get the local police to believe her was another matter, but when he started to tell her that, she was in no mood for excuses.

'I'll deal with it,' she said, and that was exactly what he was afraid of.

He found Rula in the pub, drinking ginger ale and eating crisps. She pushed a glass towards him.

'I got one for you too,' she said. 'I didn't know what—'

'Sorry,' he said. 'I don't think I've got time. Something's come up.'

As succinctly as he could, he gave her Gina's story. She listened intently, and when he had finished, she went on looking at him. Then she said, 'There's quite a lot of *Gina thinks*, in that story, isn't there? A bit short on hard evidence, if you don't mind me saying.'

'I know.' He took a swig of his drink. 'And of course Gina is my – whatever – but I do trust her instincts. She's not often wrong.'

'And you really think her granddaughter is in danger?'

'I do. She's Andrew Gray's granddaughter too, and I suppose Gina thinks Ross/Cunningham is out for some sort of posthumous revenge, but we know more, don't we? How long ago did you contact Alex Driver? Three hours? And we let Bright know we were coming, didn't we? Isn't it quite likely that they are all in contact with one another? Driver and Cunningham have known each other since school. If Driver's alerted Cunningham to what we know about Gray's campaign against them, Cunningham will know that he's in the frame for the murder. I think a man like that will do anything not to go back to prison. I think we could be looking at some sort of hostage situation.'

'Or we could be looking at a perfectly nice man, running a youth theatre.'

'We could, but my gut tells me we're not, and I can't risk it.'

'So what are you going to do?'

'Prise the officers on duty at the Perth station out from behind their desks and into squad cars for a start.'

'And then?'

'There's only one thing I can do. And if I'm wrong, it's quite likely to cost me my job.'

Chapter Thirty-Two

SOUND AND FURY

Without seeming to be much engaged, Ivan is doing an efficient job of chasing the car, and I can turn my attention to getting hold of the police. I ring 999 and, after quite a bit of negotiation, I am put through to Perth police station, where the desk sergeant admits that, yes, a superintendent from the Met has been on to them about a possible abduction, but they have not been able to *action a response* because of insufficient information.

I ask if he told them a fifteen-year-old girl had gone missing, and that she was the granddaughter of the man who was murdered in Glamis castle a week ago, and that the man who had abducted her was probably her grandfather's killer. *Yes,* to the first two, *No* to the last.

'So, you can see,' he says, 'there is very little to go on. A fifteen-year-old goes off somewhere on a Saturday afternoon. Not a police matter, even if it does happen that her grandfather's recent death is the subject of a criminal investigation.'

'She didn't *go off somewhere,*' I spit. 'She arranged to meet the man – Malcolm Ross, if you're interested – though that's not his real name – but never mind that. She arranged to meet him to do some work at the Curtain theatre. I found her jacket there, with her phone in the pocket. Tell me what teenager goes off somewhere willingly without her phone?'

'Superintendent Scott didn't mention the phone.'

'He didn't know.'

'And where are you now, madam?' he asks, and I feel that he just might now be taking me seriously.

'I'm in a car, following her abductor. I saw him leave the theatre.'

'Never a good idea to take things into your own hands, you know,' he says.

'I would very much like to put it into your hands,' I say – remarkably mildly, I think, all things considered.

'A description of the car?' he asks.

'It's very distinctive. A dark blue Morgan, vintage looking, soft top.'

'Registration?'

'I've no idea. It's too far away to see, and there's traffic.'

I can hear a furious tapping of keys, and then he says, 'Ah, now, you see, we have a problem. I have the website here, and the Morgan is a vintage-style sports car, isn't it? Open top, two-seater. Are you able to see the young lady sitting in the passenger seat, because if not –'

'This is a Morgan four-seater, and the top is up. So she is obviously in the back – or in the boot.'

There is more tapping of keys. 'Got it,' he says. 'Yes, you are quite right. There is a four-seater model. But she won't be in the boot. They have a very small boot capacity, these cars, that's why they have space to strap –'

What is it with men and their bloody cars?

I interrupt. 'So, are you sending help or am I going to have to deal with it?' I ask. 'I am her grandmother, by the way.'

'I'd better have some details of the car you are driving,' he says.

I have no idea what car I am in, of course. I didn't even notice the colour. Grey? Cream? Something ordinary, I tap on the plexiglass screen and ask Ivan if he has a hands-free phone. He has.

'Expect a call from the police,' I say. 'Nothing to be alarmed about – just tell them about the car. Give me your phone number.'

I think he might baulk at this, but I am using the *Don't tangle with me* tone which I generally found effective with recalcitrant teenage boys, and he obeys. He recites the number and I relay it to the desk sergeant. 'He's the driver,' I say. 'He'll tell you all about his car – and if you send a car out to us, he can tell the officers where we're going. Thank you so much for your help.' And I ring off.

I wait until Ivan has finished his call and then I ring David. We are still moving slowly through Saturday shopping traffic, but I have just seen a sign to the airfield, and we seem to be heading in that direction, with the blue car clearly in our sights. I can watch and talk at the same time.

There is a surprising amount of noise at his end. 'Where are you?' I ask.

'Travelling,' he says.

'By train?'

'No.'

'Well, you sound as though you're in a cement mixer. You need to get your car serviced.'

'Where are you?'

'Still in the taxi.' And I tell him about the jacket, the phone, and the Morgan. 'I'm hoping to be followed by a squad car shortly. I think your call to the station helped.'

'Where is he heading?'

'Out of Perth. He seems to be following signs to the airfield.'

'Does he know you're following him?'

'How would I know?'

'Taking diversions, overtaking, U-turns, sudden changes of speed, trying to –'

'No. He's just driving. And when he stops, we'll be on him.'

'Gina, leave it to the police. If you're right, he's a killer. If he's cornered, he'll –'

'What do you mean, *if* I'm right? You know I'm right, don't you?'

'You said you were working on a theory about how he was able to kill Andrew. Tell me – briefly.'

'Briefly, we left the door open.'

'What?'

'We left the bloody door open, David – you and I – when we hauled Andrew inside.'

'I'm sure I found it closed when I left.'

'Of course you did, because he had come in and closed it. He chatted to me outside while the rest of his party went on to the minibus. He saw what a state Andrew was in, and reckoned it was his chance to get rid of him. He probably didn't realise that Lavender was in the house, and thought we would dump him and leave him in an empty house. Andrew was pretty legless by that time, and it took the two of us to get him through the door, if you remember – neither of us thought about closing it, and Lavender – who should have done it – didn't want to be anywhere near him, and scarpered back to her bottle of wine and mindless telly. Cunningham/Ross nipped in after us. We didn't hear him – we were upstairs, and too busy manhandling Andrew. He hid – probably in the downstairs loo – heard you leave, and assumed it was both of us leaving, went upstairs and found Andrew practically unconscious. Probably he expected to smother him with a pillow or something, but there was the skien du, and he's a man of the theatre, and this was Glamis castle, so a dagger seemed so much more appropriate. You said at the start that it seemed like a professional job – straight into the eye socket – well, this was a man who had spent several years in prison, where I'm sure that sort of thing is on the syllabus. He won't have had gloves with him – unless he was still carrying them as COVID protection – some people do. I'd guess he'll have wrapped a handkerchief round his hand or something. I'd be surprised if he didn't leave a print somewhere, though.'

'I'm not sure they took his or Isla's prints. They were satisfied that they were off the premises before the murder took place. I don't think she mentioned his delay in coming back to the minibus. Do you think he got her to lie for him?'

'If he went out of the back door, he had a shorter route to the car park, and I guess he hurried back and made some excuse – said we'd kept him talking, or he needed a pee or some such. I don't suppose she consciously lied for him – she won't have suspected him – won't have thought he had any reason to be involved.'

By this time, I can see in Ivan's mirror that there is a squad car a few cars behind us.

'We're in business,' I say. 'The cavalry is here.'

'Good. Then leave it—'

'To the professionals. Yes, yes. I'll just sit here like a little old lady in the back of the car, while the big, brave policemen rescue my little girl.'

'I would really like to believe that,' he says.

He's gone, we are still headed for the airfield, and I have a composite disaster picture in my head – Cunningham/ Ross running across the tarmac to a waiting light aircraft, a drugged Freda in his arms, while I run after them with my legs impossibly heavy, as they are in dreams, screaming at him, until, out of nowhere, a single gunshot brings me to the ground. A mixture of Le Carré, Spooks and Secret Army. *For*

God's sake, nobody's got a gun, I mutter to myself, though I can't rule out the rest of it.

As it turns out, we go past the airfield, along a road of scattered houses, increasingly far apart, until we reach one with only a field – no, a golf course – beyond it, and the Morgan sweeps into its drive. I hadn't thought that we were simply following him home, but this must be it, and it is not what I would have guessed at. There is nothing stylish here – just a large bungalow surrounded by scrubby garden, its only virtue its isolation. No nosey neighbours here.

He stops the car, gets out, and comes towards us as Ivan brings us to a stop behind him. Did he know we were following him? He looks no more than slightly annoyed to see us. He walks up to Ivan's window, and then notices me and taps at my window. I wind it down.

'Mrs Gray,' he says. 'Has something happened to Freda?'

And that's it. I shove the door open, nearly knocking him over, and while he is recovering his balance, I give him a huge shove that sends him sprawling to the ground, and I think I might well have kicked him if there hadn't been a shout from the police car that has just rolled onto the grass.

I turn and shout back, 'She's in the car,' and I run towards it, pulling the back door open, and finding – nothing. I go round to the boot and tug it open, but I know she won't be there – it is far too small even for a slight teenager, and it contains nothing but some jump leads. I turn towards Freda's abductor, and I shout, 'What have you done with her? How have you done this?'

It's like a conjuring trick. I can almost believe that the car has a false floor. One of the policemen has now joined me and he takes a cursory look into the car.

'Nothing here,' he calls to the other one, who is helping Cunningham/Ross to his feet. They both look at me, and their looks say that the only crime that has been committed here is an assault. I panic. I can't be arrested – I have to find Freda, who must, I see now, be imprisoned somewhere at the theatre. The bloody man has led us on this chase deliberately – he knew exactly what he was doing – but my chances of persuading the policemen of that aren't good. Standing there, brushing himself down, Cunningham/Ross looks calm, reasonable, respectable, while I am a screaming harpy.

But now I am aware that their attention has shifted. They aren't looking at me – they're looking towards the golf course, from where, if I think about it, there has been quite a lot of noise emanating in the last few minutes. I turn to look too. A police helicopter has just landed, its blades still whirling. Out of it steps David, and I am back in movie land. This is the rescue, and I should be running towards him, except that it's not the rescue, because David should have Freda in his arms, and he hasn't.

So, I don't run towards him. I shout, 'She's not in the car, David,' instead, but he ignores me, heading instead for Cunningham/Ross and the policeman who is his minder.

'Detective Superintendent David Scott, Metropolitan Police,' he says, flashing his ID at the officer. 'I need you to arrest this man on a charge of identity theft. Charge him under his real name – Neil Cunningham?'

The officer looks startled, and I think he is going to protest, but for the first time Cunningham/Ross looks rattled. I see colour flood into his face, and his eyes go to his car as though he thinks he could make a break for it. The policeman moves a step nearer and delivers the caution. It feels absurdly theatrical.

'These officers will now search your house in your presence,' David says, and I am the only person who wants to protest. Everyone else does as he says. I don't know whether it's the impressive arrival via helicopter that does it, or the Met tag, or a natural authority which I have failed to notice over the years, but the officers jump to it, and Neil Cunningham allows himself to be marched into the house. I am appalled. As a second police car arrives and David goes to meet it, I run after him, shouting.

'She's not in the house!' I yell. 'How can she be? We followed him from the theatre. He's locked her up there. We have to get her.'

As we stop at the car, I yank his sleeve. 'This lot have got to go back to the theatre,' I hiss.

He takes hold of my arm – not gently – and steers me away from the car. 'Can you not see that you're not helping?' he mutters. 'These officers don't know me, and you are undermining my authority.'

'But don't you—' I start, but he is propelling me firmly towards Ivan's taxi.

'You are going back into town,' he says. 'I'd like you to go back to Pitlochry, but I know you won't do that, so this is the deal: you go back, and you sit in that taxi outside the theatre. These officers will search the theatre. The theatre is a possible crime scene. If you take one step onto theatre premises, I will charge you with obstructing a police investigation – and I really mean that. Do you understand?'

'I have information,' I say, with all the dignity I can manage, because I feel like crying. 'I could show them where her jacket and phone are.'

'They'll find them,' he says. 'That's what we do.' He opens the car door and waits for me to get in. Then he closes the door on me and goes round to speak to Ivan.

'You're taking Mrs Gray back to the theatre,' he says, 'and waiting with her outside the building. She is not to get out of this car, and nor are you. It will be your job to keep her safe. You are acting under police direction – and you will be paid for your time.'

I can't see Ivan's face from my seat in the back, but I can

see him go rigid. I don't know if he is most afraid of the police, possible criminals, or his hysterical passenger. This really isn't the Saturday afternoon he had planned. He manages a silent nod, and David goes off to talk to the officers in the second car. Ivan can't get us out of the drive until they have gone, so we sit in silence as they back out, and then follow them. Twisting round in my seat, I watch David return to the house. What for? I think I will never forgive him for abandoning me at this moment.

Our silence continues as we follow the police car back into town. I am bursting to vent my frustration and desperation, but Ivan is not the man for that. A message arrives on my phone at one point, and I scrabble it out of my bag with a thudding heart, irrationally convinced that it is from Freda. It is not; it is from Ellie. Ellie! Oh God!

The message reads: *Nearly there. With you in about an hour xx.* I stare at it, and I think I am going to start hyperventilating. I am having flashbacks to the last time, when my daughters descended on me like a pair of avenging harpies – only this time it is absolutely not my fault. It is not my fault, but I shall get the blame, and with that thought I start to weep fat tears of misery and self-pity.

When we get to the theatre, Ivan parks behind the police car, outside the front of the theatre, and we watch as the two officers – a man and a woman – try the door, find it locked, and shoulder it open. They disappear inside, and I think, *Sod David,* and decide to make a run for it. I wrench at the door handle, find it locked, and wrestle with it furiously while Ivan regards me in his mirror.

'Unlock this bloody door!' I scream at him.

He breaks his silence. 'Child lock,' he says, and I subside into more furious tears.

We sit and wait. Through blurred eyes I watch alternately the theatre door and the road behind us, hoping still that

David will have come to his senses and followed us. And then I see a boy I recognise – tall and red-headed – approaching the theatre. It is Alex McCleod. I bang on the window, but he doesn't hear. Instead, he goes to the theatre's wrecked door, peers inside, and then goes in. My mind is racing. What does he know? Could Freda somehow have got a message to him?

'I want to go inside!' I yell at Ivan. 'And I am going to smash this window.'

I have taken off a shoe and am battering ineffectually against the toughened glass when Alex reappears, not looking particularly worried. He hears my battering and comes cautiously to the window.

'Open this bloody window,' I growl at Ivan, but he ignores me, and I have to shout at Alex.

'Where's Freda?' I yell, and he points along the road.

Along the road?

'Where? Why?' I shout.

He puts up a hand in a *Hold on a minute* gesture, speeds off along the road, and disappears into a café a few doors along – the very café, I think, where I had lunch with Freda when she was having a meltdown about one of the McCleods being Andrew's killer. I cannot bear this one second more.

'Listen to me,' I snarl at my jailer, 'keeping me here is a crime. False imprisonment. My husband is a top lawyer, and if you don't let me out of this car right now, he will see to it that you go to jail.'

Ivan shrugs. A policeman who arrived in a helicopter has given him his orders, and he outguns any lawyer in Ivan's world, even without the knowledge that my husband is *ex* in every sense.

I vow that I will never speak to David again.

I am about to subside in despair when I see Alex come back out of the café. He waves and beckons. I raise my arms in a gesture of despair, but I am not sure if he can see me, and he goes back inside. Then he is out again, and he has someone with him – a slight little figure in paint-spattered jeans and T-shirt.

'Freda!' I scream, and Ivan turns round to look at me. 'My granddaughter,' I yell, pointing ahead, and as I look into his uncomprehending face, I realise that none of us has ever explained to him what this is all about – not I, not David, not the police. We have all ordered him about – *Drive here, Follow that car there, Wait for orders, Keep that woman in your car* – and we have never given him a reason. He has no idea what to make of me – for all he knows I am a dangerous criminal. I take a deep breath.

'Ivan,' I say, as quietly and calmly as I can manage, 'We really should have explained. The girl there – the teenager in the black T-shirt – is my granddaughter. She disappeared. The man the police arrested back at the house must have locked her up somewhere, but she's escaped. The police are searching that house because they are idiots, but she is here. And I really have to go and hug her.'

He looks at me in incomprehension for a moment, and then his dour face breaks into a smile that is almost charming.

'There is your granddaughter?' he asks, pointing to where she is standing. 'And she was lost?'

'Yes.'

'Why you didn't say?' And with that I hear the blessed sound of central locking being released.

As I stumble out of the car, I hope that Freda will come running to meet me, because my legs are so wobbly that I'm not sure I can cover the distance, but she just stands there, looking anxious, and when I get within hugging distance, she says, 'I'm so sorry, Granny. I've screwed everything up, haven't I?'

Chapter Thirty-Three

PLENTEOUS JOYS

This had to be the most embarrassing hour of her life. She had panicked and messed up, and now here was Granny, all hugs and tears, and before she knew it Mum and Ben and Nico arrived, smartly followed by Jon and Auntie Annie, and it was all tears and shouting and people throwing questions at her and not listening to the answers. And it was so much worse because Alex was there – comfortingly at her side, but looking fascinated and bewildered. *Why couldn't they behave?* Worst of all, above the hubbub she could hear Granny's voice from time to time, slightly hysterical: *'Two police cars and a helicopter! David, in a police helicopter, would you believe?'* And she knew she was in serious trouble.

As the noise reached a peak, the café manager, who had been very nice in letting her spend the whole afternoon there, drinking two diet cokes, decided to step in, politely suggesting that they might like to go outside – and order something to drink. He led them out to a yard at the back, wiped down a couple of tables and produced some folding chairs, took an order for tea all round, and suggested that, since this seemed to be a celebration, they might like to order cake as well. And then David arrived.

Freda watched him as he sketched a wave to the assembled group while scanning it for – yes – her. He spotted her, where she and Alex were sitting as far apart from the rest of the mob as they could manage, came over and put a hand on her shoulder, and she really thought for a moment that he was going to arrest her – well, you could be done for *Wasting Police Time*, couldn't you? As it was, he just said, 'Can we have a word, Freda?' and she got up and followed him back into the café, where he ordered coffee and asked her if she would like anything, which she refused because the diet cokes were still bubbling around inside her.

Then when the waiter had gone, he said, 'I'm very glad to see you. Are you all right?' And that was so kind, when she had caused so much trouble, that she felt tears threatening and she could only nod and bite down hard, determined not to be all over the place like the rest of her family.

'Can you tell me exactly what happened?' he asked.

'I'm so sorry about the helicopter,' she said. 'Will there be trouble?'

'I think I can swing it,' he said. 'We found some interesting things at Cunningham's house.'

'Cunningham?'

'Your Mr Ross's real name.'

'So I was right that he was a fake?'

'I think you had better explain.'

By this time, his coffee had arrived, plus a piece of the cake which everyone seemed to be being forced to eat.

'It's very simple really,' she said, 'and I would have been fine if I hadn't stupidly left my phone behind.'

He nodded, his mouth full of cake.

'He texted me this morning and offered to come and open up the theatre and help me move the stage blocks I've been painting onto the stage, because we're getting the sleeper back home tonight and I wouldn't get a chance to see them in

219

place. So I was pleased, and Alex gave me a lift to the theatre, but he had to drop me early because he had a band rehearsal, so I was sitting outside, in the yard behind the theatre—'

'Where we found your jacket?'

'Yes. I was sitting waiting for him, and suddenly I had the feeling that he was a fake and I couldn't trust him, and I sort of panicked. I knew he would be there at any moment, and I ran.'

'Leaving your jacket and your phone behind?'

'Yes! I couldn't believe it. I didn't exactly have a plan, but when I'd got away from the theatre, I thought I'd just wander round the shops a bit and then go to the café where I'd arranged to meet Alex if I wasn't still at the theatre when he came to pick me up. Only, in the first shop I went into I went to get my phone out of my pocket to text Alex to tell him I would definitely be in the café, and I realised it wasn't there. I'd put it in my jacket pocket, and I hadn't got the jacket.'

'A nasty moment,' he said.

'It was. It made me feel all shaky. It's like your best friend, your phone, isn't it? But I didn't dare go back, obviously, because I was sure Malcolm – Cunningham – would be there. And then I worried that Alex couldn't contact me, and I decided to just go and sit in the café because he would be bound to come there eventually.'

'Sensible.'

'It half made up for being stupid, I suppose. I worried that Mum would be sending me texts and worrying that I didn't reply, but I never thought of Granny starting a police chase. That was so – extreme.'

'Perhaps.'

'But I wasn't really in danger, was I?'

'I don't know. There's a lot I can't tell you, I'm afraid, but you weren't wrong not to trust him. You did the right thing.'

'Except for the phone.'

'Nobody's perfect.' He looked hard at her. 'Can you pin down what it was that made you feel you couldn't trust him?'

'Oh yes,' she said. 'It was the twitten.'

'The what?'

'The twitten. It's a dialect word for an alleyway. We had a lesson on dialect words in English last term, when we were reading *Tess of the D'Urbervilles.*'

'And?'

'*Twitten*. Malcolm talked about the *twitten* that led from the theatre at Pitlochry into the town. He's got this Scottish accent and I didn't think anything of it – it was like it was a Scottish word – but then when I was waiting for him, I was expecting him to come along the alleyway behind the theatre, and him saying *twitten* came into my head, and I thought that wasn't right, because I remembered Mrs O'Shea saying in the English lesson that the South-East counties don't have many dialect words now – they're more in rural areas – but there are a few, and *twitten* was one of them. She said it was still used in Sussex and leaked over a bit into Kent. It stuck in my mind because we laughed about it – *Watch out you don't meet a twit in the twitten* – stupid stuff. Anyway, I think I'd always thought he was a bit creepy, and now I thought *He's a fake,* and it somehow freaked me out, so I—'

'Took avoiding action. Very sensible.'

He looked at her as though he wanted to smile but couldn't quite. 'Your grandmother will be delighted that the English language has come to the rescue again.'

'I haven't had a chance to tell her. She wasn't—'

'Quite sane? Well, I won't be able to tell her any time soon. She's not talking to me.'

'Why not?'

'I was officious – gave her orders.'

'Blimey! How did you dare?'

'She was in danger of wrecking a police investigation.'

'Can you mend things with her?'

'I don't know.'

He drained his coffee cup, stood up, and looked down at her. 'You are so like her,' he said.

This didn't sound like a compliment.

'No, I'm not,' she said, getting up too. 'Not at all.'

'Yes, you are,' he said. 'Bright and brave, both of you.'

Chapter Thirty-Four

A SOLEMN SUPPER

He was late, and supper with the Grays and their extended family was really not what he needed at the end of what he was obliged to call a challenging day. There were other adjectives, of course – *frustrating, exhausting, infuriating* and *bloody awful* came to mind – but they were off the Met's lexicon of acceptable vocabulary. They implied too much damage, whereas whoever came up with *challenging* as the go-to word brilliantly hit on a term that was positively benign, offering a welcome opportunity to demonstrate courage and tenacity. Well, if challenges were to be embraced, he had done more than his share of virtual hugging today. And now, here he was, stepping out of a taxi outside the McCleods' house, where Aileen McCleod had gathered the family for an impromptu supper of pizza and ice cream, because he needed to talk to Gina, because he had eaten nothing but a slice of cake since breakfast time, and because, if he couldn't justify to the ACC the commissioning of a police helicopter without higher authorisation, then he would be spending more time with his family, and this was the only family he had.

The gathering round the table in the conservatory comprised almost the same cast as had gathered there eight days previously, on the eve of the wedding. Andrew was

223

missing of course, and Lavender too, and Jon's grandmother had been spared an encore with the Grays, but otherwise there they all were, not carefully placed as Aileen had arranged them on that evening, but by their own choice. Gina, he noticed, had barricaded herself with Freda on one side and Duncan McCleod on the other – no place kept for him. He was going to have to get her to talk to him this evening, though, and the prospect made him feel very tired.

The centre of the table was littered with butchered pizzas, a few flabby slices yet remaining, but Aileen had kept one warm for him, and she settled him in a seat next to hers with an appealing plateful, a bowl of salad and a glass of wine. Then she let him eat and drink in peace.

The pizza was good – hot, chewy, and cheesy – and it was a while before he stopped giving it his undivided attention and sat back to sip his wine and survey the table and the pairs in conversation: Ellie and Annie, heads together, catching up; Jon and Alex laughing; Nico in earnest talk with Duncan McCleod, probably about neolithic tombs; Gina and Freda with their private bond. Aileen was talking to Ben, on her other side, but when she saw that David had finished, started to clear away plates. He got up to help, and carried a pile of plates out into the kitchen. There the door was open into the garden, and he went across to sniff the soft, summer dusk. Aileen watched him.

'Take a walk round the garden, why don't you?' she said, 'You'll be needing a bit of peace, I imagine.'

He remembered that she had been a nurse, and thought that she must have been very good at it – competent, calm and empathetic.

'I'll just stroll down to the end and back,' he said, and stepped out into the damp, scented air.

He was not a gardener himself, nor an ardent appreciator of the natural world, but the calm of this garden in the dusk was a balm. He could almost feel his heart rate slowing as he walked down the lawn towards a rose arbour, and consciously emptied his mind of the buzzing anxieties of the day. And then he felt a sharp poke in his back, and he spun round to find Gina laughing at him.

'Call yourself a policeman?' she said. 'I could have had you then.'

'I'm off duty,' he countered.

'You're never off duty. That's your problem.'

He took a deep breath. 'I'm sorry about this afternoon,' he said, 'but you have to see it from my point of view.'

'Yes,' she said.

'I couldn't give the local officers the chance to realise that I didn't actually have any authority over them.'

'No.'

'The helicopter, the Met tag – they stunned them into taking orders, but if you started questioning –'

'Being a mere female, you mean?'

'Yes – no. Anyone. You must see that.'

'I do.'

'Really?'

'Well, not really, but I am prepared to forgive you.'

'That makes me suspicious. I assume there is a price?'

'No, actually. Well, I want to know everything you've found out about so-called Malcolm Ross, and whether you've charged him with Andrew's murder, but that's not why I'm forgiving you.'

'Can I ask why, then?'

'*Bright and brave.* Probably the nicest thing anyone has ever said about me. I don't get much in the way of accolades, you know. And Freda was very chuffed to share the praise.'

'You know I think that about you.'

'*Yes, but you don't say it.*'

'Is that a quote?'

'*The Importance of Being Earnest*. The Hon Gwendolen Fairfax. When her young man is making a hash of proposing to her.'

'I've done that once. I wasn't planning to do it again.'

She tucked her arm into his and walked him down beyond the arbour. 'What can you tell me?' she asked.

'You know there's an issue about confidentiality.'

'My lips are sealed. Come on. Give.'

It was seductive, but he had not debriefed to anyone yet – not to Rula nor to Paula, nor to the ACC, with whom there would be a sticky interview.

'We're a long way from charging him with the murder,' he said. 'Your hypothesis remains just that.'

'Has he admitted to being Neil Cunningham?'

'We are satisfied that Ross and Cunningham are the same person,' he said evasively. 'But that isn't going to satisfy the ACC that I was justified in calling up the helicopter. Only the real danger that Freda was in the hands of a killer will do that.'

'And she wasn't in his hands anyway, as it turns out.'

'The evidence pointed that way. If I can prove that Cunningham is Andrew's killer, I might get away with it. Otherwise...'

'He'll sack you?'

'Almost certainly – especially because of my personal connection with Freda.'

'Can't you get a confession out of Mr Cunningham?'

'Very unlikely. He'll know that he'll get only a few months on the false identity charge – he's got no reason to admit to murder. We'll look again at the forensic evidence, now we know who our suspect is, and I'm going to lean on the other two – Driver and Bright. There's a good chance Cunningham told them what he had done. They're in contact with one another. I'm pretty sure Driver alerted the other two·

this morning, when Rula interviewed him. That was when Cunningham texted Freda to make the arrangement for this afternoon.'

She stopped walking and looked at him. 'You mean you think Cunningham really was planning to abduct her? What for? Why get himself into more trouble?'

'He's a really arrogant guy, and I think he might have done anything to avoid another long prison stretch. He was ready to murder rather than have his career ruined again, and I think we might have ended up with a hostage situation there at his house.'

'It sounds crazy.'

'Andrew's murder was crazy.'

She was silent for a while as they walked again. When she spoke, her voice was unsteady. 'He has to be stopped. You can't lose this. Lean on Marcus Bright. Better, let me talk to him. We were friends once.'

'And then he nearly killed you.'

'He panicked. He's weak but he's not bad. I can tell him I've forgiven him – I'll have the moral advantage – tell him what Cunningham was planning to do to Freda. I'm sure I can get him to talk.'

Now he stopped and pulled away from her.

'No. Absolutely not. You must not interfere, Gina. You could ruin everything. It is so delicately poised, this, you must leave it to us.'

They walked back to the house, not touching.

'If you get the sack,' she asked, 'what will you do? The only other thing you're interested in is archaeology. Will you do that?'

'I might. I'd be away a lot. You'd see even less of me than you do at the moment.'

'Oh, I could live with that,' she said.

Chapter Thirty-Five

TROOPS OF FRIENDS

It is a week after the drama of Freda's disappearance, and we are burying Andrew with all the considerable pomp and circumstance that his brother Charles can bring to bear. We are to be in Marlbury Abbey, of course, with not just the usual choir but also the Abbey School choristers in attendance, and a sextet of Old Abbots as pall bearers. If Charles could have got the archbishop to officiate, I'm sure he would have done, but as it is we have to make do with a rural dean. I am quietly hysterical with anticipation of social disasters. For a start, I don't know where I am supposed to sit – or if I am supposed to be there at all. Is it the done thing to be at your ex-husband's funeral – particularly an ex-husband whom you have been openly bad-mouthing for the past twenty years? I have spoken to Bernice, and she intends to be there, and I know Lavender is going all out for the starring role of chief mourner, so I have been beset in past days by an irresistible image of the three of us, black-veiled, sharing the front pew, somewhere between weird sisters and Mafia widows. Hence the hysteria.

I did suggest that Bernice and I might sit together, but she says her husband is coming with her, and David, too, plans to come, though I fully expect that he will be late, and I shall get glowered at as the abbey fills up and I am saving a pew space for him. As it is, though, he phones me early in the morning to tell me that he has important news to impart and would like to see me before it all kicks off.

'Where?' I ask.

'We'll find a quiet spot in the abbey grounds,' he says.

'Lovely,' I say, imagining my smart shoes sinking into mud, because the weather has turned as we have tipped from August into September, and there has been a week of feeble but relentless drizzle.

We meet at the abbey gates and wander around until we find a convenient tree to stand under. It may be a cypress, but I'm not good with trees, so that may just be a literary fancy.

'So?' I say.

'So, the CPS have decided that there is enough evidence to charge Neil Cunningham with murder.'

'They have! What's the evidence?'

'Some forensics – specks of Andrew's blood on a black shirt. We found it in a bag at Cunningham's house. I can't think why he hadn't put it in the wash.'

'It was silk,' I say. 'I noticed it at the wedding. And you can't just bung a silk shirt in the washing machine.'

'And I guess he didn't take it to a dry cleaner because that might be traced. Too clever for his own good. But the real clincher was from Marcus Bright. He came through much more easily than we expected.'

'Really?'

'Really. Surprising, actually, because there was nothing in it for him.'

'It meant you couldn't pin it on him.'

'He knew we couldn't. He had a solid alibi.'

'Well, he's in a shaky state, isn't he? Prison did for him really. He'll have been scared of you.'

'How do you know he's in a shaky state?'

'We really ought to be going in, I think,' I say. 'People will be starting to arrive.' And I begin to edge out from under our tree.

'Gina,' he calls, 'How do you know he's in a shaky state?'

I could stall - say I just guessed he must be - but we might as well cut to the chase. I put up my umbrella - protection against rain and interrogation - and I glance across to the approach to the abbey doors, where a few early mourners are coming in. Since the ex-wife having a shouting match with her lover among the gravestones is not a good look, I lead us off in the opposite direction.

'You talked to him,' David is saying, coming after me. 'You talked to Marcus Bright when I specifically asked you not to, when I told you that you could blow the whole case. How could you do that?'

I turn on him, only just avoiding taking his eye out with the umbrella. 'Because I am not a police officer and I don't have to follow your orders,' I hiss. 'I thought it was time I forgave him. He wasn't trying to kill me when he hit me - he was after the DVD in my pocket. He used a piece of scaffolding, which was reckless - but then he is an idiot. And he's paid his debt in full - he's not a man to take prison easily - and he deserves a break. He certainly deserves not to be exploited by a charlatan in a crappy so-called language school.'

'And you were offering to rehabilitate him?'

'I happened to know that we were looking for someone to do some bread-and-butter teaching at SOAS - the stuff the rest of us don't particularly want to do. It's not exciting but it's better than what he's doing at the moment, and it might lead to better things.'

'Don't tell me - you offered to put in a good word for him in exchange for him informing on Neil Cunningham?'

'David! Of course I didn't! I didn't need to. He may be an idiot but he's not stupid.'

'But you told him that the detective superintendent in charge of the case was your – whatever…'

'I said I knew you, yes. And I said that before he applied for the job, he ought to think about tying up loose ends – making sure he had put the old life behind him before he started on the new one.'

'Christ, Gina. It's bribery. Corruption. It could certainly get his evidence thrown out of court.'

'No, it's not. You haven't bribed anyone, I am not a police officer – and anyway, the job isn't in my gift. All I can do is mention him to our head of department. I might lend him the money to buy a decent suit for his interview, but he'll have to get the job for himself. So stop being paranoid and say thank you.'

He says nothing, and deciding that the shouting is over, I turn us round to face the incoming crowd. But he is not finished.

'Why?' he asks. 'Why, when I asked you not to?'

'Why do you think?' I growl from the protection of my umbrella. 'Don't you think it might be because I love you, God knows why, and I don't want you to lose your job over that bloody helicopter?'

And then I march off, umbrella held high like a standard, to face the fray.

Inside the abbey, people are filling up the pews, leaving the front two empty for the family. I settle in one a row from the back (the very back row seems like excessive self-abnegation). I put my bag down as a marker for a space for David, though I am not sure whether he will come in or not. Looking around, I see that Bernice and Henry have chosen the parallel pew on the other side of the aisle, and we give each other a discreet, fingery wave. There is a lot of black around, I see. These are people accustomed to proper funerals – no new-fangled '*Wear something bright*' nonsense for this crowd.

Sir Nicholas and Lady Payton are here, I see, observing the conventions. Does he still have hate in his heart for Andrew, or does death cancel all?

David comes in and takes his place beside me without looking at me. He stares straight ahead, and I look at his profile for a bit. I have shocked myself. I am pretty sure that I have never before said I loved him. I don't have time for further thought, though, because the Dead March from *Saul* strikes up, and six middle-aged men in black suits and Old Abbot ties start off up the aisle with the coffin. They look like former rugby players now running to seed, and I wonder if there is to be a coronary before the ceremony is out. Well, Jon is here, so we have a doctor in the house. Then I have a thought. I lean over to David and whisper in his ear.

'Wouldn't it be a great idea to get the rural dean to announce from the pulpit that you have charged someone with Andrew's murder – and that the presumptive killer is an Old Abbot?' I say.

David merely closes his eyes, as if in prayer.

And now here is the family, following the coffin. Lavender has gone all out for her grieving widow role. She is dressed in deepest black, her skirt almost to her ankles, and she holds the hands of her boys, walking on either side of her, dressed in the uniforms of their new prep school, to which they will be dispatched next week. Charles hovers protectively behind her. She has at least resisted a veil, though I'll bet it crossed her mind. Behind her come Ellie and Ben, she looking nice in navy, he looking Italian in a charcoal pinstripe. Freda and Nico follow, both in grey – customised bits of school uniform I suspect. Freda's skirt is very short. Annie and Jon follow, he in an unexceptionable grey, she looking slightly too business-like in one of the black suits she wears in court. I look at them – my family – and I have a disorientating moment when it feels wrong that they are all out there, and I am here, stuck in a back pew, out of sight. I look across to Bernice, who is dry-eyed, and to Jeanette, Andrew's former PA, who is sitting a couple of pews ahead with her husband, and is weeping quietly into a lace-trimmed handkerchief. Everyone should keep one of those for funerals, I think.

The service is reassuringly traditional; the congregation will have looked at their order sheets and breathed a sigh of relief. Nothing happy–clappy, no home-made poems, no surprises. The hymns will be *The Lord's my shepherd* and *Abide with Me*; no-one is going to ask them to sing – or even to sit through – *Amazing Grace, You'll Never Walk Alone* or *Somewhere Over the Rainbow.* They are safe.

There are four eulogies, from the rural dean, from Charles, from the president of the Old Abbots and from the former head of Andrew's chambers. The rural dean is in a bit of trouble because he didn't know Andrew at all. Religion is one of the many topics that Andrew and I never really talked about. He, like the rest of his family, claimed an unchallenged right to celebrate christenings, marriages and funerals, as well as an occasional Christmas midnight mass, in the abbey, and I suspect that deep down he had a comforting belief that he was patently on the side of the angels, and God would see him right in the life to come. But he was not a churchgoer. The rural dean has little to work on. I suppose Charles supplied him with some basics, but all he seems to have gleaned is that Andrew was *a Marlbury man through and through.* Andrew, he told us, though there can't be a single person present who doesn't know this, was born in Marlbury, raised in Marlbury, educated in Marlbury. Though he had gone away to Oxford to study, he had returned to Marlbury, and had raised his family here. (I want to make an objection, and point out a) that he had in fact had two families, and b) that I was the person who had raised the first one, but I hold my peace.) Though his work took him all over the world, the rural dean continues, it was to Marlbury that he returned; it was in the shade of Marlbury's ancient buildings that he had rested and drawn strength to fight the good fight once again. I look round my fellow mourners to see how they are taking all this, but they look serene, letting the words flow over them. Nothing to frighten the horses here.

After him comes Charles, who is a good speaker – his skills honed by years of golf club dinners, I imagine. He talks mainly about their childhood – self-deprecating stuff about the trials of being Andrew's elder but not so brilliant brother. There is just a touch of malice as he references Andrew's competitiveness, and the congregation laughs with proper restraint. But I am feeling increasingly uneasy. There is something the matter with this occasion.

I don't go to funerals often – my contemporaries seem to be a rather hardy crowd – so I am judging by my mother's, where the church was packed and the emotion tangible as her former patients remembered her care and expertise – and, I think, relived the traumas and terrors that she helped them through. Where is the emotion in this calm and polite gathering? Jeanette, I see, still has her hanky at the ready, but I doubt she will weep again – and nobody else seems likely to. I know I shouldn't be thinking of Macbeth just now, but the words come unbidden: Macbeth, confronting the ruins of a life of compulsive striving for success and power, sees that all he has is *mouth honour, breath*. It is a good phrase, *mouth honour*, and I am afraid that it is what is being offered here.

We follow Charles's words with *The Lord's my shepherd*, which is a lovely piece of writing, and then the president of the Old Abbots speaks briefly about what a thoroughly good egg Andrew was, and we move on to his former head of chambers. He is a man with a wise old face, like a benevolent turtle, and a surprisingly strong, young-sounding voice, and as he speaks the clichés drop away. Andrew, he says, was a man who was passionate about justice, but not passionate in any other way. His heart did not bleed. He pursued wrongdoers relentlessly, with one of the keenest intellects in the legal profession, and he was fearless. He made enemies of powerful and dangerous men, and he didn't shrink from the consequences. We did not know yet what motive his killer had, and he trusted that the police would not stop until they had hunted the killer down. If he had been killed in consequence of his pursuit of justice, then that was a risk he knew he took, and he was prepared for it. He would not have wanted a better death.

And now the tears spring to my eyes, and I can see a bit of furtive wiping and throat clearing. *Go on, cry, you smug bastards*, I mutter. This is better. This is better because, with a force that nearly sends me out of my seat, I remember why I married Andrew – why, in fact, I fell in love with him. Because, you see – and this is something I never reveal to anyone – when we were students at Oxford we were exact contemporaries of the Tory boys who have been playing at running the country for the past twelve years. Yes, Andrew knew them all – Cameron, Osborne, Gove, Johnson – every restaurant-trashing, pig-loving one of them – and he could have joined their grisly crew. Marlbury Abbey School has cachet in their circles – it is the oldest public school in the country, dating from the Sixth Century, while Eton was a puny newcomer in the Fifteenth. And Andrew could debate – he could have been at the Union, posing and posturing with the rest of them. But he wasn't. While they were playing *I'm the King of the Castle* in their exclusive soft play area, he was volunteering at a free law clinic, and that's why I loved him. And if I couldn't live with the obsessional commitment that drove him to keep resisting the lure of easy money and to keep defending the defenceless, then that was my problem as much as his, wasn't it?

I am brought back to the present by the congregation rising to its feet, and I join in *Abide with me* with some fervour. Then we drone through a prayer, receive a blessing, and are dismissed with an invitation to refreshment in the school buttery. Lavender leads her mourners out, looking soulful. No-one would guess that she already has her plans for her riding school under way, or that as soon as she has packed her sons off to boarding school her good-looking young 'business partner' will be moving into Aren't We Grand Hall with her.

The rest of the congregation start to shuffle down the aisle, and we stand, like cars on a slip road waiting to join the traffic flow. David turns to me. 'By the way,' he says, 'I've read the report on Jon's mother's death.'

'Finally,' I say.

'The witness who gave the partial reg for the hit and run car also got a look at the driver.'

'And?'

'And she was sure the driver was a woman.'

'A *woman*?'

'Yup.'

'She was sure?'

'Yup.'

'Do you think Andrew had let a woman drive his car?'

'I think a woman was driving her own car. It was only a partial reg, remember.'

'Why didn't the McCleods say it was a woman?'

'They didn't know that you and Freda had cooked up your theory about its being Andrew, did they? They had no reason to say anything.'

'I must tell Bernice,' I say, straining to see if she is still there, across the aisle. 'Tell her that her faith in Andrew was justified.'

'You know she's taken over the Adita Bahader case? Prosecuting in Andrew's place?'

'Is she? Good for her. It'll be a great win for her if she can pull it off.'

We stand for a bit longer; David is ahead of me in our slip road, and he's not going to push his way out. I wonder why he chose this moment to tell me about the car driver, and decide to take it as an apology for his ungraciousness about my intervention with Marcus Bright – possibly even as a thank you for saving his career. I give him a prod in the back.

'Push a bit,' I say. 'I want to catch Bernice.'

He edges out politely, but Bernice has gone, eager to be away, I guess. We shuffle on – and then I see them.

In the very back pew, still sitting, unwilling to push their way out, are people I recognise with a great gush of affection: Farid, Ivy, Soraya, Hani and Jing Wei. With the minimum of politeness, I elbow my way across to them. Smiling, they stand up, as if in deference to their teacher – which I once was. I want to hug them all, but of course we're not doing that. Eight years ago I went into a sulk with the world and took myself off to live like a hermit crab on an unfriendly sea shore. My only meaningful social contacts were a group of asylum seekers, clinging precariously to sanctuary on that same sea shore. I gave them English lessons, and when I decided to stop sulking and move to London to a job that paid, I compensated for deserting them by giving them Andrew in exchange. I could offer them only the English language; he could offer them the right to be here. He was willing to help, as I knew he would be. He always wanted my good opinion. He did a sterling job – Border Force officials, unused to dealing with top-of-the-tree QCs, caved in and put their hands up at his approach. Farid, Ivy, Soraya, Hani and Jing Wei are all still here – as is Ivy's husband, rescued from Dover's notorious Immigrant Removal Centre. Farid – now a junior doctor – keeps me up to date with how they are doing. Life isn't easy, and they don't look prosperous in this sleek assembly, but the strain has gone from their faces, they look as though they can afford to eat, and Ivy, whose little boys died on their nightmare journey from Zimbabwe, has a tiny, sleeping baby in her arms.

'I didn't know about this,' I say, edging the shawl aside to look at the tiny, crumpled face.

'Two weeks old,' she says. 'A little girl. Our miracle. God is good.'

'It was so good of you all to come,' I say.

Farid looks at me. 'He was a good man, Andrew Gray,' he says. 'A good man.'